Redeeming
Jacob Marley

By Stephen Miller

The Santa Claus League
Volume 2

Dedication

To my friends in Kenya and Somalia. Thank you for an unforgettable year. You proved to me that hope and joy can be found in the darkest and most desperate of circumstances. May we all come together as one family, the rich and the poor, the young and the old, those of us who live in peaceful lands and those who are still struggling to make it. By His good grace, God bless us, every one.

Table of Contents

Prologue

The Back Story

To begin with, Jacob Marley was dead. There is no doubt whatsoever about that. For almost 200 years his body lay silent in his grave, but his tormented spirit wandered the earth like a vagabond—howling and weeping with each windblown step. He was a doomed soul, condemned by his riches to roam the earth in helpless misery. How long was this doom to last? I didn't know. Charles Dickens wrote about him in his masterpiece A Christmas Carol. It's not a very long book. I should have read it myself before... well, I get ahead of myself.

My name is Mason Howell. I'm a 22-year-old college senior studying at the University of Washington. I'm of European decent with blonde hair and green eyes. At five-foot 10 inches, my girlfriend Julia says it's my smile that makes me stand out in a crowd. Like many students I have a part-time job and student loan debt up to my ears. I have to fit work, study, and sleep into an abnormally busy schedule. Why am I so busy? It's simple... I'm Santa Claus.

To be clear, I'm not the only Santa Claus. Santa Claus is a title and many people share it on the earth at the same time. St. Nicholas is the conduit of all Christmas magic. He's the one entrusted with the heart-stones of Christmas, the source of all Christmas magic.

A thousand years ago the world was suffering in poverty and ignorance and it was St. Nicholas that did all he could to bring light to the world by himself; but more needed to be done. So, in an act of love, he created an organization he could share his Christmas magic with. He called it the Santa Claus League.

Every Santa Claus needs a Mrs. Santa Claus and an engineer. John is my best friend. He's two inches taller than me with wild brown hair and kind of a big nose. His ears poke out and he's skinny as a beanpole, all knees and elbows... and he was there the day I became Santa Claus.

It all started in high school when Julia was putting on a Christmas party for the kids in our town and her Santa Claus called in sick. Since I was the only one she knew who had a Santa Claus suit, she begged me to help. I wanted to impress her and to help the kids so I agreed, using the old Santa suit that belonged to my Grandpa Adams; it hadn't been worn since his death.

As John and I rifled through the ancient Santa Claus clothes I found a strange inner-suit packed up with them. It was made of an other-worldly material almost glimmering with power. I cautiously put it on... and a strange force exploded, surrounding me with magic, driving its energy into every cell of my body! And, when I came to my senses? I had all the magic of Santa Claus.

Julia Martin became my, well... my Mrs. Santa Claus. We met on the first day of kindergarten and I've been in love with her ever since. She is the most beautiful girl in three states, maybe the whole world, as far as I'm concerned. We're not married, I wish we were... but her dad stands in the way like a mountain between us.

John became my Rudolph; in other words, my engineer. Each Santa gets to pick out their own magic sleigh and John owns and maintains mine— a 1979, cherry red Chevy Nova.

Now, being Santa Claus isn't as easy as it sounds. During that first Christmas together in service to the League we fought with Snake Skin, a notorious gang leader and his whole band of criminals. We did such a good job St. Nicholas invited us to become apprentice members. Little did we know that was just the beginning of the dangerous adventures that were waiting for us.

Chapter One

Summoned by Dr. Rawlings

It was a few days before Christmas and I was sitting in Dr. Rawlings' economics class dreading how I was going to answer the last essay question of his final examination.

The professor was in his mid-50's and still dressed exactly like he did when he was awarded his doctoral degree at the unheard of age of 21. His graying blond hair was long and perfectly styled. He wore white pants and a white Miami Vice sports coat with a black t-shirt underneath. He was 80s cool and stark, all at the same time.

The words he now scratched on the blackboard seemed to steal the joy from the already depressed classroom. The course, Macroeconomics 302, was his specialty, a required class to finish up my undergraduate degree in Business Management. Dr. Rawlings was the biggest obstacle to completing my degree on time and I had plenty of reason to worry—he prided himself in seeing how many students he could flunk out each semester.

"This last essay will make up 40 percent of your grade," he said smugly, while he finished writing the question on the board. "I don't want to spend all winter break grading your tests, so what I want is a one or two sentence response, be it for or against the quotation written on the chalkboard. You will be graded for content, punctuation, and brevity. This is an economics class, not a creative writing course. Ponder your responses carefully. You may begin."

"Greed is a bottomless pit which exhausts the person in an endless effort to satisfy the need without ever reaching satisfaction," the quotation read, Erich Fromm the author. I had tried everything I could to do well on these little mini-essays, but no matter how perfect my grammar or how convincing my arguments, I almost always got back a 60 percent score or less. These daily assignments counted for 40 percent of my grade, and now the final test was based on the same model? I was getting desperate.

I knew how to get a good grade, but I couldn't bring myself to do it. Dr. Rawlings firmly believed that economic inequality was the cause of all the evil in the world. To pass his class I would have to write something against ambition and success. Everything Santa Claus is about revolves around encouraging bad children to become good and good children to become great. How could I write anything against ambition and success?

As a member of the Santa Claus League I was given magical powers to encourage goodness. I can stop time when I touch of my nose; I can see who is good and who is bad; I can even envision the past, present, and glimpses of the future for everyone I meet. The magical power that was most useful at this very moment was my ability to see the emotional state of the people in the room by the color they emitted.

When people are happy they light up in pleasant rainbow-like colors that change all the time, based on their moods. The intensity of the light they emit changes as well, depending on how excited they are. Children are especially bright.

Now, when someone is depressed, I see a person surrounded by dark filters that mute out the colors inside them. An angry or greedy person has an aura that erupts in violent displays of energy, flaming like forest fires or exploding like dark thunderbolts from a black storm cloud. Children are never as dark as adults, but when they are upset, watch out, they can turn all the lights out!

As I looked around I saw the different colors coming from everyone in the room. Some students were yellow with contentment; others were gray with boredom. Others were dark green with conflict, not wanting to betray their personal convictions, but not willing to stand up for them either.

My friend Evan Barks was the darkest of all. He had been my last fellow public defender of exceptionalism but, by the looks of him, he wasn't going to stand with me this time. He gave in to necessity, the mother of invention, but also the mother of betrayal.

I stared at my paper for a full five minutes, battling with my own convictions. My time to answer the question was almost up as dark purple sparks of impatience were emitting from Dr. Rawlings' fingertips. He always sparked like that when he was about to verbally destroy me.

I finally gave into despair and wrote my short essay, trying to be as diplomatic as I could. We all turned in our final exams and he carefully read each final sentence aloud with approving nods, until he got to mine.

"Mason Howell," he called out, raging colors swirling around his head, "explain this response! 'Laziness is the bottomless pit which exhausts the person out of sheer boredom in an endless effort to goof off without ever finding satisfaction!'"

"I think there might be a mistake, sir!" I stammered while the rest of the class froze, not daring to move.

"Is this your name?" He fumed, pointing to the top of the page.

"That's my name."

"Are these your other answers for the final exam?"

"Yes, of course," I stuttered, "but what I wrote..." At that moment I felt something I hadn't felt for almost an entire semester, a bolt of joy that caused my whole body to tingle. It hit me so hard I had to touch my nose to stop time so I wouldn't laugh out loud in front of the professor.

When I entered into time-warp (my term for the place I go when I stop time) I found my buddy John Patten standing in the back of the room frozen like a statue. He also has time-warp ability and now I realize he'd used his magic to switch out the answer on my final. To bring him into my time-warp all I had to do was touch him and my nose at the same time. As soon as I did, there he was, bent over laughing.

"That was epic!" he belted out loud, sparking like a fireworks stand on fire. "I can't believe you didn't see me take the paper, man. I out Santa Claus'd even you this time!"

"Very funny, John," I said. "Now I'm really in trouble!"

"You should have seen yourself," he hooted again. "That was the best prank I've played on you in years."

"So you flew outside of time for 300 miles, just to play a practical joke on me?"

"Sure, why not?" he grinned. "Have flying car, will travel!"

"Yeah, well you probably just got me flunked out of this class."

"Right, like he was going to like your response any better?" he laughed. "While I agree with Mr. Fromm's statement, ambition doesn't have to lead to greed. The possession of money, wealth, and power doesn't have to destroy the integrity of the individual if that ambition is directed to worthy purposes."

"You're probably right," I submitted. "I guess I was doomed anyway. Did you bring Julia with you?"

"No," he said. "She has a big social event she has to attend back in Moses Lake. We're supposed to meet her at her parents' house later on tonight."

"That's good, at least I have something to look forward to. But, do me a favor and stay out of time warp until I get done with class, will you? I'd like to graduate in the spring. You've already graduated from MIT last year, so cut me some slack."

"Fine, fine," he said. "Go back to Dr. Doom, and I'll get an ice cream. Meet me at the ice cream parlor when you get out, I'll be with the cutest girl there."

"Fine, see you in an hour," I responded and walked back to my seat, preparing myself for the Dr. Rawlings' wrath. I touched my nose, entering back into the flow of time and prepared to meet my fate. I paused for a moment, trying to remember where the conversation had left off.

"And what? Mr. Howell," Dr. Rawlings continued darkly, unaware I had ever left the conversation. "Have you lost your memory, too?"

"Not at all sir," I affirmed, gaining confidence. "I take full responsibility for what is written there. I just wished I could say more to prove that ambition is a virtue and not a vice."

"After a full semester in my class," Mr. Rawlings snarled, "I would think you'd know what kind of answer I'm looking for. I know all about you, Mr. Howell. Student by day, Santa Claus by night. I honestly don't know why you even bother getting an education with all the fantasies running through your head. Here is a worthwhile quotation from Albert Einstein you can ponder. 'Three great forces rule the world: stupidity, fear, and greed.' What do you have to say about that?"

"Isn't there a way for industrious people to contribute to society without being stupid, fearful, or greedy?" I asked, trying not to antagonize him anymore.

"Is there a way for the rich to contribute to society?" He sneered. "Since we recently studied the economic injustices of the early Industrial Revolution and the Economic Crisis of 1825, the very age your Christmas friend Charles Dickens wrote about, and since it is just a few days before Christmas, let's conjure up a Christmas Ghost and see what he has to say. Come up here to the front of the class, Mr. Howell and help me. I'll award you extra credit for this. Knowing your past test scores, you can obviously use it."

Half the students laughed and the others groaned as I stood and walked to the front of the class... uncomfortable, with nervous green sparks darting from my own fingertips. Rawlings walked over to the lights and turned them off, leaving the room dimly lit by a row of emergency lights in the back of the room.

"Since most of you here believe in fairytales and the like," he said, "channel all your spiritual powers with mine, and Mr. Howell will conjure up the spirit of Jacob Marley to guide us to the path of enlightenment."

I stood dumbfounded, not daring to do something so irreverent. He looked at me and laughed. "You really are superstitious, aren't you? Move out of the way... you're useless. I'll do it."

He raised his hands in the air, bowed his head, and with a loud voice solemnly chanted, "Hear me... hear me, ye doomed spirits of the wicked rich. Hear me and obey my commands. I summon Jacob Marley, the symbol of oppressive capitalism. I demand that he answer my solemn questions."

In an instant one of the florescent emergency lights in the room flickered on and off and stayed dark, leaving us with just one dim light. A few students in the room gasped, crackling with the blue sparks of surprise, while others emitted a dark green glow of fear. Mr. Rawlings was even more loathingly purple than before, raising his hands in the air as if he were gathering energy from the room. To my surprise, the green energy of fear began to flow to him from the students and he used it with even more effect.

"Jacob Marley," he belted as if in a trance, "did you steal from the poor?" A deadly silence filled the room—but just then the roaring sound of a car rumbling past the classroom window, growling like a doomed soul as it sped away made everyone gasp with astonishment!

"I'll take that as a yes," Mr. Rawlings continued eerily, drawing even more green power from the now-hypnotized class. "What is the fate of all those greedy capitalists who steal from the poor?"

Suddenly all of the lights in the room flickered on and off several times, causing one of the florescent light tubes to explode in its casing. Now the growling car returned, roaring past the window even louder, followed by an ear-piercing police siren. The class was clearly startled now. Dr. Rawlings continued gathering in all the student's fear energy, making himself even more powerful, although it was clear he didn't realize it.

Ignorant of why he felt so elated, Dr. Rawlings was about to speak again when a dark figure rose above him, a spirit that was seen by more people than just myself because four or five girls gave out a piercing scream! Everyone sat back in their chairs, stunned by the unnatural events.

"Jacob Marley," I commanded, taking over the frightening conversation. "Would giving up on our ambitions make the poor people of the world any better off?"

To that question all the lights flickered on and off again, blowing out another two florescent light bulbs, as the air conditioner came on, blowing out a grinding nnnnnnnooooooooo, as the air moved through the vents. "That's enough," I yelled. "Mr. Marley, I order you to return to your realm."

As if on cue all the remaining lights flickered back on as the air conditioner turned off. A huge gust of wind twirled around the room, blowing all the papers off the desks. The whole class sat perfectly still, too startled to do move.

As the dark spirit left, something cold and foreboding swept through me. "Save me," it whispered then evaporated into the ethers.

"Class dismissed," Dr. Rawlings growled, turning his purple sparks into red thunderbolts and shooting them at me. "If you think good vibrations will help you pass this class, Mr. Howell, think again. I told you not to believe in fairytales."

"Yes sir," I responded trying to catch my breath. I hurried to my desk and gathered up all my stuff. As I was leaving the room white fireworks exploded right in front of my face. I jumped back in surprise, turning around to see where it came from—Evan Barks was on fire, his countenance absolutely exploding with confidence and purpose.

The rest of the class barely moved even though the test was over. Colors of all kinds swirled around the room, clashing into each other and erupting like volcanoes. The students who admired Dr. Rawlings and his ideas were aflame with indignation and anger, while those who supported my ideas had rallied with sparking power. Even the previously bored students were taking sides on the issue.

Suddenly a red thunderbolt crashed into my chest.

"Leave now!" Dr. Rawlings boomed, sensing he had lost whatever power he had temporarily gained.

"Dare to fight for your dreams!" I yelled, closing the door and rushing down the hall to meet John at the ice cream parlor. I probably shouldn't have said that, but I couldn't help myself. Sometimes the folly of youth gets the best of a guy.

Chapter Two

Mission Control

John was just paying for a double scoop of ice cream when I walked in. I knew the place by heart as I worked in the back, cleaning up the processing plant at night. When John saw me he smiled and motioned for me to come over.

"Hey what are you doing here so fast? I didn't even have a chance to ask Barbara here on a date," he said. The girl behind the counter smiled and started helping another customer.

"He cut the final short. I guess Dr. Rawlings doesn't like differences of opinion."

"Or any opinion other than his own," John jeered. "Get yourself a cone and let' head over to Julia's."

"Something really weird happened though," I admitted a few minutes after getting my own ice cream. "It freaked me out, to tell ya the truth."

"Sounds interesting," John said with a smile, "I should have stuck around. What happened?"

"I think Dr. Rawlings may have contacted a ghost. It was the strangest thing I've ever seen."

"I doubt that... we've seen some really strange stuff, but go on, I like the sound of this."

"This was right up there with the strangest... and as the spirit was leaving it begged for my help. I'll tell you all about it on the way to my apartment. What's the plan for us to get home?"

"You tell me your secrets and I'll tell you mine," he said mysteriously. I finally gave in and explained the whole thing to him and he just gave me a shrug.

"I don't know what to tell you, that was definitely weird, but that's what I like about you. There's never a dull moment when you're around... and in honor of our friendship, I'm returning the favor."

"What does that mean?" I asked apprehensively. "We're driving home, wink-wink, and then heading over to Julia's place.

After that we'll eat more ice cream and make the finishing touches on the Sub-for-Santa lists. How does that sound?"

"It all sounds good except for the wink-wink part."

"Don't be such a baby," he chided. "I've just made a few improvements to the old Nova I think you'll like, so let's jet out of here."

It didn't take very long to grab everything I needed to visit home for three weeks—my laptop, a few clothes, and my toothbrush. After it was all piled in the trunk, John looked at me and grinned.

"Hop in," he said merrily, pointing to the front seat. "We only have a few hours before we have to meet with Julia and I want to try out some improvements!"

"Are we going hypersonic again?" I moaned.

"Maybe," he said, "but check this out, I have a new way of switching my steering wheel to flying mode. Now I can pull it up and back just like I was flying an airplane. I have new meteor shielding too, and oh, look at this! I developed a new oxygen helmet with a 3D Augmented-Reality-Heads-Up-Display. I'm even using retina-tracking. I can't wait for you to see it in action!"

"I have no idea what you just said," I admitted, jumping in the front seat of the car, buckling up like I was strapping into a fighter jet. "Will we have enough time to check it all out before we meet with Julia?"

"Sure, no problem," he said cheerfully. "We're only flying to Moses Lake. What's there to worry about?"

"Spoken like a true engineer. Where's this helmet you're so proud of?"

"It's stowed under your seat," John said. "You should put it on now."

"Won't we look suspicious wearing flight helmets?" I said, jamming the flight helmet on my head.

"Don't worry," he said. "I've got tinted windows, no one will notice anything. Relax man, and enjoy the ride!"

I expected the uncomfortable restricted vision of his old flight helmet, but instead the helmet completely disappeared and I could see everything like I was driving in a convertible. "Where'd the helmet go?"

"How do you like Augmented-Reality?" John smiled, looking at me wearing a completely different set of clothes. "Everything you see is being generated by the helmet."

"Wow, you have been busy," I said, turning my head from side to side, checking out the scenery around me. "I'm impressed, but really, you don't have to show me all your high tech gadgets... I'm good."

"Mason, Mason, Mason," he smiled deviously, flipping switches and reconfiguring the car for our flight. "You haven't seen anything yet."

John touched the side of his face and spoke to an unseen person. "Seattle Radar, Santa Claus League two zero one, Seattle Washington, requesting flight plan Sierra Juliet zero five one, hypersonic flight to Moses Lake, Washington."

"This is Seattle Radar," a crackling voice responded over the radio. "Position and hold."

"They have to get all the old men out of the way," John said, grinning ear to ear. "Some of them don't like my new sleigh, they think it's too aggressive."

"I wonder why?" I asked. "But I don't know why they are getting so bent out of shape, we're only flying to Moses Lake after all... right?"

"Right," he agreed, with a mysterious grin. "Santa Claus League two zero one," the radio crackled. "Seattle Radar, in communication with North Control Tower, cleared for takeoff, Hypersonic Flight Plan ...."

"Hallo, John," a friendly Germanic voice boomed over the speaker, interrupting the air traffic controller. "Good luck today, Yah? I'll be following your test flight."

"Thanks Rudolph," John responded happily. "If I run into trouble can you help us out before we crash?"

"Yah. Yah, no problem," he answered sincerely. "We don't want our newest League members killed in an accident."

"We're not full members of the League yet," John reminded him.

"Yah. Yah, apprentice members," he corrected.

"Why haven't we been invited to become full members yet?" John asked. "We use our Christmas magic all the time, why the wait?"

"You do ask a good question," Rudolph agreed, "but don't ask me. St. Nicholas doesn't always share his secrets. Although, maybe it's because you're not married yet, have you thought of that? You've had plenty of time, what's the delay?"

"Fear of commitment!" John blurted.

"Speak for yourself," I objected.

"I am speaking for myself," John corrected. "That's why I'm not married. I don't know why you're not married. Julia's been begging you to propose for months now."

"If it were only that easy," I complained. "Julia's dad was cool with me until he realized I might be his son-in-law. Now he barely talks to me."

"Who cares what her father says," Rudolph counseled earnestly. "You don't have to marry him. Concentrate on her. You better get your priorities straight or you might lose her completely. What do you value the most, money or love?"

"Hey, I'm all about love, but competing against a billionaire might be more than I can handle."

"I'm sorry to interrupt your love life," the Air Traffic Controller blared, taking control of the conversation. "But this is an official communication. You are cleared for Hypersonic Flight Plan Sierra Juliet zero five one. Don't hit any satellites. Seattle Radar Out."

"Now I'm worried," I said, tugging on my safety harness. "I thought we were just going to Moses Lake."

"We aren't going anywhere until you say the magic words," John insisted, pulling back on the wheel while levitating us off the ground.

"What magic words?"

"You know the ones I want to hear. Say them or we'll fly upside down the whole way!"

"Oh those words," I remembered smiling. "Now, Dasher! now, Dancer! now, Prancer! and Vixen! On, Comet! on, Cupid! on Donner and Blitzen! To the top of the porch, to the top of the wall! Now dash away, dash away, dash away all!"

"That's what I'm talkin' about!" John sang, pushing the gas pedal to the floor.

I had no idea what kind of fuel he was using, but it was powerful. We jumped forward, clearing the trees in a millisecond. With John's new technology my vision wasn't constricted and the full beautiful wonder of the world passed under and around me like a vision.

Leaving the wooded campus of the University of Washington, we flew over Mercer Island. Before I knew it we were over Lake Sammamish and heading for Okanogan-Wenatchee National Forest. Mt. Rainier was to our right in all its glorious splendor, with Mount Saint Helens not far away.

"I can almost see Moses Lake from here," I said, peering into the horizon. "I'm sorry you won't have time to test out all your other cool stuff."

"Don't worry about that," he said calmly, while beginning to turn the car round in a big arch. "We'll still get to test everything—my new fuel system, the upgraded heads up display, and energy shields."

"So why are we heading back toward Seattle?" I gasped.

"We're not," John grinned, punching us past the sound barrier with barely a shutter, "we're heading to Moses Lake, the long way around!"

Chapter Three

Meteor Strike

"The long way around?" I blurted. "You mean we're flying around the whole earth just to get home?"

"That's okay isn't it?" he snickered. "We'll get there on time, don't have a heart attack!"

Not having a heart attack was easier said than done. The openness of the flight was unsettling, like being on a rollercoaster ride without anything to hold on to. The Augmented-Reality goggles made the clouds seem to pass right through us instead of going around us. The blue sky was dotted with clouds for thousands of miles and the ground falling away fast.

John continued turning us around until we were flying straight again, pointing the car toward the sea. We were gaining speed by the second; I could barely lift my arms to grab onto my safety harness. It's a good thing I was strapped in or I would have smashed into the back window.

"We're coming up to Mach 2.5," John said happily. "Get ready for the pre-burner engines to kick in. Initiating the pre-burners on my mark, three, two, one... initiate!"

John flipped the switch and the power roared from two rocket engines located under the car. We were thrown back by the engine's thrust as it pushed us out of the atmosphere, the Chevy Nova going supernova! The car sped towards the visible moon above us, chasing the sun around the earth instead of moving away from it. As our altitude increased the sky turned darker blue and the moon became a glowing football, even though the sun was still setting in the west.

"Switching off the pre-burners and opening up the scramjet," John announced through his flight helmet. With the flip of a few more switches a mighty roar threw us back again, propelling us from Mach five to Mach ten in a steady thrust of acceleration.

I felt immediately awed and inspired by the whole thing, despite my misgivings and unnatural feeling about flying outside of my own planet in a car originally made to never leave the ground. I was struck by the beauty of our solar system and dizzy at the immensity of space at the same time.

"Isn't this awesome?" John beamed. "At this speed we'll make it to Julia's house right on time!"

"I think I'm getting motion sickness," I lamented.

"Don't puke in your oxygen mask, dude," he warned, "you might drown. Augmented Reality takes a while to get used to, I grant you, but it makes flying tons easier. Now for the second test of our mission... ramming into a low earth orbit debris field."

"You're ramming us into a debris field?" I stammered. "Now I am going to puke."

"Undo your mask and do it in a barf bag," he said seriously. "All this has to be done. You never know when you're going to hit something up here. Don't worry bro, we won't hit anything larger than a crow bar."

"Why can't we fly at subsonic speeds like Saint Nicholas?"

"Helping good kids become great! This is what great looks like ... hold tight! Here we go!"

For John following the motto of the Santa Claus League means pushing the limits of science, and he loved nothing more than discovering new ways to solve difficult problems. I just wish he'd try out some of his inventions on someone else.

John activated an energy shield that covered the whole car and it glowed a transparent blue, sparking like a bug zapper as tiny pieces of space dust bounced off the Nova's cherry red. A display came up identifying debris ahead of us as little circles covered each fragment, cataloging the location and size of the object. John flew us straight at a yellow object.

"Aren't we supposed to stay away from those?" I said in a panicked tone.

"Nah," he smiled, turning off the scramjet and coasting towards the offending objects, "The circle colors indicate how serious of a threat the rubble poses. Yellow objects should be okay to hit, but the red ones need to be avoided. Let's hit a yellow one and see what happens."

It's a good thing I was buckled in, not because I didn't want to get hurt, but because I wanted to hurt him!

The yellow object got bigger and bigger on the screen...now half a mile from us, a warning buzzer sounded, nearly scaring me to death.

"Turn away from that thing!" I yelled—but it was too late. The yellow circle crashed into an energy field just outside our bumper and flew over the car harmlessly.

"It worked!" John sang triumphantly. "If it's yellow, I can hit it. Now for something a little bit bigger."

I wanted to object, but at this point there was no stopping him. He aimed the car at a larger yellow circle and ran our car into it with the same effect. I have to admit, after the initial shock it was kind of fun.

We were dodging through the debris field hitting little pieces of yellow space junk when suddenly, a red object appeared out of nowhere. The collision alarm blared with a different tone and John made a desperate turn to the left. The baseball-sized meteor hit the rear of the car, causing us to temporarily spin out of control. But fortunately, John remained perfectly calm as he stabilized the car, finally gaining control and missing the four-foot-long rocket booster.

"That was close," he said calmly, as if nothing happened. "Are you ready to pick up Julia now?"

"Please!" I begged, barely able to breath. "How far away are we?"

"Not far, we are over the Indian Ocean right now, so about 8,700 miles away. At these speeds we'll be there in about an hour. Do you want to get there faster?"

"No, no... an hour will be great!"

"Suit yourself," John said. "I've got more juice to burn. We haven't even done a max speed test. Are you sure you don't want to see how fast she can go? We might even be able to make it to the moon with enough extra oxygen."

"Moses Lake will be fine for now, thanks! Just get me there alive and I'll be thrilled."

Meteor Strike

"Just trying to be ambitious," John said, taking us back into the atmosphere and firing up the scramjet engines.

The hour went by quickly and, with a smooth reentry, we landed at Moses Lake, drove around a wooded bend, and into a crowded private drive with a brilliantly lit house at the end. John parked the car next to a yellow BMW 4-series GC. We got out of the car and knocked on the door of the huge colonial house.

"Hello, may I help you?" a well-dressed woman said at the door, puzzled by our lack of party clothes.

"Hello," I answered, "we're here to pick up Julia. Is she around?"

"Wait one moment, please," she said politely, inviting us in and closing the door.

The house was elegant with massive chandeliers and luxurious drapes on the windows. The ceilings were tall, with enough room to put two houses in the same space, but somehow well-proportioned at the same time. Money can buy some beautiful things, that's for sure. Even though I had lived in town my whole life I had never known who lived in this mansion.

After only a few minutes, Julia came around the corner dressed in a stunning long red gown with golden beads that shimmered in the crystal lit hall. Her height was elevated by equally dazzling ruby red high heels, which gave her the stature of a beauty queen. I could barely keep from staring at her, she was so beautiful.

But then, she was always beautiful to me, even when she wasn't dressed so elegantly. Fair white skin with dark brown eyes, the color of Julia's hair reminded me of a fine piece of mahogany furniture, brown with just a touch of red. She was slender and so well put together she had to turn down modeling offers on a regular basis. To think she would want to be with me was more than I could imagine.

"Sorry to make you wait," she smiled sweetly. "Senator Walker is hard to get away from once he gets a story started. You look a little pale, Mason, are you feeling alright?"

"Hypersonic," was all I said, trying not to sound stupid.

"From Seattle?" Julia laughed.

"The long way around," I motioned, drawing a circle around my left fist with my right index finger.

"Oh dear," she frowned, "I'm glad I wasn't driving with you this time."

As we were talking, a huge man in a tuxedo came around the corner, almost touching the bottom of the chandelier with his head. He was six-foot-six if he was an inch, and built like Hercules. Following close behind him was a shorter, younger-looking man, dressed just as well, but with a more familiar face.

"This is Bradley," Julia exclaimed, pointing at the mountainous man. "Bradley, I'd like you to meet two of my best friends, Mason Howell and John Patten."

"Mason, John," he said coldly, then whispered over at Julia. "I don't know why you hang out with these losers."

"Don't be hard on my friends, darling," Julia scolded, "you've just met them."

"You already know me," the other man said cheerfully. "Bill Harper, eleventh grade calculus, do you remember?"

"Sure," I smiled, feeling at ease in his presence. "I would have never passed the class without your help. Thanks!"

Two other revelers bolted around the corner to meet us, a well-dressed woman in her early twenties and her obvious boyfriend. "Don't forget to introduce us," Julia's friend said merrily taking a picture of us with her cell phone camera. "My name is Bridget and this is my boyfriend Max. Julia and I are sorority sisters."

"Hey," Max said, raising his hand slightly.

I wasn't convinced Bridget and Max were a very good match. She was a mysterious mix of fun and purpose, and he was ... bland.

"I wish you could stay," Bridget begged, "we're having so much fun."

"I wish I could too," Julia said genuinely, "but I have a party to plan, and this is the only time we have to do it. We'll have lunch together when I get back to Boston. Would that be alright?"

"It sounds lovely," Bridget beamed, taking another picture. "You be careful now, Julia. I'll see you in a few weeks, okay?"

"And stay out of trouble!" Bradley warned, looking at me suspiciously.

"Yeah, stay out of trouble," Bill mimicked, mocking him in a deep voice. "We can't have any trouble around here."

"I'll be careful," Julia winked at Bill, as she put on a pair of fluffy white gloves. "I'll be back to school after Christmas break. Try to have a little fun without me."

"I will," Bradley smiled, his aura turning a hot red as he tried to kiss her.

Julia was quicker than he was and skillfully moved out of his way as Bridget snapped a quick picture, showing it to everyone. "Rejection!" she giggled.

"Goodbye, everyone," Julia sang, walking out of the door with John and I. "Thanks for a lovely party!"

Watching how Julia had to avoid Bradley's romantic advances was painful, like being struck by a meteor all over again. Bradley was a jerk. I looked down and saw my fingers sparking with green energy.

"Let me drive you home," Bradley complained, stepping out the door and looking at John's car down the street. "Wouldn't you rather drive in a nice BMW? You'll never make it there in that old thing. You'll breakdown on the freeway for sure. Your father wouldn't approve of you going with them anyway. Please, let me take you!"

"Don't be ridiculous," she rebuked. "Now you sound like my father. You'd be surprised how well John's car is maintained. Don't worry about me for a second."

"Bye, bye!" Bridget giggled, waving enthusiastically with her head poking out of the door. "Have fun! See you in a few weeks!"

We walked down the cold path under the watchful eyes of Bradley who didn't close the door completely until we drove away.

"I don't like him very much," John said as we headed for the main road.

"I don't hate him," I admitted. "But he might get a lump of coal in his stocking this year. What just happened back there? Is there something we need to talk about?"

"Oh, we have lots to talk about," Julia emoted, her aura becoming dark purple. "We can start by talking about Bradley. If I have to spend another minute with that muscle-bound blockhead, I'll scream."

"So why do you hang out with him then?"

"Dad set me up," she said. "He's the youngest son of one of his business partners. I've known him for years but I can't stand him."

"But your dad likes him, right?"

"He loves Bradley like a son. I've been forced to go to formal events with him my whole life. And just for the record, Dad was going to send me to a frilly prep school starting my first year of high school so I could be with him, but I didn't want to go. I like my friends, especially you."

"I didn't think you even knew my name until the night of the Christmas party," I replied.

"My mother always said boys are clueless," she said. "All through school you acted like you didn't even know I existed. Did you ever wonder why I shared almost every class with you? You are so obtuse!"

"I'm sorry, sweetheart. I didn't know."

"Will you please know this," she begged, turning bonfire yellow. "Being a billionaire's daughter is a nightmare. I wish I were middle class, like you."

I didn't even know how to react. If she wasn't so mad at me I would have burst out laughing. How many middle class folks use the word obtuse?

"You think I'm joking don't you?" she continued. "I've had to be babysat, guarded and protected every day of my life. My father only lets me hang out with you and John because he knows I'll never forgive him if he doesn't. You better believe he has other guys lined up if Bradley doesn't work out. Besides, Mason Howell, do you know any reason why I shouldn't marry a billionaire's son?"

I was too stunned to say anything. I wanted to say, you have to marry me, but I was too afraid to do it.

"Any ideas?" she asked again, waiting for a few more awkward seconds before turning away. "I thought as much," she huffed, scooting further away from me.

"I'm sorry," I finally blurted, after a few seconds of silence.

"About what?" she seethed, more purple sparks erupting from the top of her head.

"About getting so jealous."

"Do you think this is about you getting jealous?"

"Yeah," I answered confused. "My aura literally turned green with it. I had green sparks hopping between my fingertips. It was kind of creepy. Couldn't you see it?"

"No," she said, warming up a little. "For all I knew, you had indigestion. Look Mason, I actually appreciate that you were jealous... but that just confirms to me your insecurity. You don't understand my frustration."

"I probably don't, but you don't understand mine either. The thoughts of you spending so much time with a guy like Bradley drives me crazy."

"He drives me crazy, too," she frowned. "But he's the least of your problems. In fact, you should see Bradley as your best friend. He keeps all the other guys at bay. You should thank him for doing such a good job."

"I don't want you to marry a guy like Bradley," I said, "I was hoping you would want a guy who was a little friendlier. Someone more like me? Please, don't stay mad at me."

"This is not a fair fight," she frowned, drying her eyes with her gloves. "You can read me like a book, and all you have to do is flash those Santa Claus eyes at me and I'm beat. It's just as well, I guess, we have a party to plan tonight."

"That's true," I agreed, relieved that she was feeling better.

"Now we're all friends again," John said, "how do you want to get home? We can fly the shortest route to your house or we can go the long way around?"

"I'd like to be driven home with the car's tires on the ground like a normal person," she answered, snuggling into me. "Don't drive fast, just take your time."

"Whatever you want," John quipped. "Hitching up to a horse could get us there faster, but if you want wheels on the ground, we'll drive. Tally ho!"

The short ride to Julia's home was uneventful but still took us almost half an hour with the all the stoplights and annoying trucks on the road. And I now noticed the headlights of at least one car never seemed very far behind us even on the loneliest streets... Julia's security detail, keeping an eye out for her 24 hours a day. It was a good thing John always took us back to the same spot after traveling in time warp or her father would have been really suspicious. But for now, I was happy for the normal car ride, snuggling in the back seat with Julia was always a pleasure, even though John was obviously agitated at not being able to fly.

John was even more irritated at how long it took to get past Julia's security guards to park the car. Her Dad had just installed a state-of-the-art security system that surrounded the whole house, turning it into a guarded compound and his security staff were still getting used to the new protocols.

Julia's parents were out of town, so we had the whole house to ourselves, if you didn't count six security guards keeping a watch outside and security cameras monitoring our every move on the inside.

"So let's get started," Julia finally said, after getting changed into something more comfortable. "First of all, the majority of the funding for this year's event is coming from the Ebenezer Foundation. My Dad has been managing funds for this investment group for years, but this year they have liquidated the whole fund."

"Where has all the money gone?" I asked.

"Dad says it's gone to all kinds of charities: literacy programs in Central America, medical clinics in remote corners of Africa, and immunization projects in many countries throughout the world. Over a 100 million has already been distributed, and the last of those funds have been given to us."

"That's strange," I said. "How much did they give to us?"

"$130,000!" she gasped. "What's more, we have to spend every dime of it before Christmas Eve. I have to make a strict accounting for all the money, and prove it was all spent according to the mandate."

"How are we going to spend $130,000 on your little party?" John gulped. "Especially with all the other donations that have come in?"

"We can't," Julia admitted, little sparks flying from her head in frustration. "We're going to have to expand our Christmas giving to include three other parties and our Sub-For-Santa program as well. I'm getting tired just thinking about it."

"This will be great!" I said confidently, touching my nose with my finger and bringing us all into time-warp. "We can take all the time we need to prepare for it, and even take naps and relax along the way. We may only have 10 days to spend the money, but we can take all the time we need to prepare for it."

"You're right," she smiled, her temperament cooling down. "I never thought spending money would be such a difficult task."

"I may be able to help there," I comforted. "I'm already starting to get ideas for what we need to buy."

I was about to take us back into real time when something familiar and cold suddenly rushed through my chest. It was the same feeling I'd had in Dr. Rawlings class. I paused, trying to figure out what was happening when I saw a dark figure approaching, causing an overpowering metallic taste to fill my mouth as it grew nearer. The closer it got the more intense the sensation of sucking on rusty chains became.

Before I could gag, the metallic taste turned to dusty cloth, coating my throat and nose with fine, silty dust. To my horror the creature drew nearer, causing the taste of burial clothes to be replaced by the chalky grit of dry bones.

"What's going on?" Julia asked in alarm, seeing I was overwhelmed by something she couldn't understand.

"I don't know," I managed to wheeze, falling off my chair in disgust. "Give me something to drink, anything!"

Julia she raced to the kitchen while John tried to pick me off the floor. Even with his help I still couldn't control my legs, the unpleasant encounter leaving me too stunned to move. Suddenly something whispered in my ear, "Help me," it begged, "help me!"

I heard his pleas, but the taste of dry bones was so overpowering I couldn't imagine helping him.

"Go away," I demanded, gagging, coughing, and stricken with fear. "Leave me alone."

"Who are you talking too?" John asked, looking around frantically.

"Help me, please!" the phantom insisted. "Save me!"

"No," I gasped, repulsed by his presence, barely able to keep from puking. "Go away, go!"

"Hurry up, Julia!" John panicked, helping me to my knees. "He's being attacked by something."

"Leave me," I begged out loud, causing the intruder to let out a wail that made me collapse back on the floor.

"I'm doomed, I'm doomed," he cried, his face appearing before me in green misery. "Have mercy on a doomed soul!"

His face was wrapped in burial clothes, his eyes hollow and lifeless. Each time he moaned his face contorted in such painful agony, that I couldn't help but pity the tormented creature. His whole body was visible to me now as he turned away, placing his hands on his head in a gesture of complete resignation, wailing all the louder.

The horrible taste lessened as he moved away from me; instead of bone and burial cloth, all I tasted was metal chains. A horrible taste for sure, but one I could tolerate.

Another wail filled my ears, more horrible than the others as chains connected to heavy boxes lifted around his body. Unseen winds carried the heavy boxes up and slammed them into his pitiful frame, breaking one open and spilling out golden coins that once free acted like hornets, smashing and crashing into him.

"I'm doomed forever," he shrieked, turning away only to be smashed again by the heavy boxes. "I'm condemned to a relentless torture. He said you would help ... now I am lost!"

I don't know what moved me more, his pathetic weeping or the sight of his treasure crashing into him.

"I'll help!" I finally agreed, surprising even myself.

The phantom spun around and looked at me in shock, as if my approval wasn't even a possibility. His momentary pause gave the boxes the freedom to pull him helplessly around the room with the coins pelting him like stones. In a final shrieking, moaning motion, the ghost was blown from my sight, freeing me from my own torment and finally allowing me to breathe.

The encounter was very quick, but it seemed to last forever. By the time Julia handed me a bottle of orange soda the visitor was already gone.

"Are you alright?" John questioned, still trying to help me off the ground.

I didn't have the energy to reply. I took the drink and guzzled half of it down in a single breath.

"What was that all about?" Julia pleaded, helping me crawl on a couch. "Who were you talking to?"

"A ghost," I panted, my eyes still watering. "I was attacked, no, that's not the right word. What is it called when someone begs you to do something you don't want to do?"

"High school," John laughed.

"Yeah, well this was worse than that," I groaned, "I haven't had anything so painful happen to me since little Susan sat on my lap four Christmases ago."

"What do you mean by that?" Julia asked.

"I mean, when he touched me, my mouth was filled with the taste of rusty chains, burial clothes, and dry gritty bones. It was like breathing in a mummy!"

"That sounds disgusting!"

"You got that right," I agreed, taking another drink. "It was horrible. As painful as my torture was, when he asked for help I could see he was actually suffering more than I was."

"Why was he asking you for help?" Julia asked, puzzled. "What did he want you to do?"

"I don't know... he didn't say. He just begged to be saved from a relentless torture. I don't know how to describe it any better."

"You keep talking about this thing as a person," John said, looking around the room. "I was right here and I didn't see anybody. Could this have something to do with the ghost you talked about earlier today?"

"It might," I admitted. "He did seem familiar to me."

"You mean you think you've had contact with this ghost before?" Julia begged. "Why didn't you tell me?"

"I didn't think it was important," I admitted. "Anyway, I didn't think he would follow me like a poltergeist."

"You were talking to him," Julia said. "Could you see him? What did he want?"

"I couldn't see him at first, but I could feel him and hear him. He simply begged for my help."

"And you agreed, naturally," John frowned.

"No. I was so disgusted I pushed him away, but as he left, his sorrow was so intense I changed my mind."

"So you did agree to help him," Julia said.

"Yeah, I guess I did."

"You're the one with the magic," John shrugged. "What do you have to do now?"

"I don't know," I answered, "but whatever it is, it will be darker and creepier than anything we've done before."

"I like the sound of that," John smiled. "I'm always up for an adventure!"

I was weak for the rest of the night, even in time-warp. We had a good meeting though and managed to plan for three additional parties just like the one Julia had already planned for in Moses Lake. Spending that much money would be a challenge, but what else could we do? My heart was filled with excitement and doom, all at the same time. Christmas is certainly a time of mystery, and not always an easy one to bear.

The Diamond Necklace

Being part of the Santa Claus League is awesome. I get special insights into children's needs even before they sit on my lap. Using that insight, we started buying gifts that very next day with a shopping spree at Wal-Mart, (where else). As I walked down the aisles, the toys we needed to buy glowed and shimmered in front of me. I couldn't see the actual children in my mind, but I could sense their auras whispering to me.

That morning, we bought at least $1,500's worth of dolls alone. Next came bicycles and skateboards, roller skates, and soccer balls. Julia asked the store manager to assign several clerks to pack everything up for us and ship it to her house. When he saw how much money we were spending he quickly obliged.

Buying for children you haven't met is done by pure Christmas magic. Sometimes the gift makes perfect sense, like a clock radio, or a princess costume, but other times it made no sense at all. Who would want a 100-foot roll of rope... or a microscope?

We walked out of Wal-Mart having spent $35,000—at least $20,000 at a sporting goods store and another $10K at a local teen clothing outlet over the next few days. The rest of the money went all kinds of weird places. We bought fish and aquariums, kitten and puppy supplies; pots and pans, Easy Bake ovens, and all kinds of kitchen knick-knacks and odds and ends. We bought out a computer department— all its laptops and smart pads. I didn't buy any tarantula matting but I did feel inspired to get a horse blanket and new horse shoes.

It was the day before Julia's party and we still had $8,000 and change to spend. For some strange reason I felt a need to spend it at an expensive jewelry store. When we walked into Miller's Jewelry store I saw a diamond necklace glimmering with a magic glow. As I got nearer, I saw a single two-carat stone skillfully crafted in a snowflake setting with smaller diamonds surrounding it. The chain that held it was 18-carat gold and seemed to have electricity flowing around it, feeding the diamond with power. The combination of chain and stone sent rainbows of light dancing all over the room. I pointed at the necklace and smiled.

"We can't buy that!" Julia objected. "It's over $8,000!"

"We have to," I insisted.

"How will I be able to justify a diamond necklace to the foundation?" she stammered.

"I don't know, but that necklace belongs to some child. If we don't get it for her, we'll have failed completely."

"You know best," she said quietly after several silent moments. "I trust you."

"Thanks," I said kindly, trying to defuse the tension. "This isn't my idea, I promise. When I walk past something important, it jumps out at me and all I have to do is put it into my shopping cart. Someone or something is directing this money, and I don't know who it is. I've never felt such a powerful influence before. I can't wait to see how all of this turns out."

"Do you think it has anything to do with the weird experience you had a few nights ago?"

"Maybe," I admitted. "I don't know how though. I haven't felt him around at all. But I've got a mint in my pocket and a bottle of orange soda close by, just in case he does come back."

When the necklace was purchased, Julia checked her bank balance and saw that only $3.35 remained in the account. "That should be good enough," She said happily. I'm sure $3.35 won't matter."

"I don't know about that," I countered, feeling instantly uneasy. "We had better spend every penny."

I carefully walked around the store looking at earrings and inexpensive bracelets. I didn't know what Julia was doing but I supposed she was doing the same thing. Suddenly a dainty little bracelet glowed like a lightning bug over in a faraway counter. I picked it out and gave it to Todd, the owner of the store to ring up.

"That will be $23.35," Todd said.

"All that's left in the account is $3.35," Julia said confused, handing him the credit card.

"I know," I said, placing a crisp twenty-dollar bill on the counter. "We were told we had to spend every dime, but we weren't told we couldn't spend a little of our own money as well."

As we walked down the jewelry aisle, I noticed Julia glancing intently at a sparkling diamond ring. The one she looked at popped out at me too, almost as dramatically as the diamond bracelet. This ring wasn't for a needy child... I could tell that. It was for a more mature finger, a finger I instinctively wanted to place it on. I had never felt so certain about anything in my life. I was about to stop and casually look at it with Julia, but I chickened out instead, and we walked out the door together.

As we walked to the car, I should have felt energized and elated, after all, we had just spent all our money, but the very opposite was true. Somehow not stopping at the ring counter took all the energy out of the conversation.

"Why are you so afraid of commitment?" she asked casually, as if she knew I had blown my opportunity to go ring shopping with her.

"I'm not afraid of commitment," I insisted, getting into her car. "I just want to be ready when we get married. I don't want to let you down."

"That's very logical of you," she said coolly, her countenance becoming an icy blue. "But it might take more than logic to keep me around."

"I'd die if I lost you," I argued. "You have to marry me. Not right now, but soon."

"Why not now?" she frowned, pushing me away. "It's the way you keep pushing everything into the future that frustrates me. What are you afraid of?"

"Fine, fine, I'll tell you," I blurted. "I'm afraid of asking your dad for permission to marry you. He scares me, I admit it. But to be honest, the thought of losing you is worse. Being away from you this last year has been pure misery, and our time together this week has been like heaven, in fact, I couldn't imagine a heaven without you."

"Those are the kind of words I want to hear," she said, warming up to me. "Some girls would even take that as a proposal, but I want a proper proposal, complete with a ring, and yes, I'm sorry to say, my father's approval .... That was a marriage proposal, wasn't it?"

"A marriage proposal?" I chided, kissing her approvingly. "What are you talking about? I don't have a ring or your father's approval. I promise you this though, when I propose to you, it will be something you will never forget!"

"I'll believe it when I see it," she sighed. "But keep promising me you will, I like the way it sounds."

The next few days we were too busy to think about anything more romantic than chocolate. The three of us slipped outside of time more than once just to take a nap, only to wake up and work again. I was tired, and overworked, but with Julia by my side and John as my best friend, I was having the time of my life. I was only now realizing how important she had become to me. Somehow that realization changed everything.

The Mysterious Coin

The Christmas parties started three days before Christmas with Julia's yearly party in Moses Lake scheduled for Monday. The next party came a day later in Kennewick, 84 miles away. Wednesday was Christmas Eve, and it was another doozy of a day with a final Christmas Eve party in Ephrata, just a few miles away from Moses Lake.

All-in-all, we had four parties planned one on top of another.

Julia was a master party planner and she organized her many friends into an army of social media marketers. The Twittersphere exploded with excited tweets about the importance of helping children during the holidays, and Facebook friends blasted their thousands of accounts with times and dates for the upcoming parties. Bloggers blogged, and Pinsters pinned, and how they got videos posted on YouTube on such short notice, I'll never know. By the time the day of the parties came we had plenty of eager parents and anxious children wanting to attend.

Julia's party was always my favorite. Not only did it have great memories, but my Mom and Dad were in the audience this time around, chaperoning my two younger sisters. I haven't talked about them yet. My Mom and Dad are old, but cool, and still married after 25 years. I am the oldest kid in the family and have had to suffer through two younger sisters who steal my socks, wear my t-shirts and bug me to death. I guess all of that is normal though, so I can't really complain.

Somewhere between my freshmen and senior year of college my kid sisters grew up. Sage, turned 17 and insisted she was too old to sit on Santa's lap, but my youngest sister, Myia, was only 13. Luckily she heard Santa gave out good stuff so she was still enthusiastic about the whole institution. I was looking forward to seeing both of them that night.

John helped me carry in the wooden box that held my Santa Claus suit. The box was infused with just as much magic as I was and no one but me could open it. It was indestructible as well, even to fire, and decorated with carvings of ivy, elves, and a flying sleigh, that even took flight on occasion. However, as wonderful as it was to me, it didn't like John very much.

"Do you want to try to open the box again this year?" I teased, begging John to try.

"Not this year, dude," he grimaced. "I like my eyebrows un-singed thank you very much."

"Come on, John," I taunted, opening up the box an inch. "It's as easy as this."

"Yeah, right," he frowned, "then comes thunderbolts."

I lifted it up and down with my finger one last time, beckoning him to try. I don't know why he fell for it again, but the minute he put his finger on the lid to lift it up, a blue electric bolt surrounded him, leaving him nearly paralyzed.

"I hate you," he groaned, writhing in pain. "I really hate you!"

"Oh man, sorry about that," I laughed. "I always forget how painful that is for you."

"The next time we go hypersonic; I'm pushing you out the door. See how you like that!"

"Wow," I smiled, helping him up and dusting off his clothes. "Quite the Christmas spirit there!"

I opened the box easily and immediately smelled wild midnight air moving through me. The smell of pine needles and fresh peeled oranges swept past my senses, filling me with hope. Next came deep rich chocolate, one of my favorite smells of all! The suit never smelled of mothballs even though inside the box, the suit was perfectly preserved and regenerated. No matter how many children burped up on me, or how many kids with cigarette-soaked clothing whispered in my ear, it was always fresh.

The fabric of the suit was dark rich red velvet, the lapel and hem brilliant white rabbit fur. The hat was made of the same material, while the beard and wig seemed to be made of actual human hair, although it never aged or got dirty. It was a classic Santa Claus suit in every respect, complete with gold buttons, black belt and polished black boots.

When I had the whole suit on, I donned my white gloves and reached for my strap of silver sleigh bells. The sound of the bells always made me happy, especially the first time I ring them for the season. The minute I picked them up I started laughing.

"Keep it down, Santa," John warned. "It's not your turn yet. Julia is leading everyone in Christmas carols."

"Sorry," I blurted. "Sometimes I can't help myself."

"Think about something else then," he ordered, taking the bells from me and muting the, "that always works for me."

I took his advice and concentrated on taking the gold watch from its drawer and fastening it on the suit. I was still chuckling a bit, but not too bad. I was about to close the lid when something silver caught my attention, stuck in the bottom of the box.

"What's that?" I asked, still trying not to laugh.

"Another trick?" John mused.

"I'm not joking," I said finally serious. "There's something shiny in the bottom of my chest."

John took a chance and peeked into the box. His doubtful expression changed when he noticed the silver object as well. "It looks like a coin, but I'm not putting my hand into that electric fuse box. See if you can pull it out."

Doing what he said, I reached down and slid the object from under the wig drawer, and pulled it out. It was a coin. I turned it over and over in my fingers. It was dated 1778 and, even though I couldn't make out the name on the head side, it looked like King George III of England. Since we went to war against him, he's the only king I could identify in a police lineup.

"That looks like an English shilling," John stated, begging to hold it with his body language.

"It's really worn," I added, handing it to him. "What do you think it's worth?"

"Twelve pence," Julia answered, poking her head into the storage room. "Where did you get that?"

"It was in my box," I said. "I've opened it a hundred times, so I don't know why I didn't find it before."

"It's a magic chest," Julia smiled. "Who knows what might end up in there from time to time. You should hold on to it. It might bring you luck."

34

"You're right, I think I will," I answered, sliding the coin into my pocket.

I was concentrating on the coin and hadn't looked up to see Julia, but the moment I did, I gasped.

"Is anything wrong?" she said daintily, checking out her dress and spinning around to make sure everything was in place.

"Are you kidding?" I answered. "You would shame an angel if one came down to say hello. You look stunning."

She was dressed in a white chiffon dress with a fur shawl that hung off her shoulders. Her white high heels lifted her into the clouds and I wasn't sure I even wanted her to come down. Her hair was piled up high on her head in an elegant bun, with diamonds sparkling in her hairpiece. How could such an exalted creature ever want me?

"Oh, thanks," she said shyly. "I didn't get the chance to buy anything new. I think I wore this on that first Christmas party where we first really met. But hey, you look just as amazing tonight, Mason. In fact, I wonder sometimes if you trade places with St. Nicholas at times like these. You're still Mason Howell under all that wonderfulness aren't you?"

"In the flesh," I boasted, trying to pull her near for a kiss.

"Not now," she insisted, slapping my hands away from her dainty waist, "we have a hundred children ready to sit on Santa's lap. Are you ready?"

"Just keep the hot chocolate coming," I insisted, feeling hot cinnamon on my tongue just from her touch. "You know how it is out there sometimes…"

"So I've heard," she beamed. "Let's get ready for party number one."

When I walked down the hall the silver bells jingled with each footstep. The music of the bells caused my legs to move uncontrollably and I began dancing to their merry tune as a laugh built up inside my chest… I couldn't hold it in.

"Get him in there quick," John warned. "He's on fire tonight."

It was a good thing they opened the door when they did, because a rowdy, joyous laugh belted out of me, surprising even myself. The children's auras burst into flame with excitement.

"Merry Christmas!" I sang, waving my hands at all the children and laughing again. One little boy in the middle of the room was jumping up and down, lighting a round of fireworks each time he hit the ground. Julia and her social networking crew had done their job; these kids were excited.

As if on cue, the whole room of children leapt from their seats and lined up in an orderly fashion, one excited child after another. Anxious parents of older children remained in their seats while the parents of younger ones stood in line with their wiggly children.

The first child practically dove onto my lap. At her touch my mouth filled with peppermint and gummy bears. She was so full of energy; her dreams were easy to see. She wanted to help everyone and everything.

"What do you want for Christmas?" I asked, trying hard to talk with the taste of gummy bears stuck in my mouth.

"I want a horse, and a dog and a firefighting helmet," she said eagerly.

I thought for a moment I had failed her, but a vision of her future life on a farm burst into my mind. I reached down and found a wrapped gift with a horse blanket, a set of horseshoes and a firefighter doll inside, instinctively knowing she would love it.

The second little girl was just as eager. She smelled and tasted like buttered popcorn and thin mints. "I want to be a movie star when I grow up!" she said convincingly.

"So what do you want for Christmas to help you become a movie star?" I asked gently, while a vision of a costume formed in my mind.

"I want a princess dress!" she sang, jumping off my lap and twirling around in the space in front of me.

"Of course you do!" I agreed, pulling out a package with a princess dress tucked inside. "Merry Christmas!"

"Thank you Santa Claus," she said politely, giving me her finest princess curtsy.

And so it went, child after child. I never get tired of their enthusiasm and zest for life and loved spending time with each and every one of them. Even the teenagers who had the courage

36

to come sit on my lap were fun to meet. One shy teenager turned out to be Sage, my own 17-year-old sister.

Sage had snuck in line with Myia, and jumped on my lap before Myia could get there.

"Sage!" Myia complained. "I was there first, wait your turn."

"I love you," Sage laughed, blowing her a kiss.

"What would you like for Christmas this year?" I asked, pretending not to hear their playful bickering.

"I want a porcelain doll," she asked confidently, then looked down sheepishly. "I've always wanted one. I know I said I was too old to sit on Santa's lap, but you're so cute, I couldn't help myself."

"You're pathetic," I laughed, ringing my silver bells, which made me laugh even more.

"You're making fun of me aren't you?" she said, getting embarrassed.

"Not at all," I comforted, pulling out a wrapped present from my magic bag. Inside I knew was an elegant porcelain doll dressed in a dainty white dress with a sparkling crystal crown. I loved it the moment I saw it and secretly thrilled she got to have it. "I just wanted you to get the full Santa Claus experience. Thanks for trusting me, Sage, I love you."

"I love you too, Santa," she said, tearing up just a little.

"I love you too," Myia almost yelled. "Get a move on, it's my turn."

I love sisters. They laugh with you one moment, and step on your fingers the next. Myia shoved Sage off my lap and leapt in her place, giving me a great big kiss on the cheek.

"Wow, you smell good," she said surprised, tugging at my beard and inspecting my suit. "You are very convincing. Are you really Santa Claus? What did you do to my brother?"

"I am Santa Claus," I confided. "Now what do you want for Christmas?"

"I'm going to test your Santa Claus powers," she teased. "I know what I want for Christmas, but I want you to guess it. If you can give me the correct present, I'll know you're real."

"Fair enough," I said.

Figuring out Myia was about as tough as figuring out a math problem with two numbers and a plus sign. She had fish pictures plastered all over her room. Most children smelled of candy and sugary stuff, but Myia smelled of salty ocean breezes and stormy seas. Going off the hunch, I reached back and pulled out a bucket filled with nine salt water fish and a full aquarium.

"I'm sorry I didn't wrap the fish," I apologized. "It's really hard to gift wrap water bags."

"I can't believe it!" she said stunned. "You really are Santa Claus. I'm sorry for all the socks I ever stole from your sock drawer, just to tick you off. I'm sorry I hid your favorite t-shirt just to make you mad. I promise to be good, I really do."

"Just do your best," I whispered. "See you tomorrow, you little rascal."

"He's Santa Claus," she insisted to the other children still in line as she walked away from my chair. "You all better be good, because he knows everything!"

The next person on my lap was an overweight boy, named Bobby Johnson, who didn't dare even think what he wanted for Christmas.

"You can get me anything," he said shyly.

"You only get what you want," I reminded him. "Life doesn't give you anything that you aren't willing to imagine first."

Bobby wasn't unintelligent, or unable to dream, he was afraid to dream. He didn't want to get his hopes up for anything, because he was afraid what his friends might think if he failed. He was heavy for his age, and didn't want to be made fun of.

"I want a rappelling rope," he finally whispered timidly, a light beginning to burn within him. "I have all the other hardware, but I don't have the rope. But you don't have to give that to me, I'll be happy with anything."

"Don't say that," I cautioned. "A dream can only come true if you acknowledge it, believe in it, and don't betray it. Do you want the rope or not?"

"I definitely want it," he said with confidence.

"Good," I answered just as firmly, handing him a large round bulky package. "Because wrapping this thing was murder. Merry Christmas!"

"You have to be kidding me!" he exploded, his aura catching fire with fireworks shooting from his chest. "I simply can't believe it. You really are Santa Claus. My little sister said you were, but I didn't believe it. Merry Christmas, Santa. Thank you so much!"

Julia kept the hot chocolate flowing. Hot chocolate was the only thing that kept my mouth from going numb with all the varied sweet and sour tastes I had to deal with. I had a few sour children sit on my lap, but I was able to cheer them up before they left. I memorized a few addresses of some children I knew we would have to visit on Christmas Eve for a special Sub-for-Santa run. As their families were struggling and needed help. That was the case for the last little nine-year-old boy in line.

That last child at Julia's Christmas Charity Event didn't even show up until all the other children had left. I was concerned because I had a single present left in my magic bag, and no child to give it to, until he poked his head around the door.

"Come on in," I said cheerfully. "This last present must be for you!"

"My dad hates Christmas," he said shyly, not budging from the door.

"Do you hate Christmas?" I asked curiously.

"Nah, I like it, but I'm not allowed to take presents from strangers," he said shyly

"Do I look like a stranger?" I laughed, ringing my bells. "I bet you've seen Julia Martin around and John Patten as well. Mrs. Smith is helping us tonight, and she is one of the lunch ladies at your grade school, I bet you know her."

"I guess so," he said timidly. "Do you still have any presents left?"

"You bet I do," I boasted. "I think one even has your name on it."

"No, it doesn't," he frowned. "You don't know my name."

"Yes, I do," I insisted. "Julia get me a marker, I don't want Ashton Chilton to think I'm a liar."

"To Ashton Chilton, of 4017 Dusty Street, Moses Lake, Washington," I wrote in broad black pen strokes. I wrote his

The Mysterious Coin

address down in a little notebook in preparations for a secret visit on Christmas Eve. "See, it has your name on it, you have to take it now."

"Well, what is it?" he asked, still hiding behind the door.

"I can't tell you," I said. "It's a gift. You have to come sit on my lap and ask for something."

"All right," he said, coming out of the shadows and into the hall the smell of neglect filling the whole room as he got closer. Dust and cobwebs swept into my nose, forcing me to take a sip of hot chocolate to restore my ability to talk. He sat on my lap and I patted him on the back, half expecting a dust cloud to come off of him, but it didn't.

"What would you like for Christmas?" I asked kindly.

"I wish I could have a microscope," he said sadly, "but I know how expensive those things are. My dad could never get me one."

"You must like science?" I asked. "You do look rather scholarly."

"Oh yeah," he said, his whole face lighting up with joy. "I love science. I love chemistry and biology and all kinds of stuff like that. I'm going to be a scientist when I grow up. At least I could be a scientist, if I ever got a microscope."

I could see his dreams crashing back down upon themselves making him instantly the same barren, dusty boy.

"But you could be a scientist?" I encouraged him, "If you had a microscope."

"I really could," he smiled. "My grandma says I'm smart like my grandpa with science stuff."

"Well you're in luck then," I smiled, handing him the gift. "Because this present is awfully heavy."

Little Ashton Chilton grabbed the wrapped box and nearly ripped the cardboard off with the paper.

"It's true!" he cried, pulling out the microscope from the box. "I can be a scientist!"

"You certainly can," I assured him, seeing a bright future fill my mind with diplomas, and job offers, and laboratories with his name on the desk.

"Thank you so much," he said, tears welling up in his eyes. "I promise to be good, I promise to study hard."

40

"I know you will," I said, and I meant it.

The moment little Ashton left with his present, I heard the loud ringing of a coin dropping on the ground. I looked around the hall, but couldn't see anyone, or anything, so I forgot all about it.

With Ashton gone the only thing left to do was clean up and go home. The next 20 minutes were spent changing back into my street clothes while John, Julia, and Mrs. Smith, along with a few other volunteers cleaned up all the punch and cookies, putting away the chairs and sweeping the floors. As I was walking into the cultural hall, Mrs. Smith met me with a cheerful smile.

"I don't know how you do it," she said, while emptying the dust pan into a trash can. "I saw your Grandpa in action when my kids were little, and I can't tell the difference between the two of you. You look, act and talk just like him. I am truly amazed."

"That means a lot to me," I admitted, "I never got to meet him."

"Just look in the mirror," she said happily. "Dressed in his suit you look like the same man... and I know a good man when I see one!" she said loudly, so Julia would overhear our conversation. "This one's a keeper."

"You don't have to say that so loud," Julia complained. "I don't want any other girl to hear you brag him up. I've already got first dibs, ya know."

"It's a good thing you do," she warned. "I have some beautiful granddaughters in Spokane, I'd love to invite them over and steal him from you."

"You wicked woman," Julia teased. "Mason, I forbid you to meet her granddaughters."

"Does anyone know where this table goes?" I asked, trying to change the subject.

I avoided the subject on the outside but inside I was measuring how much our relationship had changed. It wasn't the same as it was even a few months earlier. Julia was always on my mind, not in a consuming or an unhealthy stalking kind of way, but more of a comfortable way. If I heard a funny story, I wanted to tell her first. If something tragic happened, I wanted to comfort her. She was becoming the center of my universe, and I liked it. And now I knew she felt the same way about me, too. If only her father was so easy to convince.

"I love you," I said softly for the first time as we pulled up to her heavily guarded home.

"Of course you do," she answered sweetly. "I love you too. Is there anything else you want to add to that?"

"Just one thing," I replied. ""How exactly do I arrange a meeting with your father? He's protected behind a 10-foot electric fence!"

"He'll be home from Sweden in the morning," she cooed, proud that I had the courage to talk to him. "Just call me, and I'll put you through."

"Sweet dreams," I said, just as John was about to drive into her compound.

"Don't bother pulling in," she called, opening the door and dancing out of the car. "It'll mess with Dad's new super security system. I can get myself in the house. See you tomorrow."

Julia ran toward the house, stocking footed, and disappeared behind the security wall.

"Dude, don't screw this up," John warned as we drove away, then taking flight in the secret of the night. "We're a team, remember? I'm your engineer, your Rudolph. But every Santa has to have his Mrs. Claus. If you don't ask Julia to marry you, she'll walk, and break up the team!"

"I'm glad you're worried about the team; I'm just worried about whether she'll be able to accept my proposal. I can get the ring, no problem, but getting her father's approval might take a letter of recommendation from Warren Buffett. I may even have to be a stockholder, who knows? And, what if he says no?"

"Then you ask him again," he insisted. "And if he keeps saying no, maybe you should steal her away and elope. Look, she's your Mrs. Claus, end of story, done deal. Stop making this so dang hard. Just do it."

"Yeah, you're probably right," I said in a daze, practically falling out of the car as he landed. "So, I'll see you around noon tomorrow for the next party. Could you keep my

Santa suit safe for me? I don't want to lug the box into my house tonight. You can go ahead and open it if you want to, no harm in that, right?"

"Nice try, but no!" John barked. "I'll pick you up tomorrow at noon."

I stood like a pillar for several minutes, going over all the terrible complications of getting married to a billionaire's daughter, when suddenly a warm thought came to my mind. Actually, it wasn't even a thought, it was more like a memory. In that moment I remembered how wonderful her kisses were... all my fears vanished. Her warmth, her charm, her grace, danced in my mind, dispelling all doubt and apprehension. The words of an obscure Christmas song rang in my ears, *I see Christmas carolers, looking more like lovers, makes me wonder where you are?*

I knew who my true love was, and where she was, and like a lightning bolt, I knew what I wanted for Christmas that year. I also knew I had to follow my own council to Bobby Johnson: a dream can only come true if you acknowledge it, believe in it, and don't betray it. I stopped walking and ran down the street to the front door of my house. I had to get to bed... I had a ring to buy in the morning.

Chapter Six

The Unexpected Haunting

The next morning, I jumped out of bed before my two sisters, with a renewed determination to secure my future. The jewelry store wouldn't open up for another two hours so I had time for breakfast. When I got downstairs Mom and Dad were already making pancakes; they noticed my enthusiasm when I asked them if I could borrow the car.

"Do you still know how to drive?" Dad kidded, handing me the keys. "I notice John does most of the driving these days."

"Yeah, well, his car has certain advantages other cars can't offer," I responded without going into too much detail.

"I can imagine," he winked, putting a finger up to his mouth.

"I remember my dad's perfectly maintained 1945 Mercury Coup," my mother reminisced. "We took more vacations in that old car than I can recall. The amazing thing was, I don't remember any unpleasant long drives. We started driving and before I knew it we were there."

"I wonder how that ever happened?" I said with a wink. "Growing up with Grandpa Adams must have been fun."

"Grandpa Adams didn't miss a thing," she smiled, almost starting to cry. "He made it to every softball game, every piano recital, and dance concert. I didn't think he even had a job, but of course he insisted he did."

"Where did he work?" I asked curiously.

"A lot of odd jobs," she said longingly. "He didn't even get married until he was in his forties. My mother married him when she was well into her thirties. I miss them both every day."

"How did they die?" I asked timidly. The details of her parent's death was never talked about in our family.

"No one knows," she said sadly, "but by the look of the crash site, it must have been horrible. The police couldn't understand how a car could make a crater in a cornfield 10 feet

44

deep. The only thing not twisted into little pieces of rubble was Grandpa's Santa Claus Box."

"Stranger still," she continued. "Mom and Dad, along with their best friend Alex Morris were dead, lying peacefully side by side not far away. I've never cried so hard in my whole life. I was only 18 when they died... I don't think I smiled a single time until I met your father. He saved me."

"It was you who saved me," my Dad insisted, giving her a warm embrace. "I would have been as old as your Dad when I got married if you didn't rescue me from bachelorhood."

"You're sweet, dear," she said, wiping away her tears. "Do I hear wedding bells in the near future with you and Julia?"

"Maybe," I stammered, "but, why do you think we're close to getting married?"

"I'd have to be blind not to see that," she grinned, placing a stack of pancakes on my plate, and pushing the syrup closer to me.

"I would have asked a woman like her to marry me after the first week of dating!" my Dad boasted.

"You would have," I joked. "You and mom dated for what, two weeks and then got engaged?"

"Two weeks was all it took," he said proudly, flipping another pancake. "I know a good thing when I see it!"

"And I was worried that you and Mom would be concerned that I was getting married to young."

"Your Mom might, but not me. I may have been 25 when I got married, son, but I would have tied the knot when I was 18 if I found your mother then. Of course, she would have only been 14 at the time, so my proposal would have been kind of awkward, but I still would have tried."

"What about you, Mom?"

"Under the circumstances, it might be a good thing," she answered carefully. "You've been dating her for a long time. Just give me at least six months' notice to get ready for the reception, that's all I ask."

"Man, am I a dope," I said, hitting my head with my hand. "In some ways I've been holding off just to please you two."

"You are a dope," she confirmed. "And now it's time to make your own decisions, away from home. 22 is young, but plenty old to start a life with someone as fantastic as Julia. And talking about a life coming together, you got your grades in the mail yesterday."

"Sweet," I said, taking the letter from her and opening it up.

"How did you do?" she asked.

"Really good," I answered after studying out the results and handing her the paper. "I'm happy with everything."

"Wow, you did terrific," she said. "All A's except for a C- in Macroeconomics. What happened there? I thought you liked economics."

"I love economics," I answered. "But a C- out of Dr. Rawlings class is as good as an A+ in my book. Thank goodness for the curve. Dr. Rawlings had it out for me right from the start. I feel really good right now. I thought I'd fail for sure."

"I'm glad things are going so well for you," my father added. "Todd Harman says you and Julia stopped into his jewelry store a few days ago. He was sure you were there to pick out engagement rings. He was surprised when you picked out a necklace instead."

"We were Christmas shopping," I answered, "picking out gifts for our Christmas parties."

"No problem," he said, pausing before placing more pancakes on the platter. "He also said she spent a lot of time looking at a particular diamond engagement set when you weren't looking. He has an eye for that kind of thing. His store is open a few hours early this morning, if that makes any difference to you. He said something about doing an inventory, but he's open for business right now if you want to stop by?"

My hunger for pancakes evaporated into thin air. I dropped my fork, took a drink of milk to wash down what I'd eaten, and rushed out the door.

"You can thank me later, son," he yelled just before the garage door slammed shut behind me.

I wanted to thank both of them, but I had urgent business to attend to. Dad was right. I was a little rusty at driving, but I managed to make it to Miller's Jewelry store without hitting anyone, even with fresh snow on the ground. Just as I approached the front door of the store, I noticed it was just swinging shut with footprints in the snow heading away from the store in the other direction. I looked around, but I didn't see anyone there. Forgetting about the footprints, I ran to the ring counter, scanning for the ring that would make me her hero.

"It's not there," Mr. Harman said sadly, noticing the blank spot where I was staring. "I opened my store early today just for you, but someone else came in and bought it just moments ago. I'm sorry. I can't order another one either, it was a one-of-a-kind design."

If a grown man could cry in public, I would have. The long elegant shape of the marquee stone and the beauty of the setting was engrained in my mind like a photograph, but it was too late. Someone else had bought my treasure.

"I have lots of other unique rings, Mason," he said hopefully. "I'm sure you can find something else she will love just as much."

"Thanks Mr. Harmon," I said sincerely. "I'll come back with Julia after Christmas, and we can pick something out together. Thanks for opening the store early though."

I walked out as dejected as any man could be. I sulked around for a few minutes, but suddenly got my courage back. I may have lost the ring, but I wasn't going to lose the girl. Hope filled me again and I pulled out my cell phone to talk to Mr. Martin.

"Hello, Julia," I said eagerly. "Could I talk to your father?"

"Hey, Mason," she responded happily. "Are you serious?"

"As the grave," I boasted. "I know he's busy, so I only want to set up a time to talk to him face-to-face. But this is a first step."

"Sure, let me get him."

Several minutes passed, and I prepared myself to talk to the CEO of one of the most successful Venture Capital Private Equity firms in the world. The longer the delay, the more my doubts had a chance to creep in. After about 15 minutes, I was ready to hang up and run away, but then—

"Hello, this is Mr. Martin, how may I help you?" her father said sharply.

"Hello Mr. Martin, this is Mason Howell. I'm one of Julia's friends... I mean, I'm Julia's boyfriend."

"Yes, yes, I know all of that," he said impatiently. "I have a deal going down right now for half the oil fields in Montana, what do you need?"

"Sorry to disturb you," I gulped, "I just wanted to set up a time when we could talk about an important matter."

The phone went dead, and stayed silent for at least a minute. "Christmas day, 11:00 am," he blurted, breaking the emptiness, and freezing the conversation all at the same time. "I'm heading out of the country that evening. But before we meet, I want you to consider a few things very carefully. I think you're a fine boy, but not ready to marry anyone, let alone my daughter. I didn't raise her with every advantage just to have her marry some local country bumpkin."

"Daddy," Julia yelled from the background, "what are you doing?"

"Being honest," he shot back. "Now let me finish this conversation, Julia. If you think he's man enough to marry you, then he'll be man enough to hear me out."

The sound on the phone became loud again, directed at me. "Do you understand, Mason? And one more thing, if you try to steal her away from me, you get nothing. No car, no money, no job or special privileges. She'll be disinherited; stricken from my will. The dog will inherit more at my death than she will. I suggest you do us all a favor, and leave her alone. Have I made myself clear?"

"Yes, sir," I said haltingly, but standing my ground. "I'll see you at 11:00 am on Christmas day."

"Think carefully," he warned, then hung up.

Julia didn't call me back and I didn't call her either. I was too shocked. I drove home in a complete fog, not knowing what to do. Maybe he was right, maybe I should just walk away from the whole thing?

By the time I got home my little sister Myia was up, and eating pancakes enthusiastically.

"Are you going to marry Julia?" she teased.

"I hope so," I answered, still reeling from her father's angry response. "That is, if she'll have me, after what happened a few minutes ago, I don't know what will happen."

"What do you mean?" she asked innocently.

"I mean, her dad almost stabbed me through the phone when I asked for an appointment to talk to him. He hates me. I don't think Julia will want to marry me after all of that."

"Are you kidding?" she blurted. "You're Santa Claus! All my girlfriends want to marry you. Every girl in school wants to marry you, even the cool eighth graders. You're all anyone wants to talk about."

"You're so funny," I laughed, feeling peace come over me again. "Did you like what Santa Claus got you at the party last night?"

"I sure did," she beamed, pointing at the aquarium bubbling cheerfully close by. "I love fish! I've named them, too. This is Dasher, this is Dancer, and here is Prancer and Vixon, they look alike. The white one is Comet, and the red one is Cupid, and the two striped ones are Donner and Blitzen."

"What about that ugly one sucking up all the gunk off the glass in the corner?"

"Oh, that's Rudolph," she beamed. "He's the most important fish of them all. Without him the whole place would get ugly and gross."

"Engineers and inventors do keep the world going don't they?"

"Huh?" she asked confused. "I'm talking about fish! What are you talking about?"

"Rudolph," I answered. "All the other reindeer laughed and called him names, didn't they? Sometimes you have to stand up for what you believe in, right Myia?"

"Sure," the 13-year-old said apprehensively; then... "No wonder her Dad thinks you're crazy!"

"Thanks for the vote of confidence," I laughed, pulling a fresh plate of pancakes near me. "Please pass the syrup?"

I spent the rest of the morning eating and playing games with my sisters. Mom and Dad joined in, and we laughed, and sang Christmas songs while Sage played the piano. Living with a family isn't always easy, but that morning was perfect, just what I needed.

John picked me up at noon and we headed to Julia's place to pick her up. Her father didn't come out to meet me but his presence was... it felt like a wet towel on a fire. Julia pretended not to be upset, but her grey aurora said otherwise. I couldn't be fooled by her pretended smiles and she knew it.

We dove into the task at hand and that helped our moods brightened up considerably. The transformation reminded me of a song by The Caroleers I learned in grade school.

It's the day before the night before Christmas and I'm busy,

busy, busy being good.

On the day before the night before Christmas, going to do

everything a good boy should.

Silly I know, but being actively engaged in a good cause made it easier for me to get control of my fears and become happy again. The activity even helped Julia's darkened aurora brighten up to its normal sparkling brilliance.

Once I donned my Santa Claus suit nothing could get me down. I was in the zone. The suit acted like it was made of Teflon the way it repelled dirt and sticky hands. No matter how many drooling babies or soggy toddlers wiped their dirty hands on it, nothing seemed to stick. A few quick wipes with a washcloth and I was good to go again.

When I'm working I never tire of seeing children's dreams. I'm constantly reminded that their juvenile inspirations are the source of next generation's wealth. Dreams don't seem very important to the politicians or investors. How can you pay for a political campaign with dreams? How can you store up a fantasy in a bank? But as worthless as their hopes and aspirations are to the rich and powerful, children's dreams fill me with joy.

* * * * * * * *

It was day two of our whirl wind tour, hosting the Christmas party in Kennewick. I was finishing up with the last child on my lap when I heard something metallic clanging on the ground nearby, it sounded like a coin dropping... then another. I'd heard that sound before at Julia's party, but this was even louder. I reached into my bag and pulled out a wrapped skateboard for the 13-year-old boy and sent him on his way. Then I heard another coin drop.

"Do you hear that?" I asked John.

"Do I hear what?" he answered.

"It sounds like a coin dropping... there it goes again."

"I think you're just tired," he said, collapsing into a chair. "And really, I don't know if I can do this another day. I'm beat."

"I'm not tired at all," I admitted, forgetting to sympathize with his superhuman effort over the last two days. "I'm going to see what that sound is."

"Knock yourself out," he said waving his hand at me limply. "I'll be sitting right here when you get back. Bring a gurney to wheel me out while you're at it!"

I touched my nose just as I heard another coin fall, and there, to my horror, was the same ghost who pleaded for my help before. He stood in front of me with outstretched hands pointing to a pile of golden coins floating in the air. He made no sound, he made no attempt to communicate, just ignoring me completely. Another coin fell from the floating stash and hit the ground, making a loud clanking sound and then evaporating right in front of my eyes.

His body was sheer and ghostly green, with white ribbons of cloth wrapped around his body. He was shackled with chains on his arms and legs connected to large boxes filled with what I could only suppose was more money. Another coin dropped, and with that last coin, he looked at me with startled eyes. I was too terrified to move, speak, or even scream. He raised both arms in my direction and floated backwards, dragging the boxes and coins after him vanishing through a window, leaving as silently as he came.

I don't have to breathe when I'm outside of time which is a good thing because I was so afraid I forgot to breathe.

Finally, after several minutes passed, I calmed down enough to finally move my arms and touch my nose. The minute I exited time-warp I fell into a chair, panting frantically.

"That's the spirit," John said happily. "Now you're acting the way a guy who just had a thousand kids barf on his lap ought to act."

"Ghost!" I stammered, pointing my shaky finger in the general area of my haunted visitor. "I just saw that ghost again!"

"I'm not falling for that one," John grimaced. "I'll fall for trying to open your magic box once in a while, but not for another ghost story. You better start thinking up something new."

"I'm serious," I insisted. "He was standing right there dropping gold coins on the floor."

"Who was dropping gold coins?" Julia asked, walking into the room after locking the door to the community center.

"The ghost from a few nights ago," I said again. "He was floating above the ground with huge boxes chained to his arms and legs."

"Did he try to scare you, or make any threatening moves toward you?"

"Not at all," I answered. "I don't even think he saw me at first. He was dropping gold coins on the ground, and when he dropped the last one, it was then he finally acknowledged my presence and floated away."

"Now you're creeping me out," John said, pulling his chair closer. "But I like it so tell me more."

"I don't know if I have any more to tell. I was too terrified to move, or talk or even scream, but somehow I think he understood my fear and left me alone."

"I love this guy!" John blurted, hopping out of his chair and giving me a man hug. "This partnership just gets better all the time."

"That's easy for you to say," I retorted. "You didn't see him."

"If he shows back up," John begged. "Take me with you. I've never seen a ghost before, and I'm dying to see one. I mean, not like I want to die to see one... you know what I mean."

"Let me know, too!" Julia pleaded. "Not that I care about seeing a ghost, but because I want to be there for you."

"Oh, the feminine touch," John complained. "A girl can take the scariest moment and turn it into a caring event. I'll get a broom and start cleaning up. You two can talk about caring stuff."

"He means well," I laughed, getting my composure back.

"No he doesn't," Julia frowned. "He's just a rascal."

"I heard that!" John yelled from the broom closet. "Still in the room. And yes, I am a rascal, thanks for the compliment."

"See what I mean," she said shaking her head. "He's incorrigible."

Women are mysterious creatures. I don't understand how they think. We were both in a great mood, laughing and joking around, when suddenly I watched her aura go from a glowing yellow to a dull grey. Something had changed in her thought processes that flipped her happiness to dread as quickly as turning off a light.

"Are you alright?" I asked hesitantly.

"Sure," she lied. "Why shouldn't I be?"

Julia looked at me like she wanted to say more, but remained silent instead. I looked into her eyes and she was almost ready to cry. A picture of her stern father popped into my head and I realized the reason for her unhappiness.

"It's alright," I comforted. "Christmas day is almost here. I'll get his permission to marry you, I promise."

"So you can read minds too?" she shrugged, getting off her chair and grabbing a broom to help the other volunteers. "I don't think your magic will work against my father. I'm not sure you'll be able to stand up to him. He's the most controlling man I've ever met."

"I've got this," I smiled, borrowing one of John's carefree lines. "Don't worry about anything!"

She smiled back at my hopeful reply, but it didn't change her color. I wished I could have responded better to her doubtful remarks, but I didn't know how I was going to stand up to him either.

I changed back into my street clothes while Julia, John, and the other volunteers finished cleaning up. Day two of our whirl wind tour was finished. I was haunted by a ghost I couldn't help and by the love of a girl out of my reach... and I couldn't tell which haunting was worse.

Chapter Seven

Drowning in Tears

When I woke up the next morning I felt tired and beat up, like I had defended the whole world from monsters all night long. My nightmares allowed doubts about being able to confront Julia's Dad to creep into my mind again and, on top of that, I didn't have the heart to tell Julia I lost the ring. My plans were being torn apart by the second. I was debating whether I should just call the whole thing off when my teenage sister Sage plopped on my bed.

"Am I going to be a bridesmaid?" she asked boldly.

"I don't know," I answered dejectedly. "That's Julia's department. She'd probably invite you if you asked nicely."

"Oh, I'd ask nicely," she grinned. "I'm much nicer to her than I am to you. I'm curious though, what does the groom's side have to do in a wedding anyway? I normally just think about the bride's duties."

"I haven't given it much thought," I admitted. "If we were married I'd have to get her the ring, of course, and pay for the honeymoon, beyond that I don't know."

"You're a dork, Mason," she challenged. "No wonder you're all messed up. How can you make decisions on stuff you haven't even thought about? It's a good thing I'm around. Wait right here."

Sage ran from the room and came back with a stack of bridal magazines. She tossed them on the bed and started sorting through the stack, organizing them by importance.

"I don't get why they don't publish a single groom's magazine," she frowned. "Half the people on this planet are male, and they all get married without a single clue to what they're doing. Unbelievable. It's a good thing I found a few articles on the duties of the groom or you'd be sunk."

"I'm glad you're here to rescue me," I laughed.

"You should be," she frowned, opening up a magazine where she had marked it. "Now the duties of a groom are not exactly set in stone. It's kind of a negotiation between the two families, but it says here that Mom and Dad would probably pay for the flowers, the tuxedos, and a rehearsal dinner or a luncheon."

"Man," I exclaimed, "that's gonna cost them a fortune with how many people the Martin's know."

"Don't worry about them," Sage stated, looking though another magazine. "Moms and Dads are supposed to go broke for their kid's weddings. It's the law. Have you even proposed to her yet?" she asked anxiously.

"Not exactly!" I complained. "I only realized I wanted to marry her a few days ago, and somebody else bought the ring I picked out. What do you suggest I do, oh wise Sage?"

"You could use a rope instead of a ring," she sang, rummaging through her stack of treasures. "I know I have an article on this somewhere. I saw it in a movie one time too, it was so romantic. Here it is," she said triumphantly, opening up a colorful article describing the details of an ancient Celtic handfasting ceremony.

"The groom takes his beloved by both her right and left hands," she began reading, "...while the officiator wraps a piece a rope around their joined hands. The groom then says I give unto to thee my heart and soul, will ye have me, my darling? To which the bride responds in the affirmative, to the end of time, my love. Isn't that beautiful?" she sniffled, brushing the tears from her eyes.

"Now I know why men don't buy groom magazines," I kidded, giving her a hug.

"Well you should," she chastised. "You screwed up the ring part already, but even you can afford a piece of rope. Get on the ball, I want Julia to be my new sister, and I want to a bridesmaid!"

"Yes ma'am," I responded, kissing her hand. "Your wish is my command."

"Put that in writing and we have a deal," Sage laughed, gathering up all her magazines. "Now get up! We're going sledding before you have to go play Santa Claus again."

* * * * * * * *

It's a good thing my Santa Claus activities are fueled by Christmas magic or I wouldn't have had enough energy to enjoy sledding at 9:00 in the morning. We had a blast, just the five of us. Mom, Dad, Sage, Myia and me, all sliding around on patched up truck tire tubes. It's the simple things that really count sometimes.

I showered up and was ready to go by noon, just in time for John to pick me up again. Our schedule was even more hectic than the day before. We had a party at 3:00 p.m. in Wenatchee, and our final party at 6:00 p.m. in our high school's rival town of Ephrata, Washington. When I entered the room in Wenatchee, all the kids shouted for joy. I was pumped up and flying on pure Christmas magic.

I had just finished filling all the requests for the first five children when a loud ringing sound filled my ears. I knew what it was, a coin had dropped. Before the next child sat on my lap, I motioned for Julia and John to come and see the ghost with me. John placed his hand on my shoulder, and Julia casually took my hand while I touched my nose.

The whole room stopped moving. Every squirmy child was suspended in time. Every sound was silenced. The only thing moving were white strips of cloth blown by an invisible wind coming from a ghost standing off to the side of the room. A handful of coins floated in the air just past his finger's reach, his gaze focused on those coins. He stood silent and perfectly motionless as we looked his way.

"I told you I saw a ghost," I whispered as quietly as I could.

"I believe you, dude," John replied. "Now what do we do?"

"We try to talk to it of course," Julia said bravely, stepping away from us to be clearly seen. "What do you want?"

The ghost made no answer, nor movement.

"Do you intend to do us harm?" I added, gaining courage.

Still no movement or response.

"Do you even know we're here?" John asked hesitantly, creeping slowly to the windblown creature.

"Don't move any closer," I warned, sensing a peaceful feeling come over me. "He's not here to hurt us. He's the same ghost I made a promise to help back at Julia's house. I'll keep you all informed if anything changes. He may not be able to see us until the night is over."

"I told you this was awesome!" John exclaimed, returning to where he had been standing before. "I love this job!"

"We're leaving time-warp," I warned. "Get ready."

The moment I touched my nose the whole room exploded back into light, color, and confusion. Julia and John went back to what they were doing without letting on we had been in a completely different dimension.

The presence of our coin-dropping ghost became our new normal, but the party continued on as usual. Some children were grumpy and tasted sour, others were over enthusiastic and filled my mouth with sugary sweetness, nothing a cup of hot chocolate couldn't fix. After four or five children I could count on having a coin drop. I touched my nose a few times just to see if he was still there, and he was, looking intently at the floating coins, but now he didn't creep me out anymore. The only reminder I had about his presence was the resounding ring I heard every half hour or so.

When the last child was praised and sent off with a gift, I touched my nose in anticipation, but the spirit was gone. John begged to time-warp with me, but he was disappointed by the absence of our ghostly visitor, too. I didn't even bother getting undressed this time, I just jumped in and helped clean up in my Santa suit and prepared for our final party in Ephrata, Washington.

The party started out just like the other ones. Excited children clapped with joy as I burst into the room, ringing my sleigh bells and wishing everyone, Merry Christmas. After a few words of encouragement, and a song, I settled in and did what I love best, shower children with gifts.

The evening was going great, the children were delightful, the ghost was dropping coins on a regular basis, and I was drinking hot chocolate and laughing with everyone.

As the party progressed, I suddenly noticed a darker than normal color coming off of several girls in the back of the line. I touched my nose to see if the color was coming from my ghost, but it wasn't. I searched the room and didn't see any one of their parents around. Strange. I decided the only thing I could do was wait to see what would happen.

The youngest sister of the three children finally sat on my lap. She was young, around five or six, and I could tell by the smell of neglect that she was in desperate need of happiness.

"What would you like for Christmas?" I asked, sensing her sorrow.

"I want a rabbit," she sighed, "but we ate the last one, so I don't think that would be a good idea."

"Maybe not," I gulped. I didn't bring a rabbit, and giving animal gifts without parental approval never went well.

"But I'd love to have a doll instead," she said happily, her aura brightening up noticeably."

"I think I can find a doll in here," I chuckled, reaching into my almost empty bag, pulling out a beautiful doll all wrapped in gold paper and blue metallic ribbon.

"Thanks, Santa Claus," she smiled and hopped off my lap.

The next little girl was just as adorable and easily coaxed into happiness with a bracelet Julia and I purchased at Miller's Jewelry store. She thanked me for the gift and moved on to be with her younger sister.

The oldest girl was a shy 12-year-old, almost a teenager, I could tell. Her clothes were simple, but clean. Her hair was medium length and straight. I couldn't tell why such a darkness surrounded her until she got on my lap. The moment she touched me I felt like I was drowning. I couldn't speak, I couldn't even breathe. I had never experienced such a feeling of doom settle over me as on that day, not even when the ghost touched me.

Julia could see something was wrong. She rushed to my side with a cup of hot chocolate, and a supportive touch, her love filling me with life again; I took a sip of hot chocolate.

"Would you like a cup of hot chocolate?" I was finally able to ask.

"That would be great," she sang. "I love chocolate."

"What would you like for Christmas this year?" I asked, trying to stay above the water that I felt rising past my chest, and lapping on my shoulders.

"I want a new father," she whispered in my ear so quietly I could barely hear her. "I'm afraid of the father I have. I don't want him anymore."

Tears filled her eyes, and those tears raised the water level above my own head, I was drowning in her tears. I could see the events she had already endured, and worse, I could sense the shadows of every horror she would yet endure at his hand. Julia had me by the hand, but not even her touch could save me. I was going to die if I didn't breathe soon, but I couldn't let this little girl off my lap without giving her hope. I would rather drown first. I had only one choice left to me, I reached up and touched my nose. In an instant all three of us were outside of time.

"Why did you do that?" Julia asked in alarm. "What's going on?"

"I can't tell you," I answered, holding little Carolyn safely in my arms. "It's too horrible. This little girl is suffering deeply, and there is nothing I can do to stop it."

"You poor thing," Julia said soothingly, touching Carolyn's hand with care.

The moment their hands met, Julia burst into tears, sharing in my powers for a moment. "It can't be possible," she cried, witnessing visions of Carolyn's past, racing across her dainty mind. "The monster, the monster! He's no father, he's a beast. Oh, you, poor little child."

"You're Santa Claus, I know you are," Carolyn sobbed. "You can do anything. Can't you give me a new father?"

I asked for guidance more intently than I have ever asked before. I knew I couldn't replace her actual father. Even her mother was browbeaten by his abuse and wouldn't come to her rescue. What was I going to do? Suddenly a flash of information came and I knew what to do.

"I chose a special gift for you," I said, reaching for a present at the bottom of my pile. "I want you to have this to remind you how special you are." I carefully opened up the package with the diamond necklace inside. As soon as the large center stone caught the light in the room, it sent colorful light dancing. Stars and rainbows painted every wall and the ceiling, sending rays of hope through all of us. I took the dazzling piece of jewelry and placed it around her neck.

"This necklace is just like you," I said. "A diamond takes millions of years to make. It starts out as black coal, but with extreme pressure and heat it becomes the most precious of all gemstones. You're no different. You're already precious because of what you've suffered without giving up. Your father may not be able to see your worth, but I can. I promise if you keep working and learning you'll rise above all your problems and shine as brilliantly as this diamond necklace."

"But it's so hard," she cried.

"I know it's hard," I said, trying to comfort her. "Just remember how much pressure and heat it takes to make a beautiful diamond. Whenever you're afraid, or in danger, think about the beauty of this necklace and what it represents."

"But I want a new father," she pleaded again.

"You can't have a new father, but remember, you do have a Heavenly one. He is eager to help you. He's never left you alone. Everything will be alright."

"But what about my father at home?" she asked. "If he sees me wearing a real diamond necklace he'll steal it."

"No, he won't," I assured her. "The necklace is enchanted with Christmas Magic. Its true beauty will only be revealed to someone who can perceive your true value. Be sure he sees it when you get home. Tell him you got it from Santa Claus. He'll just laugh and call it plastic junk. Only you will know the truth so keep it safe, and wear it whenever you need to remember who you really are. A daughter of God."

Carolyn held onto her diamond necklace and repeated the words. "I'm never alone. I'm a daughter of God. Everything will be alright."

A tear of hope fell down her cheek and then another. When the tears fell onto the necklace it burst with color and light again. Instead of a doomed future, I saw a caring husband, loving children, even grandchildren all praising her name. Her love expanded on and on, influencing generations of happy people.

Her light was so intense, my own heart was changed with it. Julia was sobbing uncontrollably, unable to contain herself.

"I expect wonderful things out of you, Carolyn," Julia said. "I wish every girl could know how precious they are in Heavenly Father's sight. This knowledge is just like getting a new father."

"It's true," Carolyn said gently. "I do have another Father. I believe it."

We held each other, for I don't know how long. I looked over at my ghostly visitor and he stood stoically, unmoved by our experience. Finally, when we had gained our composure, I returned us all to mortal time.

"You really are magic," she declared, joining her sisters. "I'll love you both forever."

At that moment a whole handful of coins fell to the ground. I heard them clatter and spin around, but I didn't even bother to look, I was too overwhelmed with joy. And now, since I was the only one to hear them fall, I simply moved on to the next child.

The rest of the night was uneventful, if you call giving the perfect gift to eager children uneventful. The last coin dropped in Ephrata as the last child was given the last gift. I went into time-warp to see if the ghost was still around, but the specter had disappeared.

"Don't you think we should call the police or something?" Julia asked, distraught after all the children and parents were all out of the room. "Carolyn's father should go to jail."

"We could try, but it wouldn't do any good," I replied. "He's already getting a truck loaded to move out of town. He sent them here so he could finish up the last few items. She'll have a tough childhood, but once she's endured her torment and abuse, she'll be made into something more precious than diamonds, you wait and see!"

"I believe you," Julia said tenderly. "You have such an amazing ability of seeing the best in people. What do you see in me?"

"Happiness," I assured her. "You're already a queen."

"You're sweet," she said wistfully.

"I'll tell you more about your future on Christmas day after I talk to your father." I said, kissing her on the forehead.

"I look forward to that," she smiled wistfully, "but, I'll believe it when I see it. Get some advice, you'll need it."

The coins started dropping again when we delivered Sub-for-Santa gifts later that night. Every toy, computer, and tool we bought ended up in the hands of a needy child.

The last handful of coins fell as we delivered presents to the family of my little neglected friend, Ashton Chilton, at Moses Lake, Washington. His house was as barren of Christmas presents as I imagined it would be, not even a strand of Christmas lights to brighten the place up, let alone a Christmas tree... but we fixed that. Ashton got a chemistry set, along with a clean white laboratory coat to go along with his new microscope. His older brother was given a longboard, while his other brothers and sister were taken care of just as well.

By the time we were done, I was exhausted. As we drove home a feeling of satisfaction came over me like I had never felt before. This was my life. I loved my work, I love my family, and I had a woman I was crazy about. What more could there be? *A wedding ring and a proper proposal!* my little sister's reminder yelled in my head. I think Julia was right, I was going to need help to figure out this proposal. We dropped Julia off at her house first, as usual, then John dropped me off at mine. A dry dusty cold wind blew through me as soon as he vanished. I ignored it, too tired to care.

Chapter Eight

The Dreaded Ghost

As I walked up the sidewalk leading to my front door, a cold and creepy feeling rushed through me once again. I had felt that ghostly presence all week, only this time, I was too tired to fight back.

"What do you want?" I said out loud, getting a rusty taste of metal in my mouth. "Tell me what you want or go away!"

I received no answer, but the silent attack continued. The overwhelming taste of rusty chains intensified, only to be replaced by the flavor of funeral wrappings, tickling my throat and causing me to cough. Just when I thought the experience couldn't get any worse, then the chalky taste of dry bones assaulted my senses.

Barely able breathe, I tried to dart inside the safety of my house, but when I reached for the screen door the button on the latch was stuck. I looked down to get a better grip on the handle only to see I was holding onto the outstretched hand of a... a ghost!

The tastes and smells intensified, causing my stomach to revolt. I looked up in dread and caught a vision of a twisted mournful face, looking directly at me from where the door knocker should have been.

I immediately let go of his hand but was so sickened by his touch, I threw up in the snowbank by the side of our porch. When I finished puking I looked up to see the rest of him standing directly in front of me.

The features of the ghost were forlorn and miserable. He had a dirty cloth wrapped around the top of his head extending to the bottom of his jaw, which held his chin up. The moment I saw him I stepped back in shock and disgust. With one hand he motioned to me and with the other he was grasping for something floating just outside his reach. I looked at the floating objects and realized they were the gold coins.

"The time has come," the phantom said mournfully. "Will you still help me?"

"I said I would," I insisted, gagging, coughing and stricken with fear.

His eyes were hollow and lifeless, but each time he moaned his face contorted in such painful agony I pitied the tormented creature. His whole body was visible to me now. He turned away from me and placed his hands on his head in a gesture of surprise and wailed all the louder.

As he moved away from me the horrible taste lessened. Instead of bone and burial cloth, all I tasted now was metal chains. A horrible taste for sure, but one I could tolerate. Another wail filled my ears, more horrible than the others as chains connected to heavy boxes lifted around his body. Unseen winds carried the heavy boxes up and slammed them into his pathetic frame, breaking one open and spilling out golden coins that, once free, acted like hornets, smashing and crashing into him.

"He said you would help ... even a soul as doomed as mine," The ghost said as if in shock. "Thank you... thank you."

His momentary pause gave the boxes the freedom to pull him helplessly around the front yard with the coins pelting him like stones. In a final shrieking, moaning motion, the ghost was blown from my sight, freeing me from my torment and allowing me to breathe.

The encounter must have been very quick, but it seemed to last forever. When I looked up again I shivered at the thought that my arrogant college professor had conjured up this tormented creature, and now that creature was following me everywhere. I quickly opened the door to my house and darted inside to safety.

I locked the door and leaned against it, hoping it would protect me from danger. As my heart rate began to lower I was startled by a crunching sound coming from behind the Christmas tree. I stood still, too sick to my stomach to move. As the horrifying gnawing and crunching continued, I sunk deeper into a corner, wishing I could disappear into the wall. In my horror I saw a menacing shadow growing larger.

"Stay away!" I yelled desperately. "Stay back! What do you want from me?!"

"Just a few minutes of your time," a large man said cheerfully, stepping into the light, finishing up a chocolate chip cookie and drinking a glass of milk. My intruder was dressed in a warm red suit edged in white fur, black belt, and big shiny black boots. He was a bit disheveled, covered all over with ashes and soot, but barely even flinched at my outburst.

"Merry Christmas, Mason," St. Nicholas laughed, instantly standing next to me. He took me by the arm, chasing all the horrible flavors from my mouth and replacing them with chocolate and peppermint. In an instant he touched the side of his nose, causing the whole room to turn that timeless glowing color I love so much.

"Merry Christmas, St. Nicholas," I replied, nearly collapsing from relief. "I'm sorry about that, you scared me half to death. I thought you were a ghost!"

"A ghost?" he smiled. "I thought I felt a wandering spirit about. They don't demand much, at least not in this dimension."

"This one's very demanding. I agreed to help him but I don't know what he wants. What should I do now?"

"That's why I'm here. It is Christmas Eve after all."

"I can't tell you how relieved I am to hear that," I admitted. "I didn't know you left the North Pole anymore, now that you have the League to help you."

"I still make house calls," he said merrily. "I'm sorry for scaring you. The world is full of mystery, some delightful and some terrifying. I'm used to both. You and your friends have done well these last few years. I've been very impressed with your work. Have you thought about becoming full members of the League?"

"All the time," I responded happily, remembering Mrs. Warner's instructions from four years earlier. "Does this mean you're inviting us to become members of the Santa Claus League?"

"Maybe," St. Nicholas tested cunningly. "You've already received the call, are you ready to be chosen?"

"I'm ready" I said confidently.

"Then why haven't you chosen a wife?" he asked, raising an eyebrow. "I see enough chemistry between you and

Julia to make a happy life together. You know every Santa Claus in my League must have a Mrs. Santa Claus."

"I'd like get married," I blushed, trying to figure out how to get marriage advice from a saint. "But it's not as easy as it sounds."

"Should it be easy?" he chuckled. "Valuable treasures are hard to find, and even harder to escape with. Now that you've won her heart, are you ready to fight for her? Her father isn't going to give her up easily you know."

"That's my problem," I replied, my confidence draining. "He hates me. How am I'm going to ask him for Julia's hand?"

"With words, I suppose?" he winked. "Is that your only problem?"

"I wish," I blurted. "When I tried to buy Julia an engagement ring, someone else bought it just before I did, now I don't even have a ring."

"Those are serious setbacks. To some, they would be insurmountable, but I have a question. Do you love her?"

"I do," I groaned. "I love her so much it hurts."

"Ah the joys of young love," he exclaimed with a smile. "I guess your cure is more pain."

"More pain?" I gasped. "I've got plenty of pain already. Besides a girl I'm afraid of losing, I have a ghost who keeps following me around. I don't need any more pain!"

"Of course you do," St. Nicholas winked, clapping his hands on his sooty red pants with decision. "Facing pain is where solutions come from. I should know, that's why solving problems have become a specialty of mine, be they among the living or the dead. In that spirit, I've decided to offer you your next level of training. It's guaranteed to be painful, are you ready for the challenge?"

"Will it get rid of the haunting ghost?" I blurted hesitantly.

"It will," he said with a chuckle, "and if you choose, it will help you find solutions to your other problem as well. But be warned, this training exercise will be significantly more dangerous than the last one."

"Can I take Julia and John along with me?"

"You'll have to," he insisted emphatically. "You'll never survive without them. Although I'll have to ask them personally to come along. There is one other team member I have to introduce you to. Are you ready to meet him?"

"Another team member?" I asked warily, "Who is he?"

"So, you haven't figured out my surprise?" he smiled with glee. "I was hoping I could have some fun with this one. When you're as old as me, a good surprise is so enjoyable. Therefore, introductions are in order. Mason Howell, I would like you to meet your newest team member, the ghost of Mr. Jacob Marley."

"Jacob Marley?" I gasped as the familiar spirit appeared, hovering in the air in deathly silence. "This is the ghost that keeps harassing me? How am I supposed to work with him?"

"From a distance," St. Nicholas suggested, handing me a mint and popping one in his own mouth. "I share your pain, believe me."

The spirits features were unchanged from just a few minutes before, as a handful of coins still hovered around him, acting like a dangerous swarm of bees. The same metallic chests looked just as heavy, as if they were bolted to the ground. The treasure was shackled to his wrists and ankles by sturdy rusty chains just as the book had described. I was almost as afraid of him as before, so I kept my distance.

"I thought he was just a character from a book," I exclaimed, still freaked out. "He can't be real, can he?"

"Like Rudolph the Red Nosed Reindeer can't be real?" St. Nicholas asked. "Rudolph Reinman would be upset if you didn't acknowledge his existence. Say hello to my guest, you're being rude."

"Sorry," I said hesitantly, taking a small step back. "Good evening, Mr. Marley."

The ghost acknowledged my presence, nodding deeply, but didn't move any closer, thank goodness.

"You've done a great deal for Mr. Marley already," St. Nicholas mused, munching on another cookie. "You accepted his mission without knowing the dangers, based on pure compassion. You also liquidated the last of his old fortune over the last few days. But you've done one more thing you don't even know about."

"What's that?" I asked.

"You found his most prized possession. You have it in your pocket right now. Do you want to know what it is?"

The coin in my pocket... I pulled it out and held it out.

"This shilling was given to me by your grandfather. He asked me to pass it on to you when the time came. It may not look like much, but don't mistake wealth for money," St. Nicholas warned. "This coin is worth everything to Jacob Marley. Hold on to it or all of this will be in vain."

"So, what do you want us to do?" I asked, taking the coin and holding it up to the light for a better look.

"You have to rob Jacob Marley's grave," St. Nicholas said mysteriously.

"You want me to rob his grave?"

"Precisely, it sounds exciting doesn't it? I've been planning this mission for years, I've just never had the right team to carry it off until you and your friends came along."

"What are we supposed to find inside... inside his casket?" I said with some trepidation.

"A fortune in gold," he whispered. "The details are thrilling. Your mission is to recover the gold and deliver it to me at the North Pole before Christmas morning. You've already promised Jacob you would help... are you willing to finish the job?"

"Grave robbing?" I queried, "It sounds creepy."

"I'm glad you think so," he chuckled happily. "But I'm a bit of an adrenaline junky. Are you willing to experience a side of Christmas you never imagined possible?"

While we were talking the sound of wind started whistling through the room. The invisible breeze had no effect on the decor, but it had a noticeable influence on Jacob Marley as the rags that covered his body began twirling around.

"You must decide quickly, Mr. Howell," St. Nicholas said, "Mr. Marley will not be able to stay long. The Winds of Doom will blow him away in several minutes. But if you accept this mission, you and your friends will be given the power to hear, see, and interact with the spirits of the dead."

"Is that a good thing?" I gulped.

"It is if you want to complete this mission," he said mysteriously. "You will learn that the term "being alive" is a much bigger idea than you ever imagined; however, I must say, you're smart to ask me questions. With this new magical power, the dead will have physical form just like you. They will be able to harm you, even kill you if you let them. Your grandfather would attest to that if he were here."

"Wow, that does sound dangerous," I gulped.

"Now don't despair, young man," he chuckled. "You won't be left helpless. Once empowered you can enter into their presence with the touch of your nose or a click of your watch. You'll be instantly taken away from their presence in the same way. Do you want to see how it works?"

"Sure," I said, eager to learn something new. "We'll use my watch this time," St. Nicholas smiled, walking over to the front window of our house. "Once your watch is fused with magic, you'll be able to do this as well."

"Like a computer upgrade…" I said, taking my watch out of my pocket.

"Exactly," he nodded. "I hadn't thought about it like that, but yes. One click takes you into time-warp, with the ability to interact with the dead. Stay close, this might be startling to you."

As soon as he clicked his watch the empty lawn in front of my house filled with a hundred people waving at me. They were all young and beautiful, with several in the crowd shining brighter than the others. I stepped back in astonishment. "Where did all these people come from?"

"They've been here all night waiting for you," he answered. "I imagine they're family and friends. I asked your Grandpa Adams to bring your Grandmother and a few of their friends over for this demonstration."

"Does that mean you can talk to the dead?"

"Yes, of course," he smiled. "They're all alive to me, and now I'm giving this gift to you. But be warned, I've only invited the righteous spirits of the dead to cheer you on tonight. The wicked spirits aren't nearly as inviting. How do you think you might like your new power?" he asked eagerly, clicking his watch a second time, causing the scene to go dark and dreary.

"It's amazing," I marveled. "I just wish I could have met my grandparents."

"Does this mean you want to tackle this new training mission?"

"Without a doubt."

"I was hoping you would say that," St. Nicholas chuckled, reaching into his magic bag and pulling out a glistening swatch of cloth. "It wasn't easy borrowing this cloak from the Ghost of Christmas Yet-to-Come, I assure you. He made me take personal responsibility for it. Without this, even he is powerless."

"What is it?" I asked.

"The future," St. Nicholas smiled, hypnotized by the mysterious cloth. "I wish I could put it on, but that would defeat the whole purpose for borrowing it. I have someone else in mind. Jacob Marley, please come forth."

The ghost came forward and I backed away, already gagging from the taste of his rusty chains as he got closer. St. Nicholas took a step toward the ghoulish phantom and handed him the cloak. As Jacob Marley opened up the cloth, it shimmered with magical waves of power. It exploded with energy as he put it on, concealing his head, his face, his form, leaving nothing visible save one outstretched hand.

"Wonderful!" St. Nicholas exclaimed, handing me a brown paper package. "Now a gift for you, Mason. Here is your next training manual. I hope you are already familiar with the story."

I didn't even have to open the package. The moment I touched it I knew it was a first edition of A Christmas Carol, by Charles Dickens. "This is my training manual?" I gasped. "Are you serious?"

"As serious as the grave," St. Nicholas said, looking over at the phantom. "Charles Dickens explains a few details about Jacob Marley in his book, but there are other things you'll need to learn before you'll be able to help him."

"Like what?" I asked as the ghost refused to even look our way.

"I can't tell you," he winked. "Isn't this exciting?"

His confidence and joy made me laugh. I didn't know anyone on earth who could share the prospect of death and destruction and make it sound so enticing. But even with St. Nicholas's enthusiasm, my own doubts crept through. He saw my concerns.

"Don't worry, my boy," he said smiling. "The Santa Claus League has a special team at our disposal to train you for missions like this. We usually use it as a recruiting tool, but not always. Now, you'd better get your courage together because you will be visited by three Christmas Spirits tonight."

"The Christmas Spirits from A Christmas Carol are part of the Santa Claus League?" I choked. "What part of Christmas lore isn't real?"

"Frosty the Snowman," he mused. "I love the song, but I still haven't figured out how to animate snow. I'm working on that. But don't worry about Frosty, you should worry about the task at hand. Your briefing is about to begin. The Spirit of Christmas Past is especially punctual."

"I've heard that," I said with a grimace, opening the package. "I've never read the book, but I've seen about a half dozen different variations of the movie."

"The book is better," St. Nicholas said intently.

The blackened Jacob Marley made no movement to even recognize our presence. He hovered in the air, witnessing everything we said and did. His dark shroud was already blowing around, but soon the gale forces became so strong it began to tear him from his solemn stance. Even the heavy boxes that floated with him were beginning to rattle on the ground, shaking and trembling as if ready to launch into the air.

"But if he's wearing the cloak of the Ghost of Christmas Future," I asked. "Why is he still being blown around?"

"He's a doomed soul," St. Nicholas explained. "The Winds of Doom are never far away. Even empowered with the cloak of the Ghost of Christmas Future they sense his presence. Now... I have a few more important instructions. Keep the book with you for reference but keep the coin and the watch with you at all times, never be without them. You will encounter the ungrateful dead tonight. It will take all your courage to survive."

"Do you think we can even complete the mission?" I asked hesitantly.

"I wouldn't send you if I wasn't sure of your success," he encouraged. "Just remember the motto of the Santa Claus League. We are here to help bad kids become good, good kids to become great, and to save the world from evil. What could be more inspiring?"

"I'll keep that in mind," I insisted.

"Wonderful," St. Nicholas smiled. "Good luck, Mason, and Happy Christmas!"

Then he was just gone.

Seconds later, John and Julia quietly knocked on my front door. St. Nicholas had obviously used time-warp to get us all together at the same time. I opened the door and let them in. They looked at me with a knowing glance as they searched the room for the wind-blown ghost.

For the second time that evening Jacob Marley acknowledged our presence, and slowly floated toward us, covered in the shroud of the future. The winds were howling through the whole room by now, lifting the heavy boxes and wrapping the chains around him, trying to blow him away.

"Pull out your watch and coin," he demanded, as the winds tossed his heavy boxes around wildly.

I pulled out my watch and coin and held them in my opened hand. In an act of power and defiance against the winds, Jacob clapped his hands, creating a vortex of magic that twirled around us like a fiery flame tongue of a tornado, spinning faster and faster until it exploded into the coin, the watch and into us, throwing us to the ground.

When I came to my senses, the last of the flaming tongues were dying down, and sparks of magic were trailing out the window. I looked around for Jacob Marley, but he was nowhere to be seen. I picked up the steaming coin and watch and slipped both back into my pocket.

"Are you alright?" I asked Julia, helping her stand up and dusting the last of the magic sparks off her back.

"I think so," she coughed. "Is getting magic always this violent?"

"It has been for me," I admitted. "How are you feeling John?"

"Awesome!" he crowed. "It's about time the sidekick gets some non-tech super powers. That was sweet! So what exactly is this super ability we were just given?" John asked, primping in a hall mirror.

"We can see dead people," Julia said timidly. "I hope it's a power we come to value. It sounds scary to me."

"I think it sounds awesome," John boasted, as the clock prepared to chime one o'clock.

"Do you really think the Ghost of Christmas Past is coming?" Julia asked hesitantly, reaching for my hand to act as an anchor.

"Yes, I do," I replied, feeling the gathering energy surround us. "And the ghost of Christmas Present and Future as well."

"Sick," John said with a grin. "St. Nicholas warned me about ghosts. He promised this would be dangerous!"

"Only you would think that's a good thing," Julia chided, grabbing his hand as well, and squeezing it tightly. "Stay close and get ready for anything!"

The clock struck one and the room burst with light, disintegrating all the matter around us. Without a place to stand, we dropped through time and space into... nothing!

Chapter Nine

A Christmas Flame

After falling for several minutes, we stopped feeling the effect of gravity giving us clues which way we were traveling. Julia held my hand tightly as we swung around each like we were weightless. John was spinning out of control and only steadied himself after grabbing onto Julia's other hand. Together, we greeted our unknown fate, excited and scared, all at the same time.

We were still floating when something familiar caught my attention, something wonderful I had sensed before. "Do you smell that?" I yelled over the whistling wind. "Something smells like oranges and chocolate. We must be getting close to an open flame."

Ever since we were initiated into the League, fire smells like our favorite Christmas memories. I smelled oranges and chocolate, John smelled greasy car parts, and Julia smelled hopscotch tiles and chalk. Smells are powerful reminders of the joy of Christmas.

"Yeah you're right about the flame," John said, still holding on to Julia's hand. "It smells great and it's getting stronger. So where do you think the flame is coming from?"

"I don't know!" I yelled back.

We didn't have to wait for long to get an answer. The swirling of smoke was replaced by a flame directly below us, and we were approaching it rapidly. The tip of the inferno crackled like a thousand camp fires. Its roar was as deafening as a blast furnace ready to explode.

"Are you still fireproof?" Julia asked in a panic. "Because if you're not, we'll burn to death for sure!"

"I've got you covered," I assured her. "You're protected by me."

The flames swirled around our bodies like bright sunshine as we passed through them. The smell was enchanting and pure, the heat cleansing and refreshing. By the time we made it through the flame, I wanted to go back. I love fire.

Our fall was quickly coming to an end. We had passed through the flame and were about to land in what appeared to be an amber lake of simmering molten glass. Julia squeezed my hand all the harder, while John let go, just in time to splash into a deep sea of wax. Julia let go of me as soon as we submerged into the hot goop. We hit the soft bottom of the lake and pushed our way back up to the surface.

No sooner had we surfaced when a giant square piece of wood, as large as a tree trunk, floated past us. One end of the branchless post was burnt and black as if it were a giant match stick.

"I'll grab onto that," John offered, swimming up to it and crawling on. After he steadied our newfound life raft, he ripped off a long loose piece of wood from the square board and held it out for Julia and me. Grabbing the stick, John pulled us both on the square log.

"Is everyone okay?' I asked.

"I'm cool," John replied, poking his stick in and out of the goop.

"I'm a little shaken," Julia answered. "But other than that I feel fine. Don't you think it's strange that that this liquid doesn't even stick to our skin or clothes?"

"That is weird," I agreed. "And even stranger, I feel completely clean, even cleaner than after taking a long bath."

"I wonder where we are?" she mused, looking around confused.

"We're inside a candlestick," John said, pointing up at the round waxy edges that surrounded the wick of the candle. "We fell through the flame up there and landed in the hot melted wax. Don't you remember the Spirit of Christmas Past is a living candle? Maybe if we row around a bit we can discover how to meet her."

"Where on earth could you find a candle this large?" Julia asked.

"Who says we're on earth?"

"John's right," I added, starting to get my bearings. "We may not be on earth at all, at least not in the dimension we normally inhabit. And as far as floating around in the melted wax of a large candle, I rather think we've been shrunk and are floating around in a very average-sized one."

"Poppycock," an ancient woman's voice ranted over the increasing roar of the candle's flame. "A large candle? A small candle? You don't know anything. Leave it to St. Nicholas to change my orders at this late hour. Who does he think I am, a miracle worker?"

"Where is that voice coming from?" Julia whispered.

"Whoever it is, she doesn't seem to be very happy," I added quietly.

"Happy? Of course I'm not happy!" the voice rang out, sending the flame of the candle blazing even higher. "For 365 days I have been preparing for a totally different person, and now I have to be a tour guide to you three? Who can put up with this kind of nonsense?"

"I'm sorry we messed up your preparations," I said. "It's just that... St. Nicholas said we would be trained by three ghosts—"

"A ghost?" a stern voice exploded, sending sparks swirling everywhere. "I am not a ghost! To be a ghost I would have had to have died! That is impossible since I have never lived a day on your earth. I am a Christmas Spirit, and the only Spirit of Christmas Past. And what are you doing young man?" she yelled at John, who was looking around the edges of the candle trying to find where the voice was coming from. "Look in the center of the wax, silly nitwit. I'm not standing outside the candle I assure you."

"She's in the flame!" Julia gasped.

I followed where Julia was looking and gazed directly into the flame. To my amazement an old woman met my gaze, completely engulfed in the fire of the candle. The wick was no wick at all, but the body of an old woman. In an instant the shape of the woman changed and she became a baby, then a child, then back to a middle-aged woman again.

"This night is not even started and I am already tired," she lamented, collapsing onto a beautiful cushioned wax chair she fashioned with the flick of her hand. "But come closer to me.

I have a job to perform. You must be of some worth or the Old Elf wouldn't have sent you to me."

As soon as she asked us to come closer, the sea of molten wax transformed into a sturdy path, allowing us to jump off the matchstick and walk on a solid surface. Her flame burned more evenly and calm filled the air.

"Come closer," she said gently, transforming into a beautiful young woman. "I want to get a good look at you. I've been tasked with preparing you for a dangerous mission and I might never see you again after this!"

"How does she keep doing that?" I asked John quietly.

"It's not polite to ignore your host!" The voice scorned. "If you have a question direct it to the Spirit who has the answers."

"Sorry about that," I apologized, walking closer to the flame. "How many women are we talking to?"

"Do you not have eyes?" she said, her flame rising hotter. "I am the same woman, presenting myself at different ages. The past has the ability to shift perspectives very quickly, you see."

John ignored her gruffness as he was mesmerized by her beauty. The Spirit was perfect in every way. Her long wispy hair was on fire, joined by her sweeping sheer outer robes. The shapely young woman surrounded by an inferno was as calm as a summer's evening. I've seen John fall for a girl before, but this display of instant affection was laughable. What was he thinking? As he drew near, he fell to his knees and just stared with his mouth open.

"What's wrong?" the Spirit asked wryly. "You act as if you've seen a ghost."

"I. I don't... I don't know what I'm seeing," John stammered. "I've never seen anyone so beautiful before."

"Those are bold words for a boy who tinkers with gears and grease all day," she smiled beguilingly. "Unfortunately, the task at hand is much more, shall we say, daring. I've never had to reveal the past of a corpse before, a rather odd request if you ask me."

"The past life of Jacob Marley?" I asked hesitantly. "Are you here to help us dig up his treasure?"

"Among other things," she said mysteriously, as she commanded three comfortable chairs to rise up from the wax. "Everyone sit, and we will learn more about our curious subject. Who has the coin?"

"The coin?" I asked confused.

"Yes, the shilling," she fumed, fire jumping from her hair. "Without the coin I am not authorized to show you anything. Do you have the coin, yes, or no?"

"Yes... of course," I stuttered, pulling it from my pocket.

"That's better," she said evenly, taking the coin from my hand and closing her eyes.

She looked calm for a moment, as if the coin's recent history was pleasant enough, but then her demeanor changed. She coughed as the flame surrounding her began to grow dim.

"It's authentic," she said, handing the currency back to me. "Apparently your Grandfather came across it at a coin show in London. It jumped out at him, as magical objects can, and I see he passed it to you. The previous owner of this coin was Jacob Marley. Now I have verified your identity, I am cleared to share with you the shadows of the past."

"Are we going to fly through London?" John asked enthusiastically.

"All in good time," she said, turning back into an older woman again, "just be patient."

The Spirit threw up both hands, causing an enormous motion picture screen to materialize from the candle wax. She sat down and, with the flick of a hand, turned on the huge monitor. "I call this Flame Vision, complete with 3D visual effects. I may be the Spirit of Christmas Past, but my search tools don't have to be antiquated. Find Jacob Marley," she said crisply.

Twenty thousand names populated on the screen. "Let's narrow that search a bit," she whispered to herself. "Jacob Marley, born around 1766, and died in 1823, London, England." The list narrowed to two.

"Do you have access to information on every person who ever lived?" John asked.

"Every person," she said studiously, transforming into a primary age school girl. "I have complete files all the way back to Adam. I have recordings for every moment of Mr. Jacob Marley's life, from his birth to his tragic death. Here we go."

The Spirit gave us a running dialogue of the search as she went with the first 3D images for Marley as a baby. "His parents were upper class, though not of nobility. His father was a partner in a successful investment banking house. Young Jacob was cared for and nurtured, lacked for nothing."

The moving picture advanced another year revealing live images of a child as he grew into a school-age boy. "He was a good student," she remarked, continuing to sort through his informative years. "Well-liked at school. Good education. Respectable family... so where is the turning point?"

She flipped through a few more years and we saw a strong and handsome, 17-year-old, Jacob Marley. He was walking down a winter path with an attractive girl on his sleeve. They stopped under the evergreen branches of a beautiful Cedar of Lebanon tree in the middle of a field, where Jacob lifted her up onto a lovely rope swing.

"Are you sure he's out of town, Sarah?" Jacob Marley asked, pushing the beautiful girl back and forth. "I don't want to cause you any trouble."

"Of course he is," she answered carelessly. "He's answering a Writ of Summons to sit with the House of Lords. He takes his appointment very seriously."

"I don't know if I'd want to be a member of Parliament this session," he answered. "Not after our recent loss to the American Colonists. The Yanks are now calling themselves citizens of the United States of America! The defeat has forced my father to rescue a dozen investors, including your father, from ruin."

"Unbelievable," she responded. "The Americans are so resourceful."

"Resourceful?" he balked. "They just walked away with a huge chunk of our empire. We've lost a fortune."

"Good for them," she smiled. "A new world needs a new government. Success should be based on merit not on nobility."

"Be careful what you say," Jacob warned, "your father is the newest member of Parliament. He wouldn't like you taking sides with the Yankees."

"Pish-posh," she said flatly, rocking back and forth, "he can think whatever he likes. It's absurd for an island to rule a continent!"

"You're quoting Thomas Paine again," he smiled, giving her another push, "but I didn't beg for a rendezvous just to talk politics, I have some wonderful news. Now that I'm finished at Oxford my father has arranged an apprenticeship with the Bank of England. I'll head home after that and you can visit me whenever you like!"

"But what about the simple life we talked about?" she asked sadly.

"A simple life with you, Miss Sarah Cave?" he chided, twirling her around. "How is that possible?"

"At least you'll be close," she grinned, gaining her balance again. "But young men are known to say unrealistic things to win their maiden's affection."

"And have I won yours?" he asked seriously.

"Of course you have, my darling," she whispered shyly. "I just don't want to leave my home. I am to become the next Baroness, you know."

"I've heard that," he said lovingly, putting his scarf around her neck. "I'll make sure you lack for nothing."

With a wisp of smoke, the screen revealed an older Jacob cheerfully enduring long hours as a bond trader for the bank. The busy schedule left very little time for holidays, but each possible moment away was spent with Sarah under the beautiful Cedar of Lebanon tree.

The seasons changed several times as the years of preparation came to an end. The scene on the monitor reformed into an elegant attorney's office with Sarah's father, Sir Thomas Cave, finishing up a stack of paperwork.

"I'm sorry for your loss," he said stoically. "Your father was a good man. He ran a prosperous banking firm, and always helped those in need. He will be missed."

"Thank you, sir," Jacob responded cautiously. "And thank you for executing his will for me. Now that my father has passed on, making me the sole inheritor of his estates."

"You have become a man of considerable substance." he noted coolly. "I pray you will be as wise with its management as was your father."

"Thank you, sir," the young Jacob answered, trying to find words to ask his next question. "Now that I am the principal partner in my father's firm, I feel financially prepared to take a wife."

"Of course, a natural desire."

"Yes," Jacob stuttered. "And that being the case, I would like to ask your permission to make your daughter, Sarah, my wife."

"Sarah? My Sarah?" he exploded. "You think you are worthy of my Sarah? Are you mad?"

"Not at all, sir," Jacob answered boldly. "I know you expect her to marry a man worthy of her. I have the means to provide for her as if she were a queen. She will lack for nothing."

"Where is your title young man?" he burst. "You are a common businessman, a dealer of bonds and banknotes. You are not fit to marry a noblewoman like Sarah!"

"But, sir," Jacob begged. "I have connections with the royal family. I could buy a title and the lands to go with it at any moment. I am worthy of her hand, you know that! Just give me a chance. I love her."

"Get out my office," he demanded. "Your father helped me out of a tight spot a few years ago but that doesn't mean you may take my daughter as a reward. I will never agree to a morganatic marriage. Take your papers and your grand inheritance and leave."

The magical screen wiped away the richly decorated office and transported us to a scene under the same familiar cedar tree with Jacob and Sarah in earnest conversation.

"He refused my request and threw me out of the room," Jacob said, "what else could I do?"

"We can elope," Sarah said emphatically, holding on to the rope of the swing, but refusing to sit.

"An elopement?" he choked. "But what about your title?"

"I don't care about my title," she cried. "All I want is to be married to you."

"But what about my father's investment house? I can't just walk out on the other partners at such a critical time."

"You can take your money and we can move to America and start fresh."

"Why can't we stay here?" Jacob complained.

"Now you're not thinking straight," she said, tossing the swing around angrily. "My father will crush you and everything you've worked for. He's a powerful member of Parliament and won't stop until you... until we are bankrupt. If you want to marry me, we must leave this very moment."

"It's too dangerous," Jacob insisted. "I don't want our escape to be discovered. Let me find a safe place for us to go. If you'll stay here and keep out of sight, I'll be back in an hour."

"An hour will be too late," she pleaded, taking a coin from her purse. "But if you must go, take this coin with you."

"A shilling?" Jacob asked, accepting the coin. "Why a shilling?"

"As a token of my love," she cried. "My father is powerful, but even he can't stop us if we act boldly. It's absurd for an island to rule a continent!"

"I'll use it to tip the coachman on the way to our honeymoon!" Jacob insisted, holding the coin up to the light and mounting his horse. "Our freedom awaits, I promise!"

Now the vision played on in fast-forward mode. Jacob galloped away only to have a stately coach pulled by four black horses approach the tree, racing with determination. When the coach arrived, a stern man confronted the woman, throwing her to the ground and dragging her into the dark interior of the carriage. When Jacob Marley returned to the tree, the swing was empty and Sarah was gone.

"Sarah!" he yelled, circling the tree in confusion. "Where are you? I'm back, it hasn't even been an hour. Sarah!"

Each morning, Jacob returned to the cedar tree and waited past dark before leaving. His robust physique became gaunt and pale as he waited in vain day after day.

One cold February morning a servant girl approached and said, "She will not return; her father forced her into an arranged marriage with Sir Henry Otway, a man of nobility. But she gave me a message to pass on to you."

"What is it?"

"Cherish my shilling," the young girl said, "I don't know what that means, sir, but those are her words."

"I know what it means," Jacob replied sadly, his aura darkening with despair. "I should have trusted her. We should have eloped when we had the chance. There were never sweeter days for me than those spent under the boughs of this cedar of Lebanon tree."

"I'll tell her," the servant said with a polite curtsey. "Is there anything else you want me to tell her before I go?"

"Yes," he said, his countenance becoming a fiery red. "Tell her I will never love another woman. My financial empire will be my only concern and I will own the House of Lords by the time I'm through. Upon my grave, I swear it."

"He was true to his promise," the Spirit of Christmas Past said sadly. "He never sought the love of another woman, never married, never had children or enjoyed the companionship of friends."

"I don't know if I would do any better if I lost you," I admitted to Julia. "I'm sure I wouldn't be any less heart broken."

"We can't let that happen, can we?" Julia whispered, taking my hand gently. "Look at how much misery came because of it!"

"You're right," I agreed. "But it's sure harder when we're the ones who have to face the consequences."

"That's very true, young man," The Spirit said with her flame diminishing to a flicker. "Her father didn't live long enough to learn of his folly. He died shortly thereafter of cholera. He never tasted Jacob's wrath, but the other members of the House of Lords knew it well because Jacob Marley created and was known for his Empire of Riches."

Chapter Ten

The Merging Empires

Jacob's business empire grew year after year and with the passing of each Christmas, he became colder and more ruthless in his business dealings. Consumed by greed, he reached a point where he was completely devoted to money, no matter the human cost.

The smoke swirled around the Flame Vision screen and curled again revealing a narrow London street. "Ah, this moment in his life is very important," the Spirit said with a frown. "The merging of two financial empires. Let's see a quick clip about that."

"Are you sure he will even show up?" Jacob Marley asked impatiently, pacing around a distinguished gentleman.

"You would have never doubted me when you were my apprentice at the Bank of England."

"That was a long time ago, John," Marley rebutted, "before you added politician to your list of accomplishments."

"That's Mr. John Smith to you," he said annoyed. "My brother is Lord Carrington. You should talk to a member of Parliament and a partner with the Bank of England with more respect. Besides, without me you would've never reached the pinnacle of success you've achieved."

"I suppose I should be grateful," Mr. Marley admitted. "I own all the other members of Parliament. They do what I say without question, but I would never think of buying your patronage. If only your friend would show up I would be even more grateful."

"He's not exactly a friend... but wait, here he comes. I would like to introduce you to a fellow business giant in the making, Mr. Ebenezer Scrooge."

When I saw Scrooge for the first time, I shuddered. He was just as rock hard as Dickens had described him. His body was already thin, and even though he wasn't older than 40, his eyes had a worn out, hollow look. He was very good at his job and it had sucked the soul right out of him.

"It's a pleasure to meet you," Mr. Scrooge said dryly. "I hear you are the force behind the London Dockland scheme. Very impressive."

"Thank you, sir," Jacob said graciously. "And am I to understand that you personally arranged the financial backing for the Coldharbour Mill in Devon, along with several other beam-steam-engine powered woolen mills?"

"That is true," he responded politely.

"What is your opinion of South America bonds?" Jacob Marley tested.

"A fine investment for fools and ignorant country bankers," Scrooge said slyly. "Do you know of any? If so I can help them purchase a portfolio full of them, as long as my fee is paid in advance."

"I think you might be right, Mr. Smith," Jacob said heartily. "He's a man after my own heart. If the arrangements can be made I would like to consider a merger. Shall we call the new firm Scrooge and Marley? It has a nice ring to it, don't you think? Let us drink to our potential partnership."

"Not tonight," Scrooge said coldly. "I will be available tomorrow morning if you like and we can work out the details. Good day to you both."

"What's gotten into him?" Marley snorted as Scrooge walked away.

"Take no offense," Mr. Smith replied. "Mr. Scrooge does not like Christmas. He is opposed to it on ethical grounds."

"I'm opposed to Christmas for other reasons," Jacob said darkly, taking a silver coin from his pocket, palming it, then returning it to his pocket again. "I think we shall get along just fine."

"Do you see the coin in his hand?" the Spirit asked. "What started out as a token of love became a symbol of financial obsession."

The smoke surrounded the fiery screen, transporting us through more years of Jacob Marley's life. To say they were successful in business is an understatement. Together they arranged the finances for the most important ventures of the

86

early industrial revolution. Millions of men and woman lost their jobs on farms and villages all across the empire as machines and factories replaced their occupations.

When Charles Dickens wrote he was a nose to the grindstone Scrooge, he must have meant the same for his business partner as well. Jacob Marley only celebrated the holiday when he had a deal to close. But no matter how important the social event, if it landed on Christmas, Mr. Scrooge never attended.

"Nothing important here," the Spirit stated, peering through images of his life. "Nothing important, unimportant. Wait! Right here… Christmas Eve, 1820. I'm afraid this will take more than just watching events unfolding on an animated screen to learn about this one. Out of your seats immediately!"

"Where are we going?" John asked, barely standing up before the chair disappeared into the wax.

"The true question is, into what dimension?" she replied, causing all the chairs, tables and equipment to melt back into the candlestick. "There are too many important things to learn firsthand. Everyone hold hands. I normally only have to tow one person around on Christmas Eve," the Spirit said sternly, turning back into an old woman, "so you'd better all hold on to each other tight. I don't know where you might end up if you let go. Once all the candle wax is burned, and the wick goes out, I won't be able to relight another candle until next Christmas."

The Spirit's hair burned with a brilliance like I had never seen before, surrounding us all in a cleansing, beautiful flame. I held on to the Spirit's hand with my right and Julia's with my left. John wanted to hold on to the Spirit's hand as well, but had to hold onto Julia's instead. The scene from the candle disappeared with a wisp of smoke and another wisp brought us to a narrow filthy street.

The glare of the candle died down, leaving the sun shining off of the snow instead. It somehow seemed less bright, even though I still had to squint to see clearly. When my eyes adjusted to the light, I saw a narrow street, with two- and three-story buildings on both sides. Some were made of wood, others of brick, and still others of more clay-like materials whitewashed with lime.

"Where are we?" Julia asked, looking around at the filthy cobbled street and glass-windowed buildings.

"I think you can figure it out on your own," the Spirit said, pointing to a sign above our heads.

"You have to be kidding?" Julia burst out laughing looking at the words.

The sign simply read, "Scrooge and Marley," and nothing more. The sign was old and worn, and just as cold as Dickens described in his book. I flipped open the old book to page 2 and read the ancient words. "Scrooge never painted out Old Marley's name. There it stood, years afterwards, above the warehouse door: Scrooge and Marley."

"Do you have the courage to enter?" the flaming Spirit asked me as an old woman, her crackling hair becoming cooler again. "You can't hide anything from me. You are afraid. You don't dare walk into the warehouse to see if either Mr. Scrooge or Mr. Marley is there. Are you going to give into your first impulse to run or go in and see for yourself?"

"Mason suffers from an acute case of paranoia when it comes to confronting powerful men," Julia added. "Sometimes the fear of the unknown keeps him from moving forward, isn't that right dear?"

"I'm not indecisive," I complained, pulling together all my courage. "Just cautious. I'll go in. They can't be all that bad, right?"

I felt for the doorknob, but my hand passed right through the door. Not wanting to seem weak, I walked through the wood and came out on the other side. When I made it through the wood I was standing inside a cold and uninviting room. The others followed, joining me in the dim light. As our eyes adjusted to the dark I noticed we were not alone. The warehouse was full of clerks and accountants all busily and silently working.

"I don't think Scrooge or Marley could see us even if they were here," Julia added hopefully. "These are just shadows of the past. Isn't that right, Spirit?"

"That's true," the Spirit said, turning into a young woman again. "Watch and learn."

"More like, watch out!" John grunted, jumping out of the way.

John's warning was too late. An energetic man bulldozed into the room, walking right through me as if I were made of smoke. I barely got a chance to see Jacob Marley but I got a good look at the man following him. He was well dressed, flamboyant and friendly, entering the building through the open door, not minding the rude behavior of the older man. Jacob grabbed a handful of keys from his desk and walked to the back of the office, sending bookkeepers fleeing in every direction.

"Scrooge!" the angry man bellowed. "I've got a client. Where are you?"

"I'm finishing up the daily accounts," a commanding voice responded, as cold and harsh as a winter's freeze.

Ebenezer Scrooge walked out of his office, just as hard and shrill as he was the first time I saw him.

"I'd like you to meet His Royal Highness, Gregor the First, Sovereign Prince of the State of Poyais." Jacob smiled cunningly.

"It's an honor to meet you, Your Royal Highness," Scrooge responded respectfully, bowing deeply. "I've read about your exploits in securing the independence of Venezuela from the Spanish Crown. Very heroic work. I'm sure you've made Clan MacGregor very proud. I also understand you were recently granted the title to an impressive new country, off the Mosquito Coast, I believe. What brings you here?"

"I have a financial venture I'd to like to discuss with ye," he said, acknowledging his accomplishments with humility.

"His Royal Highness would like to hire our services," Marley butted in. "He requires our assistance to issue 2,000 bonds with face values of one, two and 500 pounds, respectively. Of course, before we issue the bonds we must first sell land grant currencies, establish exchange rates, and a thousand other details."

"All of this sounds very expensive," Prince Gregor complained, uncomfortably. "Don't get me wrong. Me country boasts a prosperous city, deep water ports, and is rich in gold and silver and other valuable resources, but sadly short of investment capital."

"I'm afraid all of these services will be very costly," Mr. Marley said unapologetically. "But knowing how lucrative this scheme will be, we will offer Your Royal Highness our services on credit. Once the bonds are issued, we will accept Certificates of Land Rights and Poyais Treasury Bonds to settle your account. Is that arrangement acceptable to Your Highness?"

"Completely," Prince Gregor beamed. "Carry on! If I may use Certificates of Land Rights and Poyais Treasury Bonds in trade, then me resources are practically unlimited."

"May I have a word in private?" Scrounge demanded, practically pulling his partner into his office, and slamming the door. A few muffled words passed through the heavy door, but nothing more. A few minutes later the door opened widely and a hot-faced Scrooge stepped out, followed by a completely calm Jacob Marley.

"Our firm is at your disposal," Ebenezer Scrooge said in an overly sweet voice. "Be assured, in respect of Your Royal Highness, every "i" will be dotted and every "t" crossed. We will make sure Your Royal Highness does the same."

"What's going on?" I asked the Spirit as the scene evaporated from our view. "Something doesn't seem right!"

"You are correct," the Spirit said sadly, flipping her hands and covering us all in fire and smoke. "Watch on, more will be revealed."

The Cedar of Lebanon Tree

When the Spirit caused the next scene to appear, we found ourselves standing in the same crowded accounting room. Nothing had changed from the previous year, the same drab paintings were hanging on the same drab walls. Suddenly, a group of eager men and women entered into the warehouse, followed by Prince Gregor MacGregor and Jacob Marley.

"Do you have the Certificates of Land Grants ready, Mr. Scrooge?" his partner asked eagerly. "These good people would like to get back to their warm homes this fine Christmas day."

"Of course I have them ready," Scrooge shot back, creeping out of his unheated room like an unwelcome rat.

"I wish ye could've purchased these Land Grants in October," Prince Gregor lamented. "I was letting them go for only three shillings, three pence per acre then, but the market has increased their value. But no worries, even at four shillings an acre it's still a bargain. Did ye hear that we just issued 2,000 bearer bonds?"

"That's wonderful" a woman exclaimed. "We'll all be rich! But for now, please, Your Royal Highness, please tell us about the territory of Poyais one more time?" she begged. "It fills my heart with joy just hearing about it."

"It's all right here in Captain Thomas Strangways' pamphlet. "Sketch of the Mosquito Shore," he insisted, holding up the impressive leather-bound publication. "The county is a land of plenty with fertile soil and untapped gold and silver reserves. St. Joseph, the capital, is teeming with 20,000 other English settlers who have started cultivating the land, but they need the help of ye good people to become a strong and independent nation. Ye'll be remembered as fondly in the history books as Christopher Columbus is remembered for discovering America."

"I could have read it," the women swooned. "But hearing Your Royal Highness tell the story sends chills up my back. Charlie, pull out your bag, we're buying all we can."

"Ye are such a wise woman," Prince Gregor assured her. "The rest of ye may not get any land at all if ye don't get your coin bags out as well. Mr. Scrooge has all the paperwork ready. Aye, this should nae take long at all, if ye all come in an orderly fashion, one at a time please."

The whole room clamored with prospective investors, fighting each other for the best place in line. Jacob Marley smiled while Ebenezer Scrooge took money and issued the land grants to all takers. One eager customer after another made the exchange until a little girl offered up a small bag of gold coins to the clerk.

"This is my inheritance," she said shyly. "I want to make an investment. My father died and this is all he left me."

"You're a fine girl," Prince Gregor praised. "A fine girl, and one who knows a good investment when she sees it."

"Stop," Jacob whispered, taking the bag of gold from the clerk and handing it back to the child. "We don't accept money from children in this establishment. Go home to your guardian, and get an education with your inheritance."

"But with the returns on her investment she will be able to live as rich as Midas," Prince Gregor insisted quietly. "Let the girl make her investment."

"I won't have it," Marley whispered back furiously, grabbing Prince Gregor by the arm and dragging him into another room. "I'll take money from these stupid people, but not from a child."

"Then send them all away," the Prince snarled. "As far as I'm concerned, they're all children! What do they know about money, investing, or colonizing? Once they find out ye won't take money from a child, the whole mob will walk away with their money as well."

"This is madness," Jacob fumed. "Selling land grants to stupid investors is one thing, but booking them on passages to the jungle of the Mosquito Coast is a whole other matter! Can't you be happy with the fortune you've already made? Stop this foolishness. You're condemning these people to die. It'll be Jamestown, all over again."

"They know the risks," Prince Gregor said coldly. "Take her money or I'll find me another brokerage house."

"What's going on here?" Ebenezer Scrooge demanded, bursting into the room. "All the investors are ready to walk away."

"I'll take care of this," Jacob growled. "Get Miss Eliza's land grants prepared."

Jacob Marley walked out of the room and smiled to everyone. "Ladies and Gentlemen," he said cheerfully. "Do not be alarmed. I just needed to clarify a special arrangement I had made with little Miss Eliza here. We of course are eager to complete this transaction but I had to remind His Royal Highness that I had made prior arrangements to sell her land grants when the price was only three shillings, three pence per acre. Being a reputable house, I will follow through with my promise."

"That's coming out of your bankroll," Mr. Scrooge whispered, as he prepared the paperwork.

"So be it," Jacob Marley agreed, secretly putting all the gold coins back into the young girl's bag and sending her on her way with the newly issued land grants.

"What just happened there?" Julia asked confused as the vision closed up around us. "I thought he was too heartless to care."

"He had a soft spot for children," the Spirit smiled. "His one redeeming virtue. The coins you see floating, just outside his reach, are the coins he gave away that day. Without them, he would have had no hope for redemption at all. Unfortunately, other chains were forged the same day. The following scene will let you see how securely they were attached."

When the Spirit took us to the next location, we were standing on the planks of the sailing vessel, Honduras Packet. Eager settlers hugged the railing, looking out over the green swampy shores of the Mosquito Coast, the white cloth of the ship's sails billowing in the wind.

"About Ship," a voice cried over the celebration, maneuvering the ship into the harbor of St. Joseph, Poyais.

"We've made it my dear child," a mother comforted her sick daughter. "Soon we will have a solid roof over our heads and your father will be a foreman over a rich gold mine."

"I sold my business to be the royal shoemaker," a man proudly stated to another, trying to spot the promised city. "I already have 200 pounds from the Royal Bank of Poyais to help get me started."

We looked out to where the city was supposed to be, but saw nothing but rushes and unworkable land. We couldn't see a dock to put down the gangplank, or even a dry spot to let the passengers get off the ship.

"I don't see a city," Julia announced confused, looking where all the people were searching.

"I don't see one either," I admitted. "What's going on here?"

"The city of St. Joseph didn't exist," the Spirit lamented, turning ghostly and ancient. "The prosperous city His Royal Highness bragged about consisted of four broken down buildings and an overgrown cemetery. His claim that they would prosper was a lie. Of the 240 souls who risked everything to colonize this uninhabited jungle, only 50 people survived the year. The rest died of disease and starvation."

"How could this happen?" I exclaimed. "How could he send colonizers to settle a country that didn't even exist?"

"That it is what it is, I cannot change," The Spirit said firmly, remaining old and haggled. "My gift to you is light! Light is knowledge and knowledge is power. Use it wisely. Come along we have more to see."

I could not have been more relieved when the suffering cries of the stranded people faded into the past. When the new scene emerged, I and my friends found ourselves on a lonely road. The smoke didn't seem to disappear completely this time. Instead it transformed into fog, effectively obscuring the moonless night.

"Go back to the office, Mr. Scrooge," Jacob Marley demanded, holding up a single candle lantern to his face. "I don't need your services anymore tonight."

"Will you be safe?" Mr. Scrooge asked with concern.

"Yes, I will," Jacob Marley said. "Only a Grand Huntsman could have tracked us here. But if you meant to say, will the 900,000 pounds in bonds be safe? You don't have to worry about that either."

"You've always been good in business," Mr. Scrooge complimented, turning his horse around. "I'll have the room ready for the gold when you come with the wagon."

"Yes, yes," Jacob said nervously. "Get going, it's almost time."

"A secret business transaction," Julia said "I don't know what he's up to, but it can't be good."

"Scrooge is just as underhanded," John agreed. "Look how he goes along with everything he's told to do. He may not be making the deals happen, but he's sure willing to provide the paperwork."

"Shush," I said quietly. "What's that sound?"

"It sounds like galloping horses," John said uncomfortably.

"They're still a way off, but coming in fast," Julia added. "It's a good thing they'll slide right through us, because if not, I'd be afraid of getting run over."

We didn't wait long, a black coach appeared out of the darkness, sliding to a stop less than a foot away from where we stood. I jumped back, startled at the speed in which it finally made its appearance.

"Happy Christmas, Mr. Smith," Jacob Marley said cunningly as the coachman's horses complained loudly. The old man slid off of his wagon, landed on the foggy damp ground, and marched directly to the coach.

"I can hardly call this a happy occasion," Mr. John Smith, his former employer at the Bank of England scoffed as he left the comfort of his fine carriage and joined him.

"Now, now my old master. There's no reason to be gloomy. I thought we had all the details worked out. I give you 900,000 pounds' worth of South America bonds in exchange for five boxes of gold. It's a perfectly fair trade."

"How much is that worth?" I asked the Spirit.

"It's about 90 million of your current dollars," she answered easily. "A sizeable fortune to be sure."

"I'd like that in my bank account," John insisted."

"Not at this price," the Spirit assured him. "Watch."

"Why are you hesitating?" Jacob asked curiously. "When have I ever been less than honest with you? Surely you can see the advantages here."

"An advantage, you say?" Mr. Smith said with a frown. "There is little advantage in trading gold for paper assets, especially for bonds we both know can change their value so quickly."

"That's a good point," Marley conceded. "But knowledge is power. Sometimes a tiny kernel is worth more than a barrel of gold."

"Humph," is all the old master could respond. "Where is the Prince now?"

"The fool is heading to France. He thinks he can sell more land there. I told him sending settlers to Poyais was a bad idea, but he wouldn't listen. Now the hen has come home to roost. The remaining 50 survivors of his failed venture are aboard the British ship Ocean, which will make port in London around the tenth of October."

"That's less than two weeks!" Mr. Smith scoffed. "How could you possibly know that?"

"I would never attempt to make such an important trade without solid information," Marley said knowingly. "I met the captain and first mate of a Dutch clipper who passed the Ocean just two weeks ago. I paid them well to keep this information completely secret. They will not dare reveal the details if they intend to keep their lives. When the doomed ship arrives, all the bonds sold in the Poyais venture will eventually become valueless, taking the South American bonds with them. I foresee this will be the pin that pops the stock market bubble, leaving all but the biggest banks bankrupt, and a huge mess for your political friends to clean up. So there is the truth. You have a few precious days to make good on one of the greatest business opportunities of your lifetime. Use it wisely."

"And all of this because Gregor MacGregor thought to make himself a prince?" the rich banker mused. "You've made a fortune off of him already, haven't you?"

"No more than I have made off many others." Jacob Marley said callously. "If it weren't for uneducated, over-eager buyers, would any of us make our fortunes? Since you're in politics you should do something to regulate the banking system. It's in danger of a collapsing the whole economy!"

"Yes, I should... I do have some ideas for economic reforms I'd like to discuss with you..."

"Later," Jacob interrupted him, looking nervous all of a sudden. "I feel like we're being watched. We should make the trade now. The damp will kill us both if we don't."

"Very well," Mr. Smith agreed cautiously. "Let's complete the transfer."

We all watched as five heavy boxes of gold were moved from the coach to the waiting wagon. A heavy box of South American bonds was revealed and counted, including a sizeable portfolio of the ill-fated Poyais bonds.

"I wish you good fortune," Mr. Smith affirmed, getting into his carriage after the transaction was complete. "And a long life as well. But to be honest, if we keep meeting like this we will end up with neither."

"But then again," Jacob Marley shot back, pulling his silver shilling out of his pocket as he drove away. "If the reward is worth the risk, we will meet again. I may not have your royal pedigree, but I have an eye for profit. The devil will take us both in the end!"

The smoke began to swirl as Jacob Marley drove his wagon into the darkness leaving us standing in a tornado of smoke and fire.

"The fortune has been created, and its final binding chain forged," the Spirit announced, looking old and worn out. "The sinner and his treasure have been bonded together. Jacob Marley's lust for money and power have condemned him to his present torment. Quickly take my hand, I have one more vision of the past to show you."

The smoke whisked around, bringing us back to the evergreen Cedar of Lebanon tree. A dark thin man was speaking to an older woman and her servant when the scene fully formed.

"Thank you for meeting with me on such short notice, Baroness," a familiar man said courteously.

"Not at all, Mr. Scrooge," an older Sarah Otway- Cave replied. "I am curious why we are meeting here however. I have not stood under this tree since... since I was a young woman."

"That is what I am here to talk about," he replied stoically, pulling a silver shilling from his coat pocket. "I have come to return this coin to you. Alas, it was never spent for the purpose it was intended. It was Jacob's last request."

"His last request?" she gasped, taking the coin and holding it close to her heart. "What are you talking about?"

"He was murdered this morning, only a few hours ago."

Sarah gasped, fell to her knees, and burst into tears.

"I'm sorry to trouble you like this," Ebenezer continued, waiting only a few moments. "He didn't think you would still have feelings for him."

"Of course, I have feelings for him," she sobbed. "He was my only true love. I hate the man he became, but the younger man I fell in love with was as beautiful as crystal. Why have you come to torment me?"

"For reasons I cannot fully explain," he said, ignoring her grief. "I must ask if he can be buried under this Cedar of Lebanon tree."

"How can you be so heartless, sir?" her servant cried out, crouching to comfort her mistress. "Can't you see the awful state she's in?"

"This is an urgent matter," he said emphatically. "I would not trouble her grace if there were any other way."

"I can manage, Elizabeth," the Baroness said, gaining her composure and straightening her dress. "I've mourned for Jacob Marley my whole adult life. Why do you wish to bury him under my tree? Shouldn't he be given a proper burial? Isn't he highly respected in the financial world?"

"Yes, of course," Scrooge replied. "We will bury an ornate casket with full honors at St. Paul's Cathedral, in his memory, but his body needs to be buried secretly. No one can know."

"When do you plan to bury him?"

"Tonight!" he insisted. "Give your servants a night off and we'll finish up before morning."

"The Spirit of Christmas Past caused the wintry vision to unravel before our eyes. "Hold on to me children," she said, her hair glowing dimmer by the second. "We should have left sooner, but we had to stay. It was too important for me to show you everything, we had to stay."

"What's wrong?" Julia asked compassionately. "Your hair is flickering."

"The wick is almost out," she gasped. "The wax of the candle is spent, and if the flame goes out before I get you home, you will be trapped in the in-between world until next Christmas Eve. My magic is dying. Hold on to me, I think I can get us back."

Julia held onto the Spirit's hand, and John and I held on to hers. She pointed her free hand to the sky and in an instant all the ground below us was gone. The smoke swirled thicker and thicker as the moments lingered on.

"What happens to Jacob Marley?" I begged. "Was he killed on the way home?"

"I don't have the candle wax to tell you more," she coughed. "We're almost there," she coughed again. "Almost there."

"What will happen to you?" Julia cried.

"The same thing... that happens to any candle... that brings true light to the... world," she said slowly, happily, loosening her grip on Julia's hand before turning grey. "I die."

At that moment her hair went out. "No!" Julia cried.

The Spirit's fingers disappeared from Julia's hand in a puff of swirling smoke. Seconds later there was nothing left of her except for white misty ashes. Without her direction we spun upward through time and space. The smoke in the air carried us forward, becoming a thick curling river and transporting us back home.

"We're all going to die," John yelled frantically. "We're not going to die," Julia shouted back. "We might be stuck in here until next Christmas, but we're not going to die."

"Lost for a year?" he yelled in the swirling smoke. "That's almost worse!"

Up ahead I saw something colorful, something familiar... A Christmas tree. The floor was transparent and upside down but

I could see the base of the tree, wrapped presents, and the shadow of my mother's favorite couch coming up fast.

"Heads up everyone," I warned, "I think we're passing back through the floor!"

I shielded one hand in front of my face and held Julia tight with the other as the floor opened back up and threw us out of its depths like Jonah being spewed out by the whale. We lurched upward about two feet above the floor, then fell back down with a thud, right in front of my family's Christmas tree.

"We made it!" I said gratefully, panting on the floor.

"I can't believe we survived that," John groaned, picking himself up.

Julia let go of my neck, and rolled away from our dog pile. "I had her hand," she cried. "I tried to save her, but she simply faded away."

"I don't think she was worried about saving herself," I insisted. "I think she meant to save us, but I have to admit, I can't imagine why she would even want to save Jacob Marley."

"Jacob was pretty intense," John admitted. "But I didn't see any dangerous ghosts. Lame."

"You would say that," Julia smiled, brushing off a little ash from her pants and shoulders. The ash she brushed off rose into a tiny cloud, swirling and dancing in the air, until it landed on the Christmas tree. For one brilliant moment, the whole tree lit up with star dust then went dark again.

"Thank you, Spirit," Julia said reverently. "She told us these were shadows of the things that have been. That they are what they are, do not blame me. We can't change the past, but we can learn from it."

Christmas Ambrosia

It seemed to take a long time for the clock to finish ringing out twelve chimes, I counted every one. I was confused why the clock struck twelve all over again. Had a day passed or were we repeating the same long night? I looked at my cell phone, and even it said midnight. How could we have lost a whole day? I held my breath as the final chime came and went, but nothing happened. The room didn't fill up with light, the floor didn't evaporate like before, and I was left completely stumped.

"Where do you think the Spirit of Christmas Present has gone?" I asked curiously.

"Maybe he forgot," John answered with a smile. "After all, he is a Large Forgetful Spirit."

"At least in one movie he is," I said, pulling Julia down with me to the cushy couch. "I think we'll wait for him here."

"He won't come at midnight," John informed us with the book in his hand. "He'll come at the stroke of one. It says so, right here."

"Good," I replied. "That gives us a little time to figure things out."

"I like that idea," Julia agreed. "Let's put together what we know so far. Jacob Marley was a jilted suitor who became a ruthless businessman. We know for sure he only helped one small child in his life."

"We also know he was last seen hauling a fortune in gold coins in an unguarded wagon in the middle of the night," I added. "I wonder if he made it to his warehouse safely..."

"Doubtful," John said. "I'm betting Jacob Marley didn't make it back alive."

"And somehow Prince Gregor was so close to stealing the gold, he still thinks it belongs to him," Julia reasoned.

"It's still a mystery to me," I admitted. "Hopefully the Spirit of Christmas Present will shed some light on the matter."

"I'm a bit sleepy, Julia sighed, snuggling into me. "I think I'll take a quick nap. Wake me when it's one o'clock."

"I'll read a bit then," John offered, opening the book to the chapter dedicated to the Spirit of Christmas Present. I listened to him for a few minutes while he read it aloud, but fell asleep quickly, too. In what seemed like only a few moments John shook my leg to wake me up.

"It's almost one o'clock," he whispered. "Be prepared for anything!"

I opened my eyes expecting the worst, but the one o'clock hour came and passed with nothing happening. Julia was awake by now as well, waiting just as frantically.

"Wait for it," John said slowly, crouching on the couch holding a pillow as a defense. "I think I see him coming. He's huge, enormous, brace yourself!"

Julia held my hand tightly as John jumped off the couch. "He's not here!" he yelled, scaring both of us to death.

"Whose side are you on anyway?" I complained, throwing a pillow at his head.

"The bored side," he complained. "My reading didn't help at all. Right now I'm going to get myself a midnight snack from the refrigerator, Peace out!"

John annoys me sometimes. He threw the pillow back at me and sauntered off to the kitchen. He opened the refrigerator and froze, staring in disbelief. Whatever was inside that appliance made the whole room glow with light.

"Uh, guys," he said slowly. "I think you'd better come see this."

"Come in!" a hearty voice boomed out of the refrigerator. "Come in, and know me better, man!"

I ran over with Julia and peered into the ordinary kitchen appliance. Sitting on a tiny magnificent throne, right next to a pickle jar and a gallon of 2% milk was a boisterous man with curly dark brown hair and a holly wreath on his head. His green coat was edged with the most beautiful white fur, and his left hand held a torch, filling the whole room with light.

"I am the Ghost of Christmas Present," he laughed heartily. "Look upon me sitting in your well-stocked icebox! Which of you is the bearer of the coin?"

"I am," I answered boldly, taking the coin from my pocket, and showing it to him.

"A very powerful token," he mused, "full of magic. It holds both dreams and despair. What say we learn more about this man and his quest?"

"You bet," I agreed, returning the coin to my pocket.

Come, come then," he bade. "Take each other by the hand, and you, coin-bearer, take the hem of my coat."

"This is gonna be good," John said eagerly, taking Julia by the hand. "Let's get this party started!"

Julia held my hand tightly as I reached down just above the cheese and touched the Spirit's coat hem. With a roar and a flash, the whole room transformed into a giant banquet hall with foods of every variety stacked on the tables. Cakes and cookies, roasted meats, and pitchers full of delicious drinks seemed to go on forever, putting any Chinese-all-you-can-eat buffet to shame.

"See the bounty of the earth," he said, placing his cornucopia-shaped torch on a sturdy golden stand. "There is plenty for everyone! The sun shines freely every day, new children are born with fresh ideas every second."

"The world has the capacity to provide an endless feast for every person alive," he insisted, picking up a plate and filling it with all sorts of delicious foods. "There's room enough to house and feed billions and billions more of her children, so eat, eat, don't be shy! We have much to do and only a limited amount of time to draw energy from the universe to do it in. I recommend the roast beef, simply divine."

I didn't have to be told twice. I took a plate from the table and started piling food on it. As I did, the plate seemed to hold everything I placed on it with room for more. Julia was pickier than me, but even she began to wonder at the magic of our plates. John didn't notice anything. He grabbed at everything he could, sat down and quickly started shoving food in his mouth.

"What are you looking at?" he asked with his mouth full. "The Spirit said to eat quickly, and I am doing what he says."

"A wise young man!" the Spirit agreed, pulling the flesh off of a turkey breast faster even than John could eat. "Time is short, but the harvest is great, and the baked potato and sour cream is heavenly."

Julia and I sat next to each other and started to feast. The flavor and texture of each food exploded in my mouth, and I found myself eating just as vigorously as the Spirit. I looked over at Julia, and she was just as enchanted by the amazing flavors. In just a few minutes we had consumed everything on our plates and drunk all the nectar from our goblets. The large Spirit stood up and let out a hearty belch.

"That's your 10-minute warning," he sang out happily. "Eat all you can and enjoy yourselves. We have a long day's journey to attend to."

The happy Spirit continued eating and I followed his example. If the turkey was good, the Christmas ham was even more delicious, its honey-glazed meat melting down my throat. The mashed potatoes were smothered in melted butter, and blended perfectly with the exquisite country gravy. I dipped my ham in the gravy, and alternated between the meat and the potatoes until they were both gone. After that, I just went crazy, eating everything in sight.

I know eating like this sounds obscene, but the joy and pure happiness each bite brought to my soul defies description. When I started eating dessert, I thought I had died and gone to heaven.

"Try the pumpkin pie," Julia would say, and I would try it and fall in love.

"Your turn," I begged, spooning a forkful of chocolate cake into her mouth, and she would almost fall off her chair in delight. I started to get worried about the way she was downing the chocolate mousse until I had a bite. Julia and I were laughing and teasing each other, while John was eating like a bulldozer flattening dirt. Suddenly another huge belch filled the banquet hall.

"Our time to feast is over," the Spirit said happily, reaching for a sword from an empty scabbard, then raising his empty hand in the air. "Peace on earth, good will toward men!" he called gleefully. "I do that for effect, you know. I don't have a sword, nor do I need one. Peace on earth doesn't require a weapon, only the power of love. Now it's time to share our feast with the world."

I expected not to be able to stand up after eating so much food, but instead, as I slid away from the table I was bursting with energy. I wasn't a foot away from the table when without warning, an enormous belch escaped my lips and continued for 10 seconds.

"Mason!" Julia reprimanded. "Show some respect."

"Not at all," the Ghost of Christmas Present said with glee. "That's the Spirit of Gratitude. The host likes to hear a grateful belch from his guests."

"I really don't belch," Julia said embarrassed. "Not that I don't have the ability, of course, but I make it a practice to never burp in public. I don't mean to be ungrateful. Thank you for the most delicious meal of my life."

John was still sitting at the table eating everything in sight. I don't think he heard a single conversation since he started eating. "It's time to go," I chided him. "You don't have to eat everything."

"If I sat here long enough I could," John insisted, still eating uncontrollably. "I love everything here! How can I thank you enough for such a delicious meal?"

"Just pull back from the table, young engineer," the Spirit commanded. "You can thank me in the usual way."

John pulled away from the table and stood up straight, which was an incredible feat if you had seen how much food he ate. He walked around for a few moments, trying to figure out what dessert to sneak from the table, when a rumbling began inside him and roared out like an erupting volcano.

"You are most heartily welcome," the Spirit said. "I like a boy who knows how to eat and can be grateful for it!"

"I couldn't stop eating the broccoli," John confessed to me quietly. "And I normally don't even like broccoli. Now I'm hooked."

"Once again," Julia said as she scooted back from the table, "I regret my inability to show gratitude the way you would like—" Within two seconds a loud burp started from deep inside her and kept going and going and... going. When she was finally done the Spirit clapped his hands and slapped his knees in delight.

"Wonderful!" our host belted. "Thank you for the compliment!"

"I can't believe I just did that!" Julia announced in shock. Her hand covered her mouth, trying to hold back another eruption but she wasn't successful and another roar filled the air.

"You are delightfully, doubly welcome," the Ghost of Christmas Present complimented happily. He gave Julia a merry hug, John a slap on the back, and me a whispered word of advice: "You shouldn't let this girl get away. Claim her quick. She's a special one."

"What are you two up to?" Julia asked warily. "Conspiring plans for your happiness," the Spirit whispered, jabbing me in the ribs. "But we have no more time to feed the shepherds, now we are tasked to feed the sheep."

With the wave of his hand all the remaining food floated off the table and hovered in the air. I didn't realize how far the banquet table reached, or how much food it contained, until it began piling up. The pile of deliciousness grew until it became as large as a mountain before us.

"Watch this!" the eager Spirit roared, and with the twist of his wrist and the flit of his fingers a bolt of lightning shot out of his hands, energizing the whole mountain of food.

I expected to see it explode into a giant pile of ooze, but instead it turned into an equally large pile of golden dust. The dust retained all the delicious odors of the original feast without mixing together to create something disgusting.

"Into the bag," the Spirit commanded, producing a large red canvas container, ready to be filled up by his grasping hands. The dust obeyed, swirling and pouring into his outstretched bag without so much as making the strong spirit flinch. The storing capacity of the bag was magical too because no matter how much gold dust flowed into the pouch, it never filled up.

The Christmas Ambrosia roared into the bag like a raging sandstorm in a desert. After five minutes the flow stopped, except for a little stream that snuck out of John's pocket, finding its way into the bag.

"There," the jolly Spirit announced, grabbing his torch and lifting it high. "Now we are ready to feed the world."

"But isn't ambrosia the drink of the gods?" Julia asked timidly. "It's properties are supposed to grant all those who drink it immortality. At least that is what I read."

"Julia, my dear," the Spirit complimented, "you know your classics. However, Christmas Ambrosia is a slightly different variety but offering an equally important gift from the gods. It's stored as a powder then mixed into whatever food or drink is needed. We share immortal hope tonight rather than immortality. You'll find that immortal hope is a more enduring gift than simply living forever."

"I never thought of that," she smiled, "this is going to be fun."

"Right you are," he chortled. "As you are aware, the Ebenezer Foundation was liquidated recently, sending the fortune of Jacob Marley out into the world. We are tasked to use our Christmas Ambrosia to make sure the gift is received as intended... as well as giving you important clues to make your mission a success. Once again, will our young Santa Claus please take the hem of my cloak? The rest of you know what to do."

We didn't argue. I took Julia's hand and she took John's. With a little bravery I touched the hem of the Spirit's gigantic cloak and the whole room began to spin us around in circles. The refrigerator got smaller and smaller until we popped out of the center of the vortex, landing near a diner in the Midwest somewhere, by the look of the flat topography.

I looked around at the sparseness of the landscape around us and couldn't believe anyone lived here at all, let alone needed a diner. The small one-story building stood in front of us like a single tree on a vast plain, comfortable in its solitude.

The Spirit of Christmas Present pressed his face against a window and smiled broadly. "Just in time," he said, taking John by the arm and pulling him through the wall. A few seconds later he grabbed Julia and I, pulling us into the warm room as well.

"I love diners," The large Spirit said longingly. "They always have such delicious pie. But we've had our feast, now it's time for us to share it."

"Eat your biscuits and gravy, Susan," a tired but happy woman said. "My shift is about to start and I want to make sure you get plenty to eat. It's Christmas day and all the farmers are going to be hungry and happy to give big tips. Eat up!"

The nine-year-old girl was eagerly playing with a beautiful doll at the counter, but she put it down at her mother's request. "I'll eat Momma," Susan smiled happily.

"I've seen that girl before," Julia confided. "Where have I seen her?"

"She's the girl from the Christmas party four years ago," I gasped. "I'd know her anywhere. I gave her the doll while playing Santa Claus when I was just learning how to use Christmas magic. Somehow when I reached into my bag I found the doll she's holding right now. When I reached in again I found a wrapped box full of money for her mother. She used it to escape her boyfriend, the notorious Snake Skin. It happened so long ago though, I didn't think I'd ever see them again."

"An act of charity ripples like waves in a pond," the Ghost said with a smile as his torch glowed warm. "I see you are no stranger to kindness. Watch and learn what else can be done to bring joy and gladness into the world."

He reached into his cloak and pulled out his red bag full of golden dust. "Come see the power of our Christmas Ambrosia," he smiled, sprinkling a bit of golden spice on the little girl's humble breakfast.

"This is really good, Mamma," the child sang, eating with vigor.

"You must be hungry," her mother smiled. The woman left the room but soon returned with another serving.

"You try some," Susan begged. The Ghost sprinkled more dust on the second helping just in time for the mother to take a bite.

"That is good," she said, sitting down for the first time. "I don't think I've ever had biscuits and gravy so delicious. I'm going to get a plate for myself."

The enormous Spirit followed her into the kitchen where a large pot of gravy was popping and steaming. He took a generous pinch of dust from his pouch and sprinkled it into the white liquid. Just as Susan's mother finished her meal a man entered and the woman sprang from her seat to greet her first customer.

"Good morning, sir," she said happily.

"I'll have a number three, eggs over easy," he said with a thick Texas drawl.

When the waitress brought out his meal, a little bowl of biscuits and gravy was on the side.

"I didn't order this," he objected, "take it back."

"It's on the house today," she said sheepishly. "It being Christmas and all. Just try it, I think you'll like it."

"It does smell good," he admitted and took a little bite.

One bite was all it took. As soon as the next farmer came in the door he practically shoved a spoonful of gravy in his mouth. "Best biscuits and gravy in the county," he boasted. "Have the little lady get you a sample."

"I don't mind if I do," the second farmer beamed. "Heck, give me two plates of the stuff, it's Christmas today, and I've built up an appetite."

I watched in wonder as the whole cafe filled with rough, honest, hardworking men. Each one became bright and beautiful the minute they tasted the magical gravy. I saw the first man get up and leave with a wink and a smile at the busy waitress. "Be here tomorrow morning," he demanded. "I don't like being served by strangers... and to the rest of you dirt farmers, Merry Christmas!"

The whole room wished him a Merry Christmas as he left, then drove away in his old pickup truck.

Susan's mother was quickly cleaning up the table, when she found a hundred-dollar bill folded into to the credit card receipt. She held the money to her heart, tears splashing down her cheeks. She had been accepted into a new community and all would be well.

"Our work is done here," the Spirit announced, motioning us to come closer.

"Does the Christmas Ambrosia create good in people?" Julia asked, curious at the pronounced effect it had on them.

"Oh no," the Spirit said, the flame of his torch burning brighter with each burst of levity. "Christmas Ambrosia only brings out the best in people by filling them with immortal hope. These are good, hardworking men. They spend their riches coaxing grain and corn from the ground... in good harvest and bad."

"But what does all of this have to do with Jacob Marley?" I asked.

"Who do you think paid for this feast?" He said happily. "Through his torment Mr. Marley learned that money should, reinvested, helps young things grow. To value money over the hopes and dreams of the young is a terrible crime. N o w, take my cloak, we have many more tables to spice and hungry mouths to feed."

The Power of Love

The world disappeared as before, and we reappeared inside a sparsely furnished home filled to the brim with dozens of Christmas presents. The only furniture in the living room was an old couch loaded with colorful packages and a tube TV sitting inside a cluttered, broken down entertainment center. The room didn't have any pictures on the walls either, and if not for the reflection of colored lights sparkling from a fully lit Christmas tree, the room would have looked more like a jail cell.

Dozens may be an understatement, Christmas presents were stacked everywhere, piles upon piles of them. The whole room was filled, wall-to-wall with Christmas joy. Bicycles leaned against the ragged couch with bows and ribbons attached. A longboard sported a tag, proudly proclaiming its origin from Santa Claus, and a miniature kitchen set complete with a battery lit oven lamp stood by the door, left ajar as if placed there hastily. I knew it was placed that way, because I placed it there myself, and I was in a hurry.

"My, you three get around," the large Spirit smiled. "My Christmas brothers have rarely escorted such prolific givers."

"You can thank Jacob Marley for all of this," Julia said sheepishly. "He liquidated the Ebenezer Foundation and gave us the last of his money to distribute."

"I always wondered what tonight would look like," the Spirit marveled. "I know St. Nicholas has been planning the events of this evening for years. No wonder he wants me to show you where to find Marley's treasure. It all makes sense now."

"Didn't you know before?" I asked curiously.

"He probably told me, and I forgot!" he laughed heartily, his torch belching fire with him. "I'm not good at remembering the past, but when it comes to knowing the present, I am the expert! You shared Christmas magic with a whole community today, and started a chain reaction of dreams that bore fruit tonight. But I didn't bring you here just to show you a room full of Christmas presents. I'm here to show you how they are received. I'm so excited for what happens next... I love fireworks."

Moments later a bare-chested little boy came walking out of his crowded bedroom with nothing on but his pajama bottoms.

"What the heck!" he yelled, looking around the room in amazement.

"What are you screaming about?" his older brother complained, walking around the corner wearing nothing more than the first. "Where did all this come from, Bobby?" he blurted. "Is any of this stuff ours?"

"I think so," little five-year-old Bobby giggled, picking up a present. "There's a tag on it, what does it say?"

"To Tiffany, from Santa," his older brother Ashton read slowly, still wiping sleep from his eyes.

"You got a present, Tiffany!" Bobby yelled as loud as he could. "Come open it. It's Christmas! Santa Claus came! Santa Claus came! Do you have a present there for me?" he asked enthusiastically.

John, Julia, and I watched in delight as little four-year-old Tiffany walked in the room and burst into tears of joy. "Santa Claus loves me," she cried, running right for the door. "He brought me my kitchen set!"

"And now for the part I've been waiting for," the Spirit of Christmas Present chuckled, "watch this."

I expected Ashton Chilton to freak out when he saw the chemistry set and white laboratory coat. What I didn't expect was the negative way his father reacted.

"What is going on here?" he roared, from the hall. "Don't you know it's six o'clock in the blessed morning?"

"Dad's coming," Bobby whispered fearfully, hiding behind the Christmas tree. "He hates Christmas."

"What's all this crap?" he roared, looking at all the presents with disdain. He picked up a colorfully wrapped gift and threw it on the couch.

"Santa Claus came," little Bobby said timidly from behind the tree.

"There ain't no such thing," Mr. Chilton snorted, turning on the coffee machine and adding water to the pot. "Just do-gooder's trying to feel good about themselves. Don't touch a thing, don't open a present. I'm calling the cops."

"But it's a kitchen set," little Tiffany sobbed. "It's mine. I won't give it back."

"Oh yes you will!" he said furiously, dialing the number to 911. "If I can't buy it for you, you don't get it! Yea, this is an emergency," he bellowed. "Some intruders left a Christmas tree and a bunch of crap in my front room. Send out the cops, I want the place dusted for fingerprints and people thrown in jail for this."

"Yeah, I'll hold," he snarled, waiting impatiently for his coffee. "Freakin' 911 has to transfer me to the police department. I'll probably be on hold for an hour!"

The Ghost of Christmas Present took a pinch of golden dust and sprinkled it into the pot of freshly brewed coffee while Mr. Chilton paced the floor, fuming the whole way.

"Do-gooder's!" he yelled into the phone, pouring himself a mugful of the aromatic liquid. "Broke into my house and left a Christmas tree and a bunch of presents in my living room." He paused for a second, taking a drink from his Christmas Ambrosia-spiked coffee, frowning as laughter met his ears. "I'm not joking here. I want the whole place dusted for fingerprints, and I want to catch these rascals."

Mr. Chilton turned around and saw his three youngest children ripping open presents as fast as they could. He took another sip of his coffee and nodded his head in approval, not to the children, but to the amazing cup of coffee. He was about to reprimand them for disobeying him, but the coffee was so wonderful he took another sip instead.

"I want them thrown in jail," Mr. Chilton said emphatically, feeling a rush of satisfaction filling his soul. "Fine, I'll hold for the Police Chief. Finally, I'm getting somewhere."

Mr. Chilton waded through the torn wrapping paper and knocked a few wrapped boxes off the couch, sitting down defiantly. He took another sip of his coffee and closed his eyes in relief. Sensing they were being ignored for the time being,

Ashton, Bobby and little Tiffany continued opening and hiding away as many presents as they could put their hands on.

"Make a pile for Austin," Tiffany whispered. "I bet that longboard is for him."

"Finally," Mr. Chilton grunted with satisfaction. "Yeah, that's right, yes, yes. And I'm ticked off about it. They broke into my home and violated my property rights. I want them prosecuted to the fullest extent of the law."

Just then Austin, the oldest brother came walking into the room, rubbing his eyes. He stopped and panned the room, seeing the longboard in an instant.

"Don't touch that, boy," Mr. Chilton warned, "it's evidence. It's got fingerprints all over it."

"Yeah it does," Austin agreed, practically diving for the board, and picking it up triumphantly. "My fingerprints!"

"Put that down!" His father insisted. "All of you, stop opening presents! That's an order. What did you just say officer? Did you just call me a Grinch? I haven't been called that since high school. Yeah, you remember that? Good times weren't they? No, life has really sucked ever since Cindy died. If it wasn't for the kids, I'd end it all right now. They look happy this morning. I'm good, Charlie, thanks for taking my call. No I don't have to file a report. I think I'll just enjoy the day. See ya later."

"So does that mean we get to keep the presents?" little Bobby asked.

"Yeah, I guess," he smiled. "It's about time we enjoyed a little Christmas around here. Anything for me?"

"Right here, Dad," Ashton smiled, handing him an opened laptop. "I opened it by mistake, but it's yours."

"Thanks son," he answered gently. "It's just like the one I used at my last job. I wonder if I could go online and post a few resumes, who knows what might happen? I might find a job. But first, I'm getting another cup of coffee."

"We are done here as well," The Spirit of Christmas Present exclaimed, holding his torch into the air, and bringing us close together.

"What was the change in Mr. Chilton?" John asked.

"It really wasn't a very big change," the Spirit answered. "It was more a remembering. In his sadness after the passing of his wife, Mr. Chilton was afraid to let beauty return to his life. He felt guilty for feeling happy while his wife was lying dead in the ground. Our Christmas Ambrosia reminded him that his children were what his wife valued the most, and he should honor her memory by loving them. With immortal hope rushing back into his heart, he was able to do the rest himself."

We worked in the same spirit for the next 20 hours, traveling from one food kitchen to another, turning simple offerings into feasts fit for a king. We gave hope to teachers and medical care providers, social workers and emergency responders, plus every kind of charity worker imaginable. Every place we traveled, we brought joy and peace to the downtrodden and humble of heart.

What was unexpected though, was the number of artists, inventors, and computer programmers we inspired. We spent as much time fueling their creative spirits as we did feeding the poor. Our little feast seemed to give them an increased determination to continue their important creative endeavors.

We worked hard and long, yet we never seemed to tire, although I did notice the Spirit was beginning to age. His hair was turning white at the edges and the skin around his eyes started to show signs of getting old.

"So, the book is right?" I asked timidly. "You do age, don't you?"

"Yes, it's true," he smiled, grasping his torch. "I only have a few hours of life left to live and like over 2,000 of my brothers, I will die when this day is through. But I'm happy to report we just spent the last of Jacob Marley's treasure. I have been putting a certain task off, but now I know I must take you where I was assigned."

"So does this important task have anything to do with digging up a treasure?" John asked enthusiastically.

"Take my cloak," was all the Spirit said, lurching us into the night.

Chapter Fourteen

Dangerous Confessions

We landed in a new scene, right in the middle of the industrial part of London... misty fog, one-way streets, and a peculiar smell from a multi-century old sewer system made it all too clear. Of course the sign on one of the many taverns might have helped: "London's Best Fine Brew," was its invitation.

"Not exactly a place for children, eh?" the Spirit chuckled, his torch billowing flames with each laugh. "Can anyone tell me where we are?"

I looked around and the road did remind me of one I'd seen before. The four-story building was connected with the one next to it, like a trail of train cars permanently stuck on a crowded track. The glass in the windows were old, but not ancient. However, they did have a certain familiar pattern.

"It can't be," I said softly, pointing at the building. "It's called the Flying Scotsman now and the building is different, but the location is on the exact same street the Spirit of Christmas Past took us to yesterday!"

"You're right," John confirmed. "It's built on the same spot as Scrooge and Marley's old warehouse. I wonder if the ghost of Prince Gregor had any influence in the name?"

"I wouldn't doubt it," I agreed, noting the obvious reference to the Scotsman. "I wouldn't be surprised if he could also fly."

"Your skills of deduction are admirable," the Spirit grinned. "However, as we are about to enter into this unhallowed place, I offer a word of caution. Even though we are not actually visible, care must be taken. These are dangerous spirits."

"I'll be careful," Julia said smartly, "I just want to take a quick peek."

"You had better join her quickly," the Spirit urged as she disappeared through the door. "This tavern has a few nasty secrets."

Chapter Fourteen

Moments later Julia let out a bloodcurdling scream. Running to her rescue, I found her standing in a room full of drunken Christmas revelers along with hundreds of badly dressed ghosts. Each phantom was a sickening green, not altogether transparent, but having a form that appeared to have actual substance.

They were dressed in the ragged clothes of every era of English history. Some were covered in Viking-styled animal skins, others wore Roman togas, and still others dressed as simple peasants. The better part of them were dressed in somewhat more modern clothing, although they would have all looked more natural standing as displays in a historic museum.

By the look of their dirty appearance, they made no attempt to present themselves in any other way. Somehow I knew that part of their curse was the loss of any desire to improve themselves at all. They were content to look miserable and disheveled.

The mortal piano player plunked out an old English tavern song while all the drunken men sang along as best they could in their intoxicated state.

"Don't stand too close to them," the Spirit warned, "remember, this is the present. The ungrateful dead may not be able to see you, but they can sense it when something pure is present."

A snarling ghost stood up and walked cautiously toward Julia, sniffing, growling, and raising a filthy finger as if trying to touch her light. Julia backed away carefully, trying to stay outside his reach. His eyebrows raised together as he drew more certain he had found something worth pursuing. He stopped suddenly as an enthusiastic ghost bolted into the tavern.

"Happy Christmas!" the cheerful ghost sang.

"And what's so bonny happy about it?" the angry ghost bellowed, lowering his searching hand.

"Why, the holiday season always makes me happy," the colorful ghost answered hesitantly while backing up, "but it looks like you're dressed up for the wrong holiday. All Hallows Eve was two months ago. I wonder if I may have taken a wrong turn somewhere?" he coughed politely. "Is this the Hitchhiker's Pub by any chance? Now that Douglas Adams is dead, I hear he does book readings there on Christmas Eve... from time to time."

"The Hitchhiker's Pub's down the street, yeh gormless git!" the ghost yelled, picking him up and throwing him out the window. "Get out of me tavern and never come back! I thought I smelled something sweet and innocent in here. Blimey, I hate that smell!"

"It still stinks of goodness," another ghost complained. "If the stench doesn't clear out soon, I'm leavin'."

Suddenly, the jingling sound of a silver coin rolled around on the bar, drawing all the dead to their feet. In unison, the mob of greenish ghosts began crying, growling, and howling in misery. In a flash they raced to the coins, grasping at them as if they could pick them up. One spirit almost moved a coin when a large, stately-looking ghost knocked all the other hands aside and cupped the money greedily.

"This treasure's mine," the gentleman growled, pushing all the other ghosts away. "I lay claim to every treasure in this tavern. I am Gregor the First, Sovereign Prince of the State of Poyais. Yield to my demands or face my wrath!"

"There ain't no such place as Poyais," the chief ghost replied. "So why da yeh think you can claim our treasure?"

"Cause I'm the Flying Scotsman this tavern is named after," the prince lied. "I'm a Venezuelan war hero, a stock market maker and an economy breaker. I am a Prince of the New World. Ye can share in me empire or I'll send for the Hellhounds to take your souls back to the graves from where ye escaped."

"I don't want ta go back to me grave," a timid ghost with a top hat said, raising his hand. "I'll follow yeh ta where ever yeh want ta go, as long as there's treasure involved."

"Said like a man with conviction," Gregor called out enthusiastically, shouting even louder than the humans who were now singing songs and drinking heartily. "How about the rest of ye?"

A few more ghostly men agreed and stood next to the Scot. Prince Gregor MacGregor accepted their services while walking around the room, sniffing at the air.

118

"This place has the sickening smell of goodness in it," he complained. "If I didn't know better, I'd think the place was haunted by angels."

"It's just the stench of that idiot highbrow who was just here," the boney ghost complained. "I threw him out for good."

"Perhaps," Prince Gregor sniffed again. "But it seems stronger than that. It smells like Christmas."

"Christmas?" an obese ghost with a fraying waist coat said while sniffing in the air. "I like Christmas."

"Get out of me presence," Prince Gregor spat furiously, throwing the man out the door. "Christmas is me enemy. The wretched Santa Claus League have spent half of me hated enemy's treasure, and now they want to waste the other half. But I won't let them! Curse that Jacob Marley, may his bones rot forever!"

"It's the treasure of Jacob Marley yeh're referin' to?" the boney ghost asked. "Yeh're bragging about that treasure? Everyone wit' half a brain knows it doesn't exist. Go back to Venezuela and leave us alone."

"Do ye think me a powerless soul?" Prince Gregor shrieked, pulling a staff from his cloak and striking the ghost in the chest, knocking him through the bar of the pub. He flew so fast he caused paper napkins to fly off the tables and bottles to rattle on their shelves. The mortals in the room looked around in fear. One stood up, prepared to leave the pub.

"The pub's haunted," the old bartender scoffed. "You ought to know that by now. Let 'em have their fun and we'll have ours. You there, at the piano, plunk those keys or I'll find me a new boy!"

"I know where it's buried, ya pikey twit!" Prince Gregor cried forcefully. "I'm the one who murdered Jacob Marley!"

With that startling confession the Prince had everyone's attention. All the wicked spirits gathered around him, eager to hear his explanation.

"I was hidin' behind a tree when Jacob Marley finished a trade for a treasure in gold. I carefully followed after the slow-moving wagon, but me horse spooked his team and they jolted ahead in a gallop. I needed a better angle so I took a shortcut and cut him off as he was coming into the city. Then I fired off my brace of pistols, dealin' him a deadly blow that he ne're would recover from."

"What happened next?" the fat ghost asked in complete rapture.

"I was about to claim me golden prize when his galoot of a partner, Ebenezer Scrooge showed up with several armed men, surroundin' the carriage. I woulda killed all three but the morning dawn was about to break and more people were arrivin'. 'The tree, the tree,' I heard Marley beg, handing him a silly coin. 'Give this to Sarah at the tree.'"

"'He's fading fast,' I heard Scrooge yell, taking the reins and speeding ahead of the other men. "Meet me at Doctor Holloway's and bring the constable with you. Make haste! There's no time to spare, we may yet save his life!'"

"Bury my treasure with me," was the last word I ever heard from Jacob Marley. He died on the way to the surgeon, but not before clever Ebenezer took a wrong turn and unloaded all the gold back at his warehouse. When he arrived at the surgeon's residence with the blood-soaked body of his old partner, the constable, the coroner and the priest all agreed upon one fact: Marley was dead, as dead as a doornail."

"But what about the treasure?" the fat ghost asked impatiently. "What happened to the treasure?"

"I didn't know where it went," he confessed, "and I couldn't poke around trying to find it. Half of London was lookin' for me. Ebenezer suspected I was the assassin, so I had to lay low. I went to Paris and waited for the whole thing to blow over. When I returned several years later, I dug up the grave of Jacob Marley only ta find the treasure wasn't there! But then again, neither was the body of Jacob Marley. I never did find his body, nor the gold... I died a penniless man."

"I don't care how you died!" the fat ghost growled. "Tell us where the treasure's buried or we'll kick you back to Venezuela ourselves, the devil can pay the consequences."

"Have some patience, kind sir!" he said mockingly. "Some secrets just take time to uncover. What I could'na discover in life, I discovered after death. A hundred years ago I met the ghost of an old gravedigger who told me how he buried Marley with the treasure just as Mr. Scrooge promised."

"Even if yeh do know where he's buried," a ghost said timidly, "what'll yeh do about Jacob's bones? A doomed soul like Jacob Marley has his bones to protect his treasure; they're like a talisman."

"Ah, now you're using your head," Gregor congratulated. "I have that figured out as well because I have it on good word that Jacob Marley is on the road to redemption. Once he's detached from his treasure, he can't protect it anymore. The race has begun, the first one to dig up the gold wins' control over it! Once I have the gold, I'll share it with all of ye."

"You'll give us a stake in the gold?" a gaunt ghost asked greedily. "But how can we take it? We're dead! Our bodies are nothin' but bones and dirt. The treasure may be unprotected but we can't move it even if we wanted to."

"Not so," the wicked Prince bragged confidently. "I've been working on a few tricks in the last 100 years and perfected this one. Watch!"

He walked over to the dirtiest, nastiest drunk in the tavern and whispered in his ear. Next he stuck his fingers into his head and fiddled around in his brain until he flipped on some kind of invisible switch.

"Stand up, kind sir, and look at me."

The drunk man opened his eyes, stood obediently and looked right at Prince Gregor.

"What's your name good man?"

"Duane Slotham," he slobbered.

"Mr. Slotham," Prince Gregor ordered, "I command ye to be here at precisely one o'clock tomorrow morning."

"Aye, sir," he answered with a drunken slur. "I'll be right here, as drunk as ever."

"That's a good man," the prince congratulated. "And while you're at it, invite a few trusted friends to come join ye and bring along the tools you'll need for a grave robbin' party."

"Right, sir," he slobbered again. "Invite a few friends and bring along tools to rob a grave, but why?"

"You're going on a treasure hunt tonight," Prince Gregor said mysteriously. "Do you want to be rich?"

"That I do," he said greedily. "A treasure hunt sounds grand!"

"That's right. Now go back to sleep for a while and enjoy your well-deserved intoxication."

"Yes, Your Highness," the man answered, sitting back into his chair, and falling into a deep sleep.

"Jacob Marley isn't the only ghost with a mortal partner," he said triumphantly. "Our mortal labor problem has been solved! So now, I'm asking the question one last time. Who's with me?"

The whole crowd of greedy, ungrateful ghosts let out a thunderous cheer. An oppressive energy filled the tavern, the piano player piped up his tune, the drunk man woke up for another round, and the whole place became even more corrupt and unruly.

"The lust for money and power are not exclusively the traits of the rich," the Spirit of Christmas Present said sadly, "they're just as common in the poor. We should leave now, the only thing left to see here is just more drinking, singing, and plotting. Not a savory place for good folks like yourselves."

We were about to go when something bumped and scratched from underneath the Spirit's coat. He tried to take another step, but something clawed and clamored for him to stay.

"What's wrong?" I asked. "I thought you said we should leave."

"It's my children," the Spirit said sadly. "I didn't want to introduce them to you, but I suppose I must."

"I was hoping you wouldn't have to as well," John winced. "From what I've read, they might like an ugly place like this."

"You are correct, young engineer," the Spirit moaned. "My children don't want to leave this drunken establishment. Ignorance and Want are comfortable in places like this. Alcohol, mind-altering drugs, and filthy living conditions always bring out the worst in people. It makes them careless. This little boy is named Ignorance." He revealed a dirty, mostly-naked boy, digging his sharp uncut fingernails into the fair white flesh of the Spirit's leg. Faint trickles of blood seeped down his thigh, but quickly healed. I was revolted at the sight.

"And this poor child is my daughter, Want," he said, revealing an equally-gaunt little girl with the light of his torch. "She senses friends in this tavern, men who are willing to waste all their time and money, and allow their own children to suffer. As evil as my daughter may be, my son, Ignorance is more deadly."

"Any fortune gained at the expense of these two miserable children is cursed," the Spirit warned darkly. "It would be better for a millstone to be wrapped around their necks and tossed into the ocean than to offend one of these. Since each is preventing me from moving, take the hem of my cloak, Mason, and we shall rid ourselves of this wretched place."

We took each other by the hand and I reached out to take the Spirit's coat, but before I could grab it, the little boy took hold of my wrist, his bony hand impossibly strong. And now a disgusting the taste welled up in my mouth, a taste of decaying fish followed by the putrid flavor of rotten potatoes. Moldering infested meat now crawled into my mouth and I was defenseless to stop it.

"I can't breathe," I gasped, "he's killing me."

John ran to my rescue and forced my hand to grab the hem of the Spirit's cloak. As soon as I touched his cloak, mint and warm chocolate flooded my taste buds with pleasant memories. At the same instant, the grotesque creature let go of my arm and folded back inside the Spirit's cloak. I gasped, trying to catch my breath, while soaking in the wonderful tastes of Christmas. The Spirit's torch flamed higher and we all vanished into the night.

A few moments later we landed back in my kitchen as if nothing had happened... except for our guide, who now looked ancient and weak. I pushed away from his cloak, not wanting to be grabbed again by his secret cargo.

"I hope you see the challenges ahead of you," the now white-haired Spirit warned, his torch growing dimmer. "The ghost of Prince Gregor knows you're coming and he thinks he knows where the treasure is buried, with the manpower to claim and dig for it."

"Thanks for all you've done today!" I said.

"I love a grateful heart, my boy," he smiled respectfully, yet sad at the same time. "I go to meet my brothers now. My time has come. My children are grateful for your attention."

"Grateful?" I asked, confused. "How can you stand to be near them?"

"I love my children, Mr. Howell," the Spirit chastised gently. "I hope you'll learn to love them as well. Want and Ignorance will always be with you, so it's your duty to relieve their suffering, no matter how hopeless the task may seem. Don't make their torment more grievous by ignoring them or supporting those who profit them in any way. Do as you have seen me do, and bring the magic of Christmas into their lives, no matter the season of the year."

"I'll do my best," I promised.

"Good for you, my boy," he said as he handed me his magic red velvet pouch. "Here is a final gift for you. We haven't given away all of our Christmas feast yet tonight, it still holds a generous amount of Christmas Ambrosia dust to spread around. You may even need a generous portion of its life-giving properties yourself from time to time. Don't try to save it or use it sparingly. A feast like this is meant to be shared so, it will never run out."

"I'll keep that in mind," I said sincerely. "Is there anything we can do for you?"

"There is one thing I would like to try before I go," he said, pointing to the opened refrigerator. "May I have one of these metallic-contained beverages?"

"Sure," I said, pulling out a can and popping it open.

The Spirit took the drink, and in one giant long swallow emptied the whole can. "It tickles the nose doesn't it?" he said happily, his cornucopia shaped torch shooting out fireballs.

"I've never seen anyone do that," I said. "The carbonation makes you—"

"Buuuuuuuuuuuuuuuuuuuurrrrrrrrrrrrrrrrrppppppppppp ppppp," the Spirit of Christmas Present exploded. "Excellent vintage! Fare thee well, coin bearer."

"Thanks' for the compliment," I said as he faded away. "Fare thee well."

When the last light of the Spirit of Christmas Present was gone, the room seemed smaller and less alive, even though he filled only half the room. I thought about what he taught me. The poor and uneducated will always be with us, giving each generation an opportunity to feed and educate them.

Now we waited for the next visitor, the Spirit of Christmas Future, the ghost I feared the most.

The Black Future

The clock in the dining room struck one for the third time in our long night, sounding out its mournful tone. I knew that at the end of its eerie echo, the Ghost of Christmas Yet to Come would appear in my living room. When the chime fell silent I held on to Julia's hand, sensing she was just as nervous as I was.

We didn't have to wait long as the foreboding spirit walked through the front door, replacing the clock's ringing sound with the moaning and howling of a tormented soul. The Spirit of Christmas Future was a familiar sight to me by now, although instead of being wrapped in burial cloth, he was shrouded in a deep black garment, the same one St. Nicholas had given him to wear at the start of our bizarre adventure. His cloak sometimes shimmered with energy, yet still concealed everything inside completely. Black or not, I knew beneath that opaque robe was old Jacob Marley, our final guide.

"Are you sure this is the same ghost?" Julia whispered.

"The same one," I confirmed. "You should have seen him on my door knocker," I added, "up close and personal."

"You should have left him there," John lamented. "Look at what's coming out of that creepy robe!"

I looked down and saw heavy chains wrapped around and around, connected to five heavy metal boxes, boxes I had seen transferred into Jacob Marley's wagon on the night he was murdered.

"Do you know who I am?" the ghost moaned directly at me.

"Yes..." I stuttered, Julia still taking cover behind my back. "You are, or were, Jacob Marley."

"That is true," he moaned. "In mortality I was that man. Do you have the coin?"

"Yes," I answered, pulling the token from my pocket.

As soon as he saw the silver shilling he let out a mournful shriek so loud it rattled the plates in the cupboard. "Hide it, hide it from me," he demanded, the cloak letting off an eerie vibration that electrified the air. "The sorrow is too great!"

"I... I'm sorry," I stuttered, putting the offending coin back into my pocket. "I don't mean to make your misery worse."

"That is not possible," he howled into the night, shaking his chains furiously. "I'm a doomed soul. It is required of every man, that the spirit within him should walk abroad among his fellowmen, and travel far and wide; and if that spirit goes not forth in life, it is condemned to do so after death. It is doomed to wander through the world -- oh, woe is me! -- and witness what it cannot share, but might have shared on earth, and turned to happiness! Do you know why I am here now?" he moaned, still in agony.

"Redemption," I answered.

"Yes, redemption!" he sighed, shooting rays of hope from beneath his black robe.

"How were you able to warn your business partner, Ebenezer Scrooge, so many years ago?" I asked.

"By a Christmas miracle," he answered. "After my murder I wandered the earth in helpless agony for many years until one dark Christmas morning I noticed a man delivering gifts to sleeping children. My heart was gladdened by his generosity, so I followed him around for most of the night. He was no ordinary man. His sleigh was magical and pulled by reindeer, and he worked entirely outside of time. His movements were so fast, I had trouble keeping up."

"Suddenly, he stopped," the ghost continued. "He looked directly at me and asked, 'What is your purpose following me around all night? The ungrateful dead aren't concerned about anything more than mourning their own pitiful existence.'"

"I was gladdened by your service," I answered, speaking for the first time in a decade. "I am not able to serve those whom I ignored in life, and it makes me happy to see you able to help."

"Who would you serve if you could?" the man asked curiously.

"All men," Jacob answered, "but especially children."

"To help a child would be a reward indeed," the man said. "It is unfortunate you only took the opportunity to help one child in your entire pitiful life. However, you did save the one child didn't you? Curious. There may be a glimmer of hope for you after all. If I gave you the opportunity to help one person on this earth, who would it be?"

"I would be happy to help even the most despicable, undeserving wretch on this planet."

"And you would spend your one chance helping a person of my choosing?" the Giver asked curiously.

"Anyone!" I pleaded.

"By now the Winds of Doom had rattled my chains and caused my metal boxes to crash into each other, alerting the other spirits of my location. As soon as they noticed the mysterious man the other tormented spirits seemed to be drawn to him as well."

"My name is St. Nicholas," he said before the other spirits arrived. "Meet me here at this same hour next year."

Jacob Marley's story was so intriguing; I hadn't noticed how his clothing was being blown around by the Winds of Doom. The metallic boxes started scooting away in the hurricane forces as well, but Jacob stood his ground, pulling them back.

"Were you able to return the next year?" Julia asked, still hiding behind me.

"Yes," Jacob moaned. "And I was given the task to try to redeem the foulest, most despicable, and wretched man on the planet."

"St. Nicholas meant to save Ebenezer Scrooge, didn't he?" I inquired.

"No!" he cried, his chains rattling so loud the roof nearly shook off its walls. "St. Nicholas intended to redeem me; the most undeserving doomed soul who ever roamed the earth. I pleaded for him to choose anyone else. I begged him to select anyone but me to be redeemed. I deserved my fate. I fell to the ground in misery, I wanted to be forgotten. He got out of his sleigh, lifted me up off my face and simply instructed me to do what he asked... and if I did, all would be well."

I felt a peaceful spirit settle over the room. Even though the Winds of Doom tore at his black cloak, I felt cleansed of any ill feelings I had for him. He was the vision of a monster, a horrific phantom that struck fear into my heart, but at the same time I was filled with such pity I could not hold back my own forgiveness.

"It's obvious you did what he asked," Julia said softly, pointing to the worn book in my hand. "Charles Dickens records you were willing to help your old partner, thus freeing part of your own bondage. Where is the treasure buried now?"

"London, England. That is all I can tell you," he moaned. "His Royal Highness, Gregor MacGregor has spies everywhere, they are soon to swarm around us."

"So how do we get to London?" I asked. "Do I touch your cloak?"

"No!" the ghost screamed, pulling back his robe. "That would bring certain death. I'm not a redeemed spirit. I am a doomed soul and not capable of carrying a mortal. No, I believe your engineer has a form of transportation that will suit your needs."

"Are you talking about my Chevy Nova?" John asked with glee.

"Do you have anything faster?" Marley groaned over the violent winds. "Fly to my old office in London and meet me there. I will send a messenger to help you. Do as he says, I don't have time to say more."

The Winds finally won over Jacob's ability to withstand their forces, picking him off the ground and spinning him in a circle. The metallic boxes crashed into each other, spilling the contents of one of the boxes into the air. Hundreds of gold pieces flew about the room, crashing into him like a swarm of wild bees. He responded with a wail that shook the whole house, allowing himself to be blown through the window in the front room, leaving behind half the gold coins still twirling around in the kitchen.

The activity in the room was frantic, the remaining gold coins acted like a child left behind at a gas station. They darted through us and around us, trying to find their tormented victim. Finally, one coin darted out the same window Marley had exited, and the rest followed. We looked at each other in shock, waiting for the last coin to dart away.

"Well, my lust for gold is gone now," John blurted. "I've heard of seeking for riches, but I've never heard of riches seeking for you."

"Especially not with the intention of beating you to death," Julia added, still shaken by the strange display.

We bundled up against the cold and walked out of my parent's house and over to John's car.

"This mission gets harder all the time," Julia sighed as I helped her into the back seat. "But we can't turn back now. Jacob Marley gave us strict instructions to meet us at his old warehouse office. Does anyone know how to get to Scrooge and Marley's in London?"

"No, problem," I answered, sliding into the seat next to her and buckling myself in. "All we have to do is find a tavern called The Flying Scotsman."

"That shouldn't be hard," John said. "Let's Google it." John took out his smartphone, and entered a search. Moments later he got back 58,200 results. "The Flying Scotsman," he announced, reading off the top listings of the search. "The roughest tavern in London."

"That figures," Julia said "Does it show an address?"

"Sure," John replied. "4 Caledonian Road, King's Cross, London, N1 9DU. I have no idea what all of that means, but if I put it in Google Maps, and wait a second, there it is, picture and all. Anyone want to go on a road trip?"

"Without the scramjets!" Julia insisted, hitting John on the arm. "I still get sick just thinking about what you did to me. I don't ever want to fly hypersonic again!"

"Hey, that was last year," John said, only to get a threatening sneer from Julia.

"Fine, fine," he lamented, "have it your way, we'll just go supersonic. All I'm trying to do is speed things up a bit. Just prepare for a longer ride."

On our transatlantic flight John pushed us to Mach 2.5. Even at those speeds it took us a few hours to get to tavern. We passed the time by reading Charles Dickens' book together. St. Nicholas was right, the book was better, especially now that we had met almost all the characters in person.

130

We left Moses Lake, Washington just after one o'clock in the morning, which should have put us in London around 9 o'clock a.m. I didn't know how would we ever be able to dig up a treasure in broad daylight, even if it was Christmas day. Instead, when we arrived in London it was still one o'clock in the morning. Somehow St. Nicholas was able to manipulate time and space, turning back the clock for us, leaving plenty of time for grave-robbing. The darkness of night was still ours.

John decided to stay in time-warp as we approached London. Even at one o'clock in the morning the city was alive, although at a slower pace, and John didn't want to raise any suspicions. We opted to find a parking spot on the street, not far from the Flying Scotsman where we could appear and not be noticed. We flew around for a few minutes, darting around cars until we found an empty street, free of traffic and people. "Do you see any cars on the road?" John asked.

"I don't see any," Julia replied. "How about you, Mason?"

"No cars," I agreed. "But pull forward a bit, I think I see someone walking around the corner."

"Good eye," John praised, pulling ahead and putting the car in park. "I'm turning off the engine now, make sure we're still in time-warp with your powers, okay, Mason?"

"No problem," I answered.

John put the Chevy Nova in park, and turned off his time-warp generator. I kept us firmly in time-warp, while we all piled out of the car. I was about to take us out of time-warp when someone bumped into me.

"Pardon me," an average-looking man said. "I didn't expect to cause any disturbance. I normally pass right through."

"P.p.p.pass right through?" I stuttered, looking around, making sure I hadn't accidentally touched my nose, and taken us out of time-warp.

"It was my mistake," he said cheerfully. "I assumed you were mortal, but I see you must have passed into this dimension recently."

"No worries," I replied, trying not to sound as alarmed as I was. "We're just trying to find the Flying Scotsman. Could you point us in the right direction?"

"Aye, I could, but you look a little young for that kind of entertainment. They have a bad reputation in both dimensions, both the living and the dead."

"We're supposed to meet someone there," Julia begged. "I don't think we are going in."

"Oh, I see," he winked. "If that's the case, I'll take you there myself. This is a dangerous part of town, and anything can happen."

The old man took Julia by the arm as gently as a warm breeze and started walking toward the tavern.

"Are we out of time-warp?" John whispered frantically.

"We're not," I gasped. "This is the same fellow I saw down the street a few minutes ago. He shouldn't be able to move."

"Do you think this is the ghost Jacob Marley said would meet us here?" John asked.

"I don't know. I'll find out." I ran ahead and took Julia by the other arm. She glanced at me with a look of terror.

"So where do you live?" I asked the kind old man with all the courage I could muster.

"Where do I live?" he answered laughing. "Now that's a good one. I haven't lived for quite a while. My bones lay not far from here, but I don't like it much there. Too crowded for my taste."

"So you leave your bones at home and go walking at night?" I asked hesitantly.

"Well, of course I do. What else can I to do with them? I can't very well take my bones with me now, can I?"

"Yes, I see your point," I said, confirming I was indeed speaking to a wandering spirit.

"Ask him!" John whispered, pulling me back for a second. "Stop beating around the bush."

"Be quiet and let me do this," I insisted, catching back up with them again. "Do you walk these parts alone often?"

"Aye, I walk every street alone," he said sadly. "I haven't helped a living soul in years. I should have spent my life helping others instead of amassing this fortune that now haunts me. In my current condition I can only watch the needy from afar. It's a horrible torment. But now that you're here, things are looking up for me. I've come with an important message."

"I told you he was the one," John bragged. "Ask him to take us to Jacob Marley."

"Just a second," Julia said suspiciously. "How do we know we can trust you?"

"I have a similar problem," the man paused. "I have a message to deliver from a mutual acquaintance, but I can't deliver it until someone shows me a coin."

"Here it is," I offered, pulling the shilling out my pocket.

"T'is a pretty thing, isn't it?" he smiled. "Now I can trust you, and you can trust me. My name is Henry Bessemer, in life I dallied in iron production, but alas, I took little care in anything else. I've come with a message from Jacob Marley. You were wise to test me. I'm not the only spirit looking for you tonight."

"What's the message?" Julia gasped.

"My time is short, so listen carefully. Prince Gregor suspects someone is coming to dig up the treasure before he can get to it. He knows you are coming, and dressed the way you are, he will discover you immediately."

"What's wrong with our clothes?" Julia asked.

"It's not your clothes that will tip him off, it's your light," he explained. "You are clothed in so much light I could see you miles away. You must concentrate on hiding your light so as to not bring suspicion to yourselves."

John closed his eyes and concentrated on dimming his light but nothing happened.

"How did I do?" he asked, still as bright as before. "Not well," Mr. Bessemer said "There's a trick to transfiguring spirit matter. Imagine you are covered in something dark, a blanket, a deep mist, or anything black. See what happens."

John tried again, this time fading his color to a ghostly green.

"That's it," our escort grinned. "Now for the rest of you. Others of my kind are coming, you must act quickly."

Julia closed her eyes, and the light and color surrounding her dimmed to a dull grey. When she opened her eyes, she was pleased by the transformation. "I just thought about being covered in a dark fog," she whispered. "It really worked. It's your turn, Mason."

I closed my eyes, pretending I had just fallen into a coal bin, and was covered in black coal dust. When I opened my eyes, I could barely see my own hand.

"Very impressive," the ghost complimented. "That is not an easy shade of black to fake. By the looks of you now, I'd guess you were dead at least six months. You may be able to dig up the treasure after all."

"Have you come to show us where the treasure is buried?" I asked.

"Oh, no," he said. "I only came to teach you how to hide your mortality and escort you to meet Jacob Marley. Let's go before we run into someone less friendly."

"I have a few more questions," Julia insisted, following the ghost as he marched us down the street. "How can you see us in time-warp? How can you touch us? You're dead?"

"I may be dead but I'm not as helpless as you think," he answered, checking for other ghosts as we crossed a street. "You're a visitor in this dimension, but I live here. In my realm I have as much solid form as you do. If you were in the mortal dimension I could pass through your physical body with ease, but with you sharing this dimension I'm stopped by your spiritual body."

"So our spirits make us tangible to you?" Julia asked timidly.

"Yes!"

"Doesn't that put us in danger?"

"Grave danger," he frowned. "That was supposed to be a joke not a prediction. Look over there... we've got company."

As promised, a nasty-looking ghost materialized where we had just crossed the street. Two more joined him, and by the time they got near us, six disembodied spirits were walking right for us!

"Here they come," Mr. Bessemer said softly, pulling near a parked car so the rough group could pass us by. "Just act natural."

"The light came from right around here," a short spirit with a limp insisted.

"I don't see no light," the obvious leader snarled. "But keep a close look out. Newly dead spirits haven't learned how to keep their fresh deaths hidden very well. If we see them, we'll have a little fun. Right, boys?"

"That's right, Jake," the short one guffawed. "We'll knock their lights out for sure!"

"Forget about looking natural," Henry panicked. "Think dark thoughts and maybe they won't know who you are."

The haunted gang was about to pass us by when their powerful leader stopped, looking right at us. "Are you coming or what? Or do me and the boys have to rough yeh up a bit to give yeh the courage to join us?"

"No," I stuttered. "We're coming?"

"We left a good poker game for this," Mr. Bessemer growled, turning dark and nasty. "This better be good."

"You got that right," the ornery leader spat. "If I don't get to cause some mischief tonight, I'm outta here." We joined the rough looking ghosts and walked towards the Flying Scotsman. Up ahead a group of equally unhappy phantoms materialized, joining another group as they went. They had all the makings of an angry mob.

Some spirits had enough light to look alive, which is how we must have fit in, but others were much darker. I noticed Mr. Bessemer wasn't the only ghost burdened down with bank deposit boxes and other earthly treasures.

"Stay close to me," Mr. Bessemer begged. "This wasn't in the plan. We'll have to wait for it to get over and meet with Mr. Marley after that."

"We'll follow your lead," I answered, trying to blend in as best as I could.

As we approached the large group a shrill voice rose above the crowd, causing the hair to stand up on the back of my neck.

"This is bad," Julia warned, trying to find a way to escape. "Do you hear who that is?"

"It can't be him," John lamented.

"It is," I confirmed. No matter how badly I wanted the leader of the mob to be someone else, I couldn't change the fact that His Royal Highness Gregor MacGregor was at the heart of the riot.

"I thank ye for coming on such short notice," Prince Gregor yelled to the rowdy crowd. "I know I took ye from cold tombs and familiar hauntings tonight, but I have a question for ye. How would your lives have been different if ye were born rich?"

"I would'a been happy," a man growled, followed by a hundred grunts from the crowd.

"Aye," Sir Gregor smiled cunningly. "Ye would've been happy, I'm sure. What if ye'd been born with a silver spoon in your mouths? Would your stomach's have been gnawed by hunger? Would your wee ones have died of sickness?"

"Nay," another man cried. "Nay, we would've lived like kings."

"Aye," he shouted. "That's for true. But since we canna turn back the clock, what if ye were rich today? Imagine yourselves surrounded by gold coins? How would that make ye feel?"

"Happy, powerful, safe," were the words the crowd roared out in approval, sending a circle of green energy swirling around the well-dressed ghost.

"To be happy ye have to want gold worse than anything in your lives," Prince Gregor taunted. "You deserved to own a fortune when ye were living souls, but now you're dead, ye deserve it even more!"

The crowd exploded with even more green energy. It wisped around them, making the simple ghosts even more greedy. The allure of riches was tantalizing, causing all the ghosts around us to succumb to his hypnotic words.

"Gold's a lovely thing," Prince Gregor chanted. "Gold is good. I promise ye a treasure tonight, but a treasure must be fought for, and we the people of this land must the ones ta do it!"

The whole mob burst into cheers of pent-up joy. Old ugly poltergeists hugged each other like they had just won the lottery. Younger ghosts pranced around in a reckless frenzy. The more excited they became the more greenish plasma they created.

136

"This guy is brilliant," John whispered, "look how he's controlling the crowd."

"And tells them what they want to hear," Julia agreed quietly.

"Quiet," Mr. Bessemer warned. "Don't say anything that goes against him. He'll sense your disapproval."

"What did ye say back there?" Prince Gregor yelled over the cheers of the crowd.

"It's too late," he moaned. "Look away. Don't look at him."

Julia looked behind her and to the side, but Prince Gregor's gaze was fixed on her. "I asked ye, lass, what was it ye just said?"

"I didn't say anything important," she responded anxiously, diverting her gaze from him.

"I'll decide what's important," he said manically. "And look in my direction when ye speak to me. I canna understand your strange English when ye don't. Come closer so I can get a better look at ye. My spies told me to expect conspirators. I believe ye and your friends might be the ones I've been waiting for."

The Flying Scotsman

The crowd roared their approval, clearing a path for us to be interrogated by the pretended prince. Prince Gregor stood his ground, not coming any closer to us in a display of superiority.

"Now what do we do?" John whispered, "I don't think we can trick our way out of this one."

"I'm thinking," I said frantically.

"Don't look at me," Henry Bessemer gasped, "I was just supposed to be a guide. I don't know what to do."

"We don't have a choice but to stand before him," Julia said. "We can't turn back now."

"Then I guess it's time to meet His Royal Highness," I agreed, taking Julia by the arm to answer our summons.

As we began walking through the unruly crowd, an invisible wind began to kick up. Moans came from all around us as heavy treasure boxes and carpet bags of money rose above our heads, tugging at their owners.

Mr. Bessemer was walking beside us, but was soon having a hard time walking a straight line as something under his jacket began tugging him around.

"What's wrong with you?" Julia begged. "We're being summoned."

"I know that," he said as a chain rose up from his clothes and pulled out a heavy box of money. "I'm having a bit of trouble with the Winds. Can you hold on to me?"

"Why didn't you tell us you were a doomed soul?" Julia panicked, doing everything she could to keep the ghost from being blown from our presence.

"I was hoping if I did something good it might forget me this time," he said, "I guess I was wrong. But hold on to me. Don't let me go!"

Mr. Bessemer's voice was choked off the chain wrapped around the old man like a snake. We tried to hold on to him, but no matter what we did, it was impossible to hold him down. His body was lifted off the ground, dragging us along with him. We floated around with him, crashing into ghosts as we went.

Other ghosts were just as tormented. Scores of them were wailing and crying in the Winds of Doom. In a final gust, the tormenting winds ripped our guide loose, swirling him around our heads in a powerful vortex.

"This was my leap of faith," he cried as his moneybox smacked him across his face. "I hope we meet again, my road to redemption has begun. Happy Christmas." The whirlwind spun the old ghost faster and faster until he was swept away from our view.

"He's gone," Julia panicked. "Now what do we do?"

"He's given me an idea," I whispered, "follow my lead," I said as my twirled body around. "Act like you're being blown away by the Winds and let's get out of here!"

We held on to each other as our clothes flipped around in the whirlwind. We fit right in with other spirits who were trying to resist the Winds of Doom as well. Their riches strangled and smashed into them just as violently as they did with Mr. Bessemer, so and we took advantage of the distraction.

We scooted around in circles, howling and moaning just as pathetically as the other ghosts until we pretended to be blown around the corner. Once we were out of sight, we circled back and hid under a Land Rover parked on the street while we waited for the winds to stop.

No matter how intense the Winds of Doom roared, Prince Gregor withstood their forces, although he grimaced every time they blew through and around him. The other ghosts didn't fare as well. Even the ones who weren't blown away screeched in pain as they blew by. Finally, after a few more pathetic souls were taken away, the Winds died down leaving Prince Gregor standing triumphantly.

"It's too bad my three friends couldn't withstand the Winds of Doom," Prince Gregor MacGregor said after gaining his own composure. "I thought maybe they weren't dead at all. Their spirits were far too bright for my tastes."

Some of the ghosts laughed at his remark, although most were still in too much pain to acknowledge anything. The Winds had taken about 50 from the group, but that still left over 200 greedy-looking male and female spirits.

"Many wonder how I can withstand the Winds because of my former riches," Prince Gregor continued. "When the Winds began to sift the wicked from our midst, did you see me tremble? Nay! Did you see me worried in the least about my standing before the Winds of Doom? Nay again! Isn't this proof of my virtue? Doesn't this prove I died innocent before the judgment seat of man?"

From what I had seen the spirits were all too busy suffering their own grief at the time to see how obviously affected he had been by the Wind's tormenting blasts. Nonetheless, bit by bit the green energy of the people's combined power swirled around McGregor once again as the crowd rallied to his cause.

"I died a pauper," Prince Gregor cried. "Aye, it's true. I was penniless when I was buried in a grave of honor by the grateful country of Venezuela, a country I helped to liberate. Are ye the honored dead as well? Can ye withstand the Winds of Doom?"

"That's it," Julia whispered so quietly John and I had to strain to hear. "The Winds of Doom only carry away those who died with large amounts of money that was never put to good use."

"What do you think it does to the poor people?" I asked quietly.

"I'm not sure," she admitted, "but it certainly has an effect. Maybe it causes them to regret their squandered opportunities. Even Prince Gregor was tormented by the Winds, although he won't admit it."

We remained hidden under the Land Rover while Prince Gregor MacGregor continued working up the crowd. In our concealed position we could see and hear everything he did. He had the mob riled into a frenzy by this point. They cried at the memory of their former lives of poverty and affliction, and were angry at those who took away their easy riches. As the crowd surged from sorrow to anger, the greenish energy swirled around them. Prince Gregor breathed it in deeply, harvesting the energy to increase his own power.

As the Prince stole their energy, I noticed a remarkable change in their spirit forms. Many of his followers started out brighter than others, but with each wisp of energy stolen from them, their countenances darkened. As the green energy of the group intensified, gathering force, gaining power.

"And what do I ask of ye now?" he continued. "Nothing! I only come with a gift. I come to share my gold with ye! Aye, it's my gold, and only I know where it's buried. Me enemy Jacob Marley stole it from me and now I have the power to take it back. Are ye ready to commit to me noble cause?"

The mob roared its approval.

"If that be the case, behold," he yelled, leaping into the air and disappearing into a black fog. "I am transformed into your angel of vengeance!"

The mob fell back, astonished and afraid. The dark mist circled above them, causing all the ghosts to tremble and groan. Suddenly, a black warrior with glowing green armor emerged. He floated above them raising his arms triumphantly.

"I am your champion," he boomed over his minions, shooting a green fireball from each hand. "Once ye have proven yourselves worthy, I will make you captains of your own fate. I will clad you in dark armor that ye may bring wrath upon your enemies. Once empowered ye will fly at my command! Who is with me?"

The crowd roared its approval, chanting his name, over and over again.

And now," he announced all the louder, reaping more green energy from his frenzied army, "here come our mortal conspirators. When they come out of the pub, follow them to the cemetery!"

"I've seen enough," Julia whispered over the roar of the crowd. "Let's get out of time-warp!"

"I think she has a point," John agreed, taking Julia by the hand. "Get us outta here."

I took Julia's hand and clicked my watch. As soon as I did we were transported back into mortal time, the night becoming very dark and quiet and free of Prince Gregor MacGregor and his mob of cutthroat thugs.

"Whew," Julia exclaimed. "We got out of there just in time. Now what do we do?"

"I don't know," John whispered. "But, I don't think we're out of the woods yet. Look, the pub door is opening!"

As if on cue, four of the dirtiest-looking men I had ever seen walked out of the pub. I recognized the foulest of them, Duane Slotham, the same man Prince Gregor conspired with while we eavesdropped with the Ghost of Christmas Present. Julia gasped at his sight. True to his word, he had brought three other men with him.

Each man had an unholy glaze in his eyes, not one of spiritual possession, but of an unquenchable fever for gold. The foul men walked our way, heading directly for the car we were hiding under.

"Follow me," I whispered in a panic, crawling backwards out from under the Land Rover and creeping into a dark business stoop where we couldn't be seen. Julia and John trailed me into the shadows, trying not to make any noise. I don't know why I was worried, the men from the pub were so drunk they could barely even walk straight.

"Where's the treasure?" one of the four drunken man asked unhappily, using a key to open up the trunk of the boxy Land Rover Defender. "Don't brass me off."

"Like, what Gavin said, mate," the second man slurred.

"Tell us the plan or I'm goin' back ta the tavern for another drink."

"All in good time, Billy," Duane insisted. "I'll show yeh the map when the time is right."

"Show me the map now," Billy Clubbard demanded.

"Why? So yeh can steal it from me?" Duane snarled. "No Billy, I'll show it to yeh when I'm good and ready."

"Yeh might want to reconsider that," Gavin Roberts threatened, lifting up a shovel from the back of the vehicle. "If Billy, Tuug, and me bashes yeh over the head, it might get blood all over your precious map, and then what would yeh do?"

"All right," the leader said "But just to make things clear, I'm still the leader. If yeh do as I say, yeh'll each get 100 solid gold coins."

"And what'll you get?" Billy complained.

"It's none of your business," Duane retorted, handing over the treasure map. "It's my scheme."

"This ain't no treasure map," Billy complained. "It's a map of Highgate Cemetery. I wouldn't step a foot in that haunted place again for a thousand pounds!"

"Well ain't that grand," Duane sneered. "Because that's where the gold is buried, if yeh don't want yer share. I'm sure Gavin or Tuug will be glad to take it off yer hands."

"Not so fast," he complained. "I just said I wouldn't do it for a thousand pounds, that's all. Gold's an entirely different matter."

"I'm glad we got that settled," Duane said gruffly. "Are we all ready to go now?"

"Not yet," Tuug Qabri, the dark-skinned East African said in his thick Somali accent. "Where exactly is the treasure buried? There is no mark on the map to show the exact site of the grave, there is only a general circle of sorts, up in the corner by the Circle of Lebanon. The forest is thick up there, we will never find it."

"I know how to get it," Duane said spitefully. "Do yeh think I'm so stupid I'd let yeh know exactly where it is? Shut up and get in the car before I give yer share ta Billy."

We watched them all pile into the old grey Land Rover and turn round on Caledonia Road to take a right, then they disappeared into the night.

"I'm kind of freaked out here!" I whispered in the shadows. "No wonder St. Nicholas needed younger League members to work on this mission. This could get very dangerous."

"Talking about dangerous," John pointed out. "Did you see Prince Gregor's armor? He looks ready for battle!"

"There has to be a way to beat him," Julia said, trying to build our courage. "That being said, I've never seen anyone drain away people's dreams and replace them with vengeance and greed like that."

"I have," I admitted. "I saw Dr. Rawlings do the same thing in my economics class. Somehow he was able to harness the energy of his students to give himself more power, but Prince Gregor has taken it to a whole new level."

"I was surprised at how miserable the ungrateful dead were when the Winds of Doom came through," Julia added. "It's as if it has as much influence on the greedy poor as on the ones who were blown away!"

"Maybe that's what the Ghost of Christmas Present was talking about," I offered. "People who are never willing to take a risk to improve their lives are the real victims of Want and Ignorance. I have to admit, I felt the poor people who bought land from Prince Gregor were foolish, but now I'm not so sure."

"At least they did something good, even if it was foolish," Julia agreed. "Maybe success can't be measured by positive outcomes. Maybe the true measure of success is the willingness of a person to take a chance for a better life!"

"So you're cursed if you chase after money and you're cursed if you don't?" John asked. "How is that fair?"

"I don't think chasing after money is bad at all if it builds you dreams," Julia answered. "It's the love of money that's wicked, not whether you have it or not. It's obvious the doomed rich should have used their fortunes to help other people, but maybe the doomed poor didn't take advantage of the opportunities they had to progress. Regret is a powerful tormentor."

"I'm cool with that," John agreed. "And as for Prince Gregor, he was the rottenest apple in the barrel, but he died penniless, so the Winds can't blow him around at all... although I'll bet he's only pretending not to feel the pain of his misdeeds."

We waited in the darkness for a few more minutes as the damp English fog started creeping around us and under my coat, making me shiver. We huddled together until John was too eager to wait any longer.

"Shouldn't we follow them?" he asked eagerly. "We don't want them to get too far ahead of us."

"Not yet," I answered. "We don't even know where Jacob Marley is buried."

"I agree," said Julia, clearly shaken by what we had just seen. "I'm glad Jacob sent the old man ahead to show us how to blend in, but wasn't he supposed to take us to meet Jacob Marley?"

"How could he do that?" John asked. "The whole place was swarmed by ghosts."

"The only thing left to do is wait," I suggested. "Mr. Bessemer said Marley's ghost would meet us here. Maybe he's still coming."

Julia nodded in agreement, not offering up any more ideas. The three of us stayed hidden in the shadows as lights from cars shone in the distance, driving closer, and then passing us by, uncaring. John was getting antsy again when a low familiar voice vibrated from the shadows.

"The pretended Prince of Poyais doesn't know where I am buried," the unseen Spirit moaned. "His men don't know either. He hopes to discover the location from you, and order them to steal it."

Jacob Marley appeared inside a business display window, speaking to us from behind the glass. The window pane didn't inhibit his volume in the slightest. I was happy he chose to appear to us from there. I didn't like being too close to him.

"Why didn't you tell us Prince Gregor could control the mortal world," Julia demanded. "How do we fight against that?"

"There wasn't time to explain then, and there isn't now!" the ghost moaned, shaking the window pane with its force. "You must learn as you go. The powers in play are far beyond your comprehension. I have but few ways to prepare you for what is to come. Mason Howell, keep your grandfather's watch close by and do not lose the bag given to you by the Ghost of Christmas Present. It may be important to you in the future."

I dug into my pocket and pulled out the golden watch, making sure I had it handy. I could feel the coin was still there as well. I reached in my coat pocket and found the magic bag filled with the dust of golden Christmas Ambrosia from our delicious feast, making sure I could get to it in a hurry.

"Prince Gregor MacGregor thinks he is invincible," boomed the dark-hooded ghost. "But he is mistaken. His arrogance will be his undoing. He also believes you will lead him to where the treasure is hidden."

"Is that true," I asked. "Will we lead him to the treasure?"

"Yes," the Spirit moaned.

"If you know we'll lead him to the treasure," I asked confused. "Why don't we wait until he's gone and dig it up then?"

"Some things can only be done on Christmas Eve!" he groaned. "For everything there is a time and a season on this earth. Do not question the timing. You must find the treasure, dig it up, and take it to St. Nicholas by morning."

"By morning, I get it, so where is your grave?"

"I can't tell you," he groaned. "I'm not allowed to reveal the location."

"What about Sarah, your former fiancé, or Ebenezer Scrooge?" I asked. "They were there. They know where you're buried."

"Sarah only knows the general location," Jacob Marley cried, the Winds of Doom howling through his clothes again. "And Ebenezer is not allowed to reveal it either,"

"This is not his redemption! You are my champions. I have to use my own resources through you, or we will all fail tonight."

"So if Ebenezer can't tell us, and you can't tell us," I complained. "Who can?"

"Elizabeth Jackson," he whispered. "You need to find Elizabeth Jackson, the first person interred at Highgate Cemetery. Find her, and she will lead you to my grave!"

The window rattled again, not from his screams, but from the winds dragging him from his perch. "I will help you all I can," Jacob Marley yelled over the gale, his boxes of gold and heavy chains swirling in the air. "I will send for help." As in the times before, he let out a final scream of anguish before being blown from our presence.

"So the treasure is buried in Highgate Cemetery just like Prince Gregor's men said," I repeated aloud.

"And we have to find Elizabeth Jackson, the only person who knows where he's buried," Julia added.

"But to do that we have to fight off an army of crazy ghosts and an armored black knight to boot," John interjected. "This is fantastic!"

We were still talking when a stern man dressed in a black police uniform appeared in front of the business opening with a bobby stick in his hand.

"Alright now," he said gruffly, tapping the heavy stick on his rough hand. "Come out of the shadows, and keep your hands where I can see them.

"Is there a problem, officer?" Julia said innocently.

"Yeah, there's a problem," the officer shot back. "It's past one o'clock in the blessed morning, and little girls like yourself should be back home with their Moms and Dads. What are you three doing walking about this time of night?"

"Just a little sight-seeing," John replied.

"Oh I see," he said, drawing nearer. "An American agitator from the Colonies. Look here, I have a long list of complaints tonight about windows being rattled, and strange happenings all over the place. Some of our best residence are so scared they won't venture out to our side of town for an innocent Christmas drink."

"We are just leaving," I offered. "If that's alright with you, officer."

"No, as a matter of fact it's not alright with me," the officer said, reaching for his radio. "I'm taking you in for questioning. Officer Swain, requesting back up on Caledonia Road, King's Cross, please respond."

"Officers on their way," the radio responded. "Now then, put your hands up, turn around and place them on the wall," he demanded. "I overheard you saying something about digging up a body at Highgate Cemetery? We don't approve of wacko's disturbing our local cemeteries and digging up our dead. This isn't fairytale land, and we don't appreciate your disrespect, so again, up with your hands.

"Charlie, send a crew out to Highgate Cemetery, I think there may be a pack of vandals preparing for another tomb raiding party tonight," the officer said into his radio.

"Roger that," Charlie, replied.

I was terrified of meeting a 100 angry ghosts if we went back into time-warp, but something had to be done, and I was the only one able to do it. I took Julia by the right hand, and John took her left, and we raised them up together, leaving me free to click the golden watch. In a flash the world took on that golden magical hue again.

Officer Swain froze like a statue. I looked into his open mouth and could count his silver fillings and crooked teeth. The police officer wasn't the only thing in suspended animation, the whole street was frozen. The only moving objects were John, Julia, and me. I scanned the street fearing the worst, but it was free of angry ghosts as well. Luckily they must have all followed the Land Rover like Prince Gregor ordered and stopped looking for us.

"You just resisted an arrest!" John blurted, putting his hands down. "That's a criminal offence!"

"I'm sorry," I stammered. "I didn't know what else to do."

"No, man," John said, slapping me on the back. "That was epic. I didn't know you had it in you. I don't think any of the old guys in the League would have done that. Maybe that's why Jacob Marley chose us in the first place. Beside the fact that flying over an 18-foot fence and digging up a dead guy is kind of out of their League."

"Very funny," Julia groaned, not appreciating his clever play on words. "This is getting so complicated. Maybe we should just turn ourselves over to the police."

"You're kidding, right?" John smirked. "How are we going to explain all of this to our parents, let alone the police?"

"Oh, I don't know," she huffed in frustration. "I thought doing the right thing would be a lot easier."

"I know," I agreed, putting my arms around her "But we're young and kind of dumb... at least that's what my dad keeps telling me, so maybe we just have to do the best we can."

"Touch your nose and see what he does," John begged.

"I'm not doing that," I balked.

"Come on," John insisted, "it would be funny! I want to see him reanimate. Do it!"

"Enough already," Julia interrupted. "This isn't a game. We'd better get out of here before we start getting visitors of a deadlier nature."

"I suppose you're right," John sulked, taking the policeman's hat off his head and putting it back on backwards.

148

"But I would love to see the expression on his face when he thinks we've disappeared into thin air!"

He laughed about it as we ran up Caledonia road where we parked the car. When we arrived we found an awful surprise that took the grin off his face.

"No way," John fumed, pulling the neatly-placed ticket off his window.

"What does it say?" I asked. I had never seen a British parking ticket before.

"It says bla bla bla, bla bla bla, you owe 120 pounds' payable to the Ministry of Transportation. I don't know how much that is in dollars, but it's more than what I want to pay. I hate tickets!"

"You're going to hate this too, then," Julia said shyly pointing down at the passenger side front tire of the car.

"They put a boot on my tire?" John complained. "Why would they do that?"

"We're in London," Julia pointed out. "They drive on the other side of the street remember? I guess we parked on the wrong side of the road, not to mention the fact that you have Washington state license plates.

"Terrific," he said bitterly. "I didn't even think about that. Now we're really messed up. With my plate number, they can pull up all my personal information. As soon as we leave, the cops will notice my car is missing and have everything they need to track us down. This is just grand."

"We'll sort it out later," I suggested. "We better get going or Prince Gregor's men will get to the cemetery before we do."

"Yeah, you're right," he sighed. "At least we have a grave to dig up and a treasure to rob."

"You're so weird," Julia smiled, kissing John on the cheek then piling into the backseat of the car with me.

John heaved a sigh a relief when he started up the engine and flipped on the anti-gravity generator. At least something was going right. "Next stop, Highgate Cemetery!" he called.

The car rose straight up in the air with the boot on the tire spinning around, banging helplessly on the wheel well. John grimaced every time the metal boot banged into his car but flew us northwest, directly over King's Cross railroad terminal and past well-lit roads and sparkling lights without stopping.

We flew past buildings large and small until we came to a dark foreboding land. Strangely enough the forest glowed with small animals and sleeping birds of all kinds. The west part of the cemetery was a de facto nature preserve, and we could see the rainbow of colors below us. I was convinced John had found the right spot.

"There's no use trying to drive around right now," John bristled. "Stupid boot! With this thing jacking us up, we won't be able to fly supersonic or engage the meteor shields or anything. I have to figure out a way to get it off. Until then, we might as well park by the front gate and start asking for help."

"Ask for help?" Julia coughed. "Who do you plan on asking?"

"The dead people who live here, of course," he blurted. "Who else can we ask? Someone has to know Elizabeth Jackson."

"That'll be interesting," I said. "How do you suggest we do it? Knock on a tombstone, and hope someone friendly answers?"

"Sure," John confirmed. "Unless you can think of something better?"

"Sound's good to me," Julia conceded.

John set us down right in front of the main entrance to the cemetery and eagerly said, "Let's go knocking on some tombstones."

Chapter Seventeen

The Power of Imagination

Strange things can happen in an ancient cemetery on Christmas Eve. Highgate Cemetery is the first of the Seven Magnificent Cemeteries that encircled London in the early 19th century. The cemetery is divided into two sections, the West, which is mostly closed to the public, except for private tours, and the East section which is open to the general public and still receives new internments.

Bordering the two cemeteries is a lovely park with a pond, gardens and several large open grassy areas. We aimed for a parking spot just outside the cemetery gate, next to the park.

We hadn't set our wheels down on the ground for two seconds before an eager-looking young man with a broad smile knocked on John's window. He was dressed in early 20th century motoring clothes, complete with grey flannel coat, round flat hat, goggles, and striped pants. From his translucent appearance, he was obviously a spirit.

"Valet service?" he asked.

"Valet service?" John responded after rolling down the window, trying not to act too surprised. "Do I need to move?"

"As a matter of fact you do," the parking attendant insisted cheerfully. "We have a coach-and-four arriving in just minutes and we need to clear the road for them."

"I'm sorry," John said politely, but I don't let anyone drive my car, not even my best friend."

"That's true," I confirmed. "He's afraid I'll blow it up."

"Ha, I don't blame you," the ghost agreed. "Your bonny car has clean aerodynamic lines. I'd wager she's fast to boot. I like fast cars."

"So do I," John belted, sticking his hand out the window to greet a fellow speed freak. "My name's John Patten. It's nice to meet you."

"Likewise," the ghost smiled, shaking his hand vigorously. "My name's Percy Lambert, but you can call me Pearly."

"It sounds like you know something about cars."

"That I do," the attendant responded. "I once had a bonny black Talbot. I called her the Talbot Star. In 1913 I was the first man to drive an automobile over 100 miles an hour. For a while I was the fastest man alive!"

"What happened then?"

"I crashed her into the wall at Brooklands Speedway defending my title and died. It was a fantastic death! Bad luck, that, but what a triumph!"

"Wow!" John awed. "That is amazing. Good for you!"

"Thanks, mate," he said happily.

"Ask him about Elizabeth Jackson," Julia insisted. "We're in a hurry."

John looked a bit uncomfortable, but followed her instructions anyway. "Would you have anyway of contacting a woman named Elizabeth Jackson for us?"

"Elizabeth Jackson?" he mused. "I've heard of her, but she travels in circles far above my social status. I'll ask Mr. Wombwell while you park somewhere else. He knows everyone."

"No problem," John said. "Where should I park?"

"Hmm, park her next to the spaceship over there," he answered cheerfully. "Douglas Adams won't mind as long as you don't ding his paint job with your car doors."

"His ship reminds me of the Heart of Gold," John said, looking at the large spherical spaceship. "Did this Douglas Adams write science fiction by any chance?"

"Yes, it sounds like you've heard of him," Pearly answered. "His most famous book is called A Hitchhiker's Guide to the Universe. But since his burial here in the cemetery he hasn't stuck around long enough for me to ask anything else."

"The ship doesn't look very stable," Julia noted. "It looks like a giant ball."

"Don't worry," the young man confided, "she won't roll over on you. He may not stick around anyway. He explained it like this, 'the probability of me remaining for the lectures is infinitely large, so I'll most likely be leaving.' He's a clever one, that, but I can't understand a thing he says."

"He's awesome," John replied. "I love his stuff."

"Ah, there is one more thing," the young man said hesitantly, "I don't want to act like a nosey parker, but you're dressed rather informally for a formal occasion such as this. I suggest you change into something more dignified. Try something from the mid-19th century. Maybe something like this."

In an instant the man changed his clothes to a long black cloak with a proper top hat and a cane in his hand. "Mr. Michael Faraday prefers this mode of clothing at his annual Christmas Lecture, so we try to make him happy. You can wear whatever you please at the party afterwards... Oh dear, here comes Mr. George Wombwell, the guest lecturer. He's not only arriving with his coach, but it looks like he's bringing his whole menagerie, how exciting."

"I guess I'll park next to the Heart of Gold," John agreed, as the parking attendant ran frantically to help the long train of exotic animals find a place to land. "I hope I get to meet Douglas Adams," John said eagerly. "I didn't know he was buried here. He wrote some important episodes of one of my favorite television shows. I wonder if he travels with the Doctor?"

"Dr. Who?" Julia said with a smile.

"I'm glad you got the joke," John said while levitating the car, parking it next to the large spherical orb with red brake lights on the rear in the shape of a heart.

Unfortunately, the craft disappeared the moment he set the car down. The solitude didn't last long though as a large carriage pulled up next to us, filled with the sounds of a joyous man so jolly I thought it might be St. Nicholas.

"Take the horses and stock them with the other animals," he ordered his coachman cheerfully. "Happy Christmas," he belted our way, opening his carriage door with exuberance.

"Merry Christmas," John answered, getting out of his car without turning it off, for fear of having it seen in the mortal world.

"You are strangely dressed," the joyous man observed. "This is a formal occasion, weren't you informed?"

"Not until just a few minutes ago," John answered.

"Well, don't you worry," he said. "Just copy the style of my clothing and we can be on our way to the lecture. I'm the guest of honor, you may have heard? Very excited, very, very excited indeed."

"We didn't bring any formal clothing with us," I said hesitantly while helping Julia out of the car.

"But you did bring the sunshine, didn't you?" he smiled, looking at Julia with admiration and bowing deeply. "Mr. George Wombwell, showman and animal trainer extraordinaire, at your service."

"So pleased to meet you," she responded elegantly, followed with a curtsy. "My name is Julia Martin."

She was used to meeting important people, so I wasn't surprised she was able to charm him like she did.

"My name's Mason Howell," I added, trying to sound dignified. "And this is John Patten my best friend."

"It is a pleasure to meet you all," he said politely. "I hate to intrude on your business, but I was just visited by a rather tormented friend, burdened down with boxes of gold. He rather desperately asked for my assistance. Would one of you possibly be carrying a silver token?"

"I am," I said, showing the coin quickly then putting it back in my pocket.

"Then you three must be agents of the fabled Santa Claus League," he said quietly. "Am I correct in my assumption?"

"Yes sir," Julia confirmed.

"Say no more," the jovial man whispered, stepping back into his coach and bidding us to come in with him. "Come, come and join me. I have important news for you."

I didn't know if we were supposed to follow him in but we did anyway. He had a peaceful spirit about him, a lovely, kind spirit that won my trust immediately. Julia followed after me, unafraid and unbothered by being surrounded by a carriage that didn't even exist in the material world. John was a little more hesitant, not because he was afraid of the unknown, but because he didn't like leaving his car unattended with the keys in the ignition.

"Michael Faraday, Robert Grant, and I are members of the Santa Claus League, the British Chapter. We are committed to helping you in any way we can. Charles Dickens and Ebenezer Scrooge are unfortunately tied up with other matters at the moment, or they would be here as well. Both men give their apologies."

"So you know Charles Dickens and Ebenezer Scrooge?" Julia asked.

"Who doesn't?" he chortled. "Fine men, the both of them."

"Then you know about Jacob Marley and his treasure?" I whispered.

"Of course I do," he chuckled, his body rocking back and forth with laughter. "It's only the living who don't know about his buried fortune. Every spirit around believes it's buried in the West section, but to this day it has never been found. Do you know where it's buried?"

"Not a clue," I responded. "But we know the name of the woman who does."

"My, my," the old man regaled. "Tonight is the night after all. How exciting. And I thought I would steal the show with Nero, my wild African Lion. Alas, I have been upstaged again, but no mind. My friend Pearly mentioned something about contacting Miss Elizabeth Jackson. Does this have anything with her?"

"Yes, it does," Julia whispered. "Could you introduce us to her?"

"Yes, of course," Mr. Wombwell whispered even softer. "But why would you ever need to find her? She is the last woman anyone would think to contact. A charming woman; yes, and firm; certainly, but shy; unused to causing trouble. I've known her for years. Why her?"

"Elizabeth Jackson was entrusted with the true location of Jacob Marley's grave," Julia answered.

"Miss Jackson... a secret bearer?" Mr. Wombwell blurted, then holding his hand over his mouth. "Unbelievable, that sly woman. No wonder she's had such a beguiling look about her all these years, as if she was guarding a secret. And by George, she is!"

"She was the first one publicly buried in the cemetery," Julia explained. "But with the tens of thousands buried here, how will we ever find her?"

"Leave that to me and my men," he said soberly. "I'll have my most trusted friends assist you. For now, change into more formal clothing and pretend you're going to the lecture."

"Changed into what?" I asked. "We didn't bring any other clothing with us."

"I was told you already knew how to transfigure spirit matter," Mr. Wombwell stated curiously.

"I can turn my aura a darker color if that's what you mean," I offered.

"Excellent," he cheered. "If you can do that anything is possible. Let me teach you how to transfigure matter. The first thing to know is matter can be changed into whatever form you choose in this realm. Just imagine what you want to wear, drive, or a tool you may need, and you will have it."

"That sounds awesome," John said, closing his eyes in concentration. "Let me try it."

To my amusement, in his first attempt all he managed to create was a pile of rags. He looked at the frayed material and frowned. Undeterred, he stared at the pile of fabric with a look of intense concentration, causing the random fabric to come together to form a fine silk top hat. John was so pleased with the results he followed it up by created a traveling coat with silver buttons. When that was done he made himself a pair of striped pants and black spats for shoes.

"Very nice," Julia gasped. "My turn."

She didn't even close her eyes and her button- up-shirt and levis transformed into a stunning evening gown with a hat that tied under her chin. Her dress was long and covered everything except for her dainty feet, which were shod in black button-up boots. She was the picture of fashion.

"It's your turn," she said, looking at me with curiosity.

I closed my eyes and envisioned a black Victorian Santa Claus tuxedo. At my command my current clothes transformed into a formal coat with white fur on the lapels, Santa Claus red

156

cummerbund, leather straps, and golden buttons. I had a large red silk tie, a button up white collared shirt, and a top hat just like John's. My pants were wool with a sharp crease along the front with shoes, shiny and black.

"You three clean up nicely," Mr. Wombwell complimented. "It takes most of us several years to master the art of transfiguration as well, but then you are part of that special League aren't you? You are dressed perfectly for the occasion."

"I have a question," John asked curiously. "How is all of this possible?"

"With the power of imagination of course," he smiled. "How else is anything created?"

"I just never thought of imagination as such a literal power," John said amazed.

"Nothing given to man comes by chance, my boy," he smiled. "That's why the League is so determined to encourage children to use and develop their power of imagination. My, you really don't know very much about the League, do you?"

"We're still in training," John explained. "We're not fully vested members yet."

"Not fully vested?" Mr. Wombwell blurted, standing up, and bumping his head on the ceiling of the carriage. "I thought St. Nicholas would have sent seasoned professionals for this kind of mission. Have you really so little experience?"

"We just passed the first level of training a few years ago," I admitted. "But we have learned a lot in the process."

"Great Scott!" he exclaimed in surprise. "This changes everything. Mr. Marley was correct; our assistance will be necessary. He asked me to organize military forces to assist you, but I didn't think that would be necessary. I'll have to apologize to him the next time we meet for being so flippant. If you will excuse me, I need to invite a trusted advisor to assist us."

We sat anxiously on plush seats for a few minutes as hushed voices bled through the walls of the coach. When Mr. Wombwell returned, he brought a stately man with him. He was tall, dignified and dressed in a military uniform with a large ornate cross on his chest.

"I would like to introduce you to Mr. Robert Grant," the animal trainer said politely. "Mr. Grant is a highly decorated war hero, honored policeman, and a longtime member of the Santa Claus League. He has come to offer his assistance this evening."

"How do you do?" he bowed deeply, looking at Julia with appreciation. "And who do I have the pleasure of meeting?"

"This charming light-of-the-dawn is Julia Martin," Mr. Wombwell said, "and her two friends are Mason Howell and John Patten. They're all members of our illustrious League, the American Chapter. And all mortal, if you hadn't noticed."

"Very well disguised," he complimented. "I would have guessed only newly dead. It is a pleasure to meet you."

"They have come to unearth Jacob Marley's gold and deliver it to St. Nicholas," Mr. Wombwell whispered.

"I see," Mr. Grant pondered. "This task will not be easy. As soon as their spades hit the dirt every spirit who resides here will be aware of their efforts. The spirits of the ungrateful dead will resist."

"My thoughts exactly," Mr. Wombwell confirmed. "That is why I need an experienced commander to lead this expedition. Would you take on this daunting task?"

"It would be my honor," Mr. Grant said humbly, "If things are as you say, we may need to take our forces into battle."

"We may," Mr. Wombwell replied solemnly. "As a Senior Officer of the Santa Claus League, I grant you the rank of Lieutenant General and Protector of Highgate Cemetery."

"Thank you, Mr. Wombwell," Mr. Grant said, bowing reverently. "I accept the responsibility."

"Would you also be willing to help them find Miss Elizabeth Jackson?"

"Why of course," the military leader answered. "But why Miss Jackson?"

"She is the key to unlocking the treasure," Mr. Wombwell said mysteriously. "She's the only one who knows the location of Jacob Marley's grave. She's kept it a secret for almost two centuries and hasn't even hinted at her knowledge. If only the Queen's army could have spies so dedicated."

"Indeed," he replied. "I shall call for her immediately. She's a friend of mine."

"Thanks for your help," I said. "Can we fly into the cemetery now?"

"Now?" Mr. Grant asked. "Heavens no... much to dangerous."

"Why's that?" Julia asked.

"The whole place is crawling with Marxists, that's why." Mr. Wombwell answered. "If Karl Marx knew what we were up to he'd burn the whole place to the ground."

"Karl Marx?" I gasped. "Why will he be here?"

"He's buried here, my good man," Mr. Grant insisted. "Regrettably, we all have to live with that unfortunate fact."

"Very true," Mr. Wombwell agreed. "His enthusiasm is cyclical and I'm afraid this is one of his more active years."

"Terrific," John complained, "then how will we be able to fly my car in there without being seen?"

"Stratagem," Mr. Grant said cunningly.

Just then a quiet knock interrupted our secret meeting. Mr. Grant stepped outside for a moment then stepped back in.

"It seems fate is on our side," Mr. Grant announced. "MacGregor's mortal accomplices have a flat tire. That should slow them down for a few minutes and give us time to get ready for them. I have a plan. Mr. Wombwell, do you have a copy of tonight's itinerary?"

"Yes, I do," the animal trainer confirmed, handing Mr. Grant a rolled parchment.

"We'll build our strategy around tonight's scheduled events," Lt. General Grant began. "Mr. Faraday is scheduled to open the lecture series a few minutes from now. The chorister will lead us in singing "God Save the Queen," followed by Cardinal Nicholas Wiseman who will offer the invocation. Mr. Faraday will then say a few kind words of introduction; after which you will begin your lecture."

"And as always," Mr. Wombwell added, pointing to an emphasized paragraph. "We have scheduled for Mr. Karl Marx and his mob to interrupt us sometime during the evening."

"Precisely," Mr. Grant said. "We shall allow Mr. Marx to empty the riff raff from the cemetery and engage with us as he always does. Only this time we'll cause a distraction. We will fight Karl Marx and his men, drawing all their attention away from my three young friends. They should be able to fly into the cemetery without being noticed."

"It's a splendid plan," Mr. Wombwell said enthusiastically, standing to leave the carriage. "Mr. Grant, please keep these three safely inside my carriage until it's time to make your move. One more thing. If everything goes badly, and I expect they will, remember the living have power over the dead. Godspeed to all of us. Pray for our success."

"He doesn't seem very confident" I whispered to Mr. Grant.

"He is concerned, but resolute," Grant replied calmly. "But do not worry, Mr. Wombwell has entrusted you to my care. I will not fail you. But if you will excuse me, I need to step outside and keep an eye out for the mob. You never know when Karl Marx and his men will strike. I bid you adieu... m'lady."

Julia nodded in return, more reverently than Her Royal Majesty, the Queen of England could herself. I knew at that point I had a lot to learn about taking care of someone as charming and beautiful as Julia. "Thank you, sir," she said shyly. "You're very kind."

"Yeah, he's kind," I said, after he had closed the door, "but what about Karl Marx and his band of raving lunatics?"

"Look on the bright side," Julia comforted. "At least we can blend in now. We know how to manipulate our clothes and even build tools with just our minds. Thirty minutes ago we didn't have a single ally."

"And we have a plan," John added. "That's more than we had before."

Just as they finished their words of inspiration a rumbling vibration shook the whole carriage. I always get comfortable too soon, but now my heart skipped a beat as a hundred hands slapped the outside of the carriage, rocking it back and forth.

Chapter Eighteen

Meeting Elizabeth Jackson

"Death to the rich! Workers unite!" the ranting mob chanted together in an impossibly loud voice, crushing past us. "Death to the rich! Workers unite!"

"Just let them pass," Mr. Robert Grant whispered appearing inside the coach. "They interrupt Mr. Faraday's lectures every year. Engaging them in an actual battle will be a huge surprise. But don't worry for your safety, I've sworn to protect you!"

"We'll do whatever you say," I answered quietly as the mob continued stampeding past us.

"Fight, you oppressed creatures," Karl Marx yelled. "All you have to lose are your chains."

"How dare you interrupt my lecture," Mr. Wombwell rebuked from a distance. "I won't stand for it this year. Men of Highgate! Men of science! Defend yourselves!"

The ensuing battle rang out like a thousand gongs. Mr. Grant waited another 15 seconds and poked his head out the carriage window to see how the fight was going.

"Right then," he said, pulling his head back in with a smile. "Our distraction is working. All's clear. Let's make this fast."

Mr. Grant bolted out of the carriage with lightning speed and we followed him out as fast as we could move. The peaceful park had been transformed into a noisy battlefield. Hundreds of Michael Faraday's guests were fighting like they were on a suicide mission, causing so much noise a bomb could have gone off unnoticed.

John opened the door to the Chevy Nova and we all piled in without being seen, then he put it in gear and flew straight up and over the cemetery wall.

"I don't think anyone saw us," Julia announced, looking back at the battle. "This is insane. I didn't expect any of this to happen tonight."

"That is exactly what I was hoping for," John laughed. "It's freaking awesome!"

"I question your sense of awesome," I complained. "We've already faced an angry mob of ghosts, and we haven't even met up with Prince Gregor MacGregor's army yet."

"Think happy thoughts," Julia encouraged. "We'll get through this night, just watch and see!"

"That's the spirit," Mr. Grant praised, directing John's flight. "Don't overthink the task at hand, just do what needs to be done, one step at a time. Our allies are apprised of the situation. The fight will continue for as long as needed to provide for your safety. Furthermore, we have posted guards all over the cemetery to warn us of any approaching spirits. If they come, we'll know about it and defend you at all costs."

"What about the four mortal thugs he's bringing with him?" I asked.

"You'll have to deal with them yourself," Mr. Grant insisted. "It's that madman Prince Gregor I'm worried about!"

"Wow," John said. "How do you even know about him?"

"He has a very bad reputation," he responded warily. "In our dimension we call people like him scavengers. He steals emotional power from his victims to fuel his own evil designs."

"I never thought being dead would be so complicated," John mused, looking below for a landing spot. "I could enjoy a place like this."

"Don't get so excited to join us just yet," Mr. Grant interrupted him. "You have a lot to live for, including chocolate, don't forget chocolate. Chocolate is the only thing a spirit can smell... I don't know why. There isn't a ghost in a million who wouldn't return to mortality just for another taste. Do you see that clearing? Fly over there."

"All this talk about chocolate makes me hungry," John mused, following Mr. Grant's navigation suggestions. "Mason, look back there in my backpack, and get me something to munch on."

"Sure, John," I responded, grabbing his bag and pulling out a bag of potato chips, a few packaged lemon cookies, and four almond chocolate bars."

As soon as Mr. Grant saw the chocolate he turned pale. "Are you insane?" he whispered. "Put those back! Get them out of sight, or we'll have the whole cemetery population crashing in on us. Nothing, and I repeat nothing, is more tempting to spirits than chocolate. In fact, I can't be in the same car as you right now. Park over there at the fork in the road. I'll go ahead and find Miss Jackson."

"But how are you going to get down?" John asked, hovering over the cemetery.

"I'll fly," he said, opening the door. "Prince Gregor isn't the only one who can do it." The man flew to the earth and landed like a cat, dusting himself off, and running toward the dark tombs.

"Set her down where Mr. Grant said," I suggested. "We'll wait a few minutes, and if he doesn't come back we'll start looking ourselves."

"You're the boss," John responded cheerfully, landing where he was told. "We've been hanging around the park outside of the cemetery for the last hour. Now we finally get to be among the tombstones past midnight. I can't wait."

The wheels of the car touched down exactly where Mr. Grant told us to park even though it was a tight fit. The cemetery was a popular burial site for a hundred years, but after the best spots were taken they started burying people anywhere they could find an open space. Pauper's graves were created to literally bury one person on top of another in unmarked graves.

Of the 170,000 people buried there, only 53,000 had grave markers. 53,000 headstones crammed in such a small space made landing the car a near miracle without crushing tombstones and getting out of the car was even tougher.

We waited inside the car for Mr. Grant to return. I've never been in a cemetery at night, let alone in a cemetery where I can see, talk to, and be touched by all the residents and I was a little rattled by the whole thing. Julia, on the other hand, was looking through every window, stunned by the beauty she saw.

"What kind of place is this?" she asked in amazement. "Have we landed in a fairytale land? I don't think Officer Swain knew what he was talking about."

I didn't know how to answer her question since I hadn't really looked around yet. But now as I gazed I saw the whole cemetery was green open fields, cities built into mountains and trees.

"Do you see the little country cottages spread out among the underbrush?" she asked astonished.

"I sure do," I answered. "I thought the tombstones would be dreary and spooky but they look more like crystal monuments, floating above the ground."

"Not everything is beautiful," John added. "Some of them are busted down and ugly. Look over there, it looks like a wicked old witch lives there, with a crooked falling down house and dead fields all around it."

"But you can see the beauty too, right?" Julia asked.

"Sure I can," John answered. "I'm just trying to figure this place out."

"No problem," she smiled. "I just wanted to make sure you were seeing what I'm seeing."

While dark acres of wild brambles were scattered over the cemetery, the overall effect was a patchwork of beauty as far as the eyes could see. Apparently the righteous spirits of the dead could change their physical size and enjoy their own resting places. I couldn't step anywhere without crushing something beautiful on my side of the car. But when John opened his door, below him was a dreary wasteland.

"Do you think we can we step here?" John asked timidly.

"Go ahead," Mr. Grant said, appearing on a piece of dry land. "One of Karl Marx's lieutenants is buried here. He may have been rich in life, but look at his real net worth now!"

John got out of the car, stepping on the dead spot, then onto the road without disturbing any of the greener graves. Julia and I did the same thing. The road was the only consistently dark space in the whole cemetery, and even it glowed with the green grass underfoot growing in patches.

"Follow me," Mr. Grant commanded. "Miss Elizabeth Jackson is attending a Christmas party on Egyptian Avenue this year. She doesn't want to reveal herself until absolutely necessary."

"Why can't we take the car?" John complained. "I hate leaving her parked like this. We can fly above the cemetery and Miss Jackson can hop up and talk to us in the car and—"

"A lady never hops into a stranger's car," Julia reprimanded.

"The young lady knows what she is talking about," Mr. Grant agreed. "Elizabeth Jackson is far too proper to be treated so casually. She's not too far away, but we must make haste, I don't want any of Prince Gregor's spies seeing us."

We ran down a curved road, passing plot after plot of absolute beauty. After running for a few minutes, Mr. Grant stopped and pointed at a dark gate, encased with four enormous Egyptian columns, two on each side of the opening. Inside, the tunnel was a combination of light and dark doors. The light ones held the good people, enjoying their eternal rest, while the others were vacant, their owners most likely roaming the earth in misery.

"Don't be alarmed if we meet a few spirits," Mr. Grant warned. "This is our home you know. Try and stay calm, and don't let them know you are mortal, if possible."

As we got closer to the gate, I noticed people darting in and out of lighted doors. We politely greeted each one as they socialized between massive parties going on inside the crypts. I could hear music at each one, a level of merriment I wasn't used to hearing at any party I had ever attended.

Several times a cheerful chap would stop and say hello to us, then whisper a few quick words to Mr. Grant and briskly walk on. With each report, I could see both the messenger and the receiver become more frantic.

"What's going on?" I asked, getting concerned.

"Intelligence updates," Mr. Grant said quietly as a young couple walked past us, the lady with a parasol in her hand.

"Could you be more specific?" I whispered frantically.

"Yes, surely," Mr. Grant answered quietly. "I just received word that Prince Gregor's four mortal accomplices have almost fixed their flat tire. Once back on the road they will arrive in 10 minutes at most. His legion of thieves and vagabonds are holding back for some reason. On a positive note, I have word that Elizabeth Jackson has agreed to help us, she will meet us West of the Circle of Lebanon, by the Jerusalem tree"

"Where is that?" I asked confused.

"It's just down the trail," he explained. "The old tree growing on top of the circle is a cedar of Lebanon tree. It predates the cemetery by more than a century."

"Of course," Julia exclaimed. "It all makes sense now! Jacob Marley was secretly buried under a cedar of Lebanon tree. Could Elizabeth Jackson be the same trusted servant we saw at that last meeting with Ebenezer Scrooge?"

"One and the same," a beautiful woman answered, stepping out of the shadows. "But how would you know that?"

"Christmas magic," Julia answered, giving her a respectful curtsey.

"Thank you for your assistance, my Lady," Mr. Grant said, bowing deeply at her presence.

I bowed too, as did John. Who wouldn't bow? She was dressed in a diamond studded gown. Her gloves were white and went past her elbows. She wore a splendid necklace that sparkled like sunlight and her hair was braided up and held together by a golden clasp. Each element of her being radiated royalty, yet in life this woman was nothing but a servant, and a spinster, who died without love or fortune. She must have died with a heart full of goodness though, because in her new life she was divine.

"It is a pleasure to meet you." I said. "Thank you for your help."

"I'm not helping yet," she said apprehensively. "I only agreed to an initial meeting. How do I know I can trust you?"

"I can help with that," I said, pulling out a silver shilling from my pocket. "Does this look familiar?"

"Oh my giddy aunt!" she gasped. "Then it is true! Tonight is the night! The Baroness will finally be at peace knowing her Jacob may someday be redeemed."

"Then you'll help us?"

"To the ends of the earth," she replied. "I don't know why Mr. Scrooge entrusted this information with me in the first place. I was certainly not special in any way."

"Everyone who lives a good life is special," Julia said.

"You're too kind," she said humbly, changing her beautiful party clothes into working apparel. "Now, you've guessed the correct location of his burial. He is buried under the Jerusalem tree but I'll have to show you exactly where!"

As we headed back to the car, we were greeted by a group of 10 very large men. Each man was protected by a padded uniform with a double-breasted coat and bright silver buttons running down both sides. Their shoes were made of thick leather, polished black, and their baggy pants looked ready for heavy work. To protect their head's, they wore heavy silver helmets with a strap under each of their chins.

"I would like you to meet a few of my friends," Mr. Grant said quickly. "May I introduce you to the heroes of the London Fire Brigade. They have volunteered to help us in our cause. Please meet Mr. Thomas Ashforth, Mr. Henry Berg, and the rest of their men."

"Thank you for your assistance." I said sincerely.

"We are honored to defend you," Mr. Ashforth said crisply. "All these men died in the line of duty. Each is powerful in their own right; together we are a formidable team."

"As are we," the impressive leader of another group of 50 men announced, marching out of the shadows. "My name is Lieutenant Colonel Charles Edward Earl, Officer in Command of the soldiers from the Commonwealth and Screenwall Brigades, at your service." Each man was dressed in a WW I uniform, decorated with service medals of valor.

"Thank you for your help," I said happily, as a feeling of hope rushed over me. Maybe we could win this war after all. By the time we arrived at the car we had another 200 volunteers ready to defend us.

"Meet us at the Jerusalem tree," I called. "If you know anyone else willing to fight, we could use their help!"

"Yes, of course," Lt. Col Earl saluted, gathering in his men to give his orders. "Private Sewell, see how many other soldiers we can find willing to fight for the cause of Christmas."

"Yes, Sir," the Private responded crisply, disappearing with the other ghosts into the night.

The Chevy Nova launched straight up again into the dark night. Mr. Grant was sitting in the front seat, guiding John to the tree. As the car rose above the tree line, a strange green blob glowed in the distance a few miles from the cemetery. I had a sickening feeling the plasma was coming from Prince Gregor MacGregor and his army.

"Park on the east side of the tree," Mr. Grant suggested, giving John parking directions. "And don't park to close to the edge. We don't want your car to fall off."

The Jerusalem tree was encircled by a large concrete edge, making it look like a tree growing in a massive decorative pot. Beyond the edge was a drop off of at least 12 feet that ended in a path on the ground. On the lower level, ornate tombs were cut from granite, circling the whole structure. The final effect made it look as if the tree were planted on top of scores of tombs, when in fact it was the other way around.

John followed Mr. Grant's directions, setting the car down with its nose hanging close the edge. The back of the car pointed toward the base of the tree, with just enough room to get around it. John, Julia and I piled out of the car, being careful not to step off the man-made cliff.

"Miss Elizabeth," Mr. Grant called reverently. "It's time to show us the grave."

"He's buried here," she said solemnly, pointing to an exact spot under the tree. "His bones are below us now, resting in a roughhewn pine box. The Baroness begged me to witness where he was buried, and swore me to secrecy. A secret so solemn, I've not revealed it until now."

"Help me unload the picks and shovels," John asked. I ran to help him while Miss Jackson continued her mournful story. I worked quietly, listening carefully as we made things ready to dig.

"His servant dug the grave that night," she continued, "and stuffed the body of my Lady's true love in the top section of the pine box. With the casket in the ground and the body tucked inside, Mr. Scrooge and the gravedigger loaded five heavy boxes into the coffin, and nailed the lid down tight. I suspected the boxes must be filled with something valuable, based on how heavy they were, and how they jingled when they moved, but it didn't matter. He made me swear again, to tell no one. Not even the dead! Sarah knew, of course, but no one else."

"How was the Baroness able to keep the grave from being discovered?" Julia asked.

"That was simple," Miss Jackson said slyly. "What better place to hide a secret grave than in a cemetery! With her beloved gone, the only thing she wanted to do with the land was turn it into a place of mourning. To her great satisfaction, she demolished her father's home, the Ashurst House and had St. Michael's Church built in its place."

She continued her explanation. "Her dear friend, Stephen Geary, was the architect for the most important features of the cemetery. She made sure the tree was not to be disturbed by convincing him to design a protective stone circle around it, making it appear to be higher and apart from everything else. She lived until she was 93, much longer than I did. I don't know anything more than this. Good luck tonight!"

"Thank you for your help," I said sincerely.

"I feel so relieved now my secret is revealed," she said smiling. "But I can feel the heat of war approaching... I suggest you three get digging!"

"I agree with Miss Jackson," Mr. Grant insisted. "We can keep watch, but we can't help you dig."

Just then a spirit interrupted our conversation. "I'm sorry to be a bother, sir, but I have urgent news."

"Report!" Mr. Grant ordered.

"Yes, sir!" he said with precision. "I bring bad news. The flat tire is fixed and the grave robbers are on their way. To make matters worse, Prince Gregor MacGregor has negotiated a union with Karl Marx and his mob. Their earlier delay was only to gain more followers. Mr. Marx and a few loyalists are still on their way to St. Paul's, but the bulk of his men have sided with Prince Gregor. The madman has at least a 1,000 souls at his command. Sound the alarm, the war has begun!"

Grave Robbing

John left the car running to keep it in time-warp. He turned on a battery-powered lantern and hung it from the evergreen tree while Julia and I pointed our shovels to the earth and dug in as hard as we could. The ground fought back, nearly throwing the shovels right back at us. We tried again, but with the same result. The glowing soil didn't move so much as an inch.

"Maybe the ground is frozen," John suggested, grabbing a pick and thrusting it into the cool soil. The loose dirt didn't even move.

"Maybe time-warp has everything frozen," Julia suggested.

"You know what will happen if we unlock time?" I reminded her.

"Yes, I know," she said cautiously. "We start the clock ticking, giving us even less time to get this done."

"It's not just that," I insisted. "Remember the policeman back at the Flying Scotsman, and all the back-up he requested?"

"It doesn't matter," John interrupted. "We don't have a choice. Look, half the dead people in London are protecting us from the other half. We do this now and do it fast. So let's get our Santa Claus on, and get digging."

When John is right, he's right. What other choice did we have?

"Be careful out there in the mortal world," Mr. Grant implored. "We don't want to wake up the neighbors, and don't worry about Prince Gregor, we have him routed at the gate. He won't step a foot onto these sacred grounds if I can help it. As for his four mortal grave robbers, I can't help you. I'm afraid you're on your own. Good luck. If you need to come back into our dimension, we will be here protecting you."

We waved at the scores of defenders willing to help us, and held each other's hands. Then John hopped in the car and prepared to turn off the time-warp generator as well. "Ready or not here we come," I said bravely. "Turn off the car!" The moment he did all the magical light and color left the world.

The winter night was cold, damp and completely still, with hardly a glimmer of moonlight behind the clouds. The famous London drizzle had begun, causing us to work all the faster with the only light to be seen was John's electric camp lamp hanging on a limb of the ancient tree.

"I never thought I'd be a grave robber," I said quietly.

"I know," John said laughing, throwing the pick into the cold ground. "Ain't it cool! And think about that policeman with his hat on backwards and no one to arrest? I wish I could have seen that!"

Before we got very far we had to come up with a place to put the dirt. The outer edge was only fifteen feet from the center of the tree. Because of the tight quarters, the only place to put the dirt was on the edge of the grave or on the road twelve feet below us. We decided to put as much of the dirt on the road as we could. I felt bad about that. Man, were the caretakers going to be upset!

The digging went fast. We knew the casket was less than three feet wide and about six feet long, buried six feet deep. I thought the tree roots would get in our way, but they avoided the coffin and the space above it completely. I guess even a tree knows a doomed soul.

It didn't take long before we had to dig in shifts. John and I took turns digging and throwing the dirt and rocks from the grave and shoveling it up to Julia. Julia dug into the pile we made and tossed the dirt over the edge, and down to the road. We had excavated down to about four feet when Julia motioned for us to stop.

"I hear a car coming," she said in a hushed tone.

"Does it sound like a police car or a Land Rover?" I asked quietly.

"How would I know that?" she muttered. "Maybe you should ask Mr. Grant what's going on."

"That's a good idea," I replied, touching my nose.

Going into time-warp may have not been a good idea. As soon as I went in a spear grazed past my face, almost taking my ear off. What I saw was even more devastating. The whole cemetery was a battlefield. Quaint cottages in the distance were on fire, women in Christmas party dresses were screeching and running in all directions. A secure perimeter line was being formed around where we were working, with Mr. Grant calling the orders.

"What are you doing here?" Mr. Grant yelled back at me. "The outer wall is under attack. Prince Gregor, the flying demon, is circling the battle lines and breaking down our defenses. We're holding our own here in the center, but it's hand-to-hand combat further out. Get back to your own dimension or I can't protect you."

"What about the mortal grave robbers?"

"They are already here," he groaned, thrusting his shield to block a darting arrow. "But you're safer with them than with us. Now get out of here or we're all doomed."

I touched my nose again, entering back into the dark peaceful world of the living.

"Well, what did Mr. Grant say?" John asked curiously. "It didn't look like you were gone for more than a millisecond."

"A millisecond is all it took," I said stunned. "Prince Gregor is swooping down and making holes in their outer defenses, and his forces are pouring in. It's all-out war everywhere as far as the eye can see."

"Oh dear," Julia said, moving dirt around even faster. "And what about the grave robbers? What did they say about them?"

"They're here," I answered, "but the war is too hot to find out more. We're on our own."

"I wouldn't be saying that," a dirty man whispered, clicking back the hammer of his revolver. "I'd say yeh had good company."

It was Duane Slotham. He was standing on the lip across from the Circle of Lebanon. There was a gulf between us but he was close enough we couldn't hide or run away. Down below us, on the street his three henchmen leaned a ladder against the wall. A few seconds later, his henchmen circled around us like rabid wolves.

"I had a hunch I'd find yeh here," Duane said coarsely. "And my boys say I was crazy ta bring a ladder. Do yeh think I'm crazy now, Billy?"

"Of course I think yeh're crazy," Billy Clubbard replied, "It just so happens I like your kind of crazy."

"I'll take that as a positive thing," Duane said, spitting brownish tobacco on the ground. "I've heard about buried treasure my whole life. It's good ta finally have a go at one."

"Well by all means," John said sarcastically. "Come here and dig for it. So far we're doing all the work."

"You're doing a good job, Laddie," he smirked. "You can keep digging. This will be the easiest grave robbing job I've ever done. Watch 'em boys, while I join yeh."

As soon as Duane disappeared into the night John acted as if he wanted to fight them off. Billy pulled out his own gun and held it menacingly.

"You'd best to be good boys and girls," he snarled. "No use anybody gettin' hurt just now."

"I don't like this," Tuug said "Does this mean we have to share our cut with them since they're doing all the work?"

"Share the treasure?" Duane growled from below as he climbed up the ladder. "Of course not yeh daft idiot. We'll let 'em dig up the grave, and they can even open the coffin, but they ain't getting a single coin. When we drive away we're leaving 'em behind, maybe dead or maybe alive, dependin' on how eager they are to help us. That's the power of Revolver Democracy."

"Oh, right," Tuug smiled as Billy concealed his own weapon. "Revolver Democracy."

"Yeah," Duane said, joining them on the raised circle. "Revolver Democracy, I just made that up. It's the kind a democracy where the guy holding a 38 Special gets to make the rules."

"Your nothing but a thug no matter how you try to justify it," Julia accused. "Stealing never helps anyone, not even the thief."

"Shut yer trap and keep workin', little Miss," Duane growled. "How can me and me boys be thieves if we're stealing from you? I'd say you were the thieves and we're the rescuers."

"Then let us go," I said, hopping out of the half dug grave. "We don't want any trouble."

"Get back in there and keep digging," he demanded, kicking me back into the hole. "If yeh don't shut up, I'll shoot all three of yeh now and fill the grave up with your bones. How'd yeh like that?"

"Calm down," John said casually. "We'll keep digging."

"He's right, Mason," Julia added. "Just do what they say. Are you alright Mason?"

"I think I have a bloody nose," I said, touching it with my right finger.

At the touch of my finger the world changed and I was back in the war zone again. Prince Gregor MacGregor and his thousand men were pushing against the line, while countless others were fighting with Robert Grant to keep them at bay.

"I see you've been surrounded by enemies of your own," Mr. Grant yelled over the battle. "Don't give up. Never give up. Remember, the man who knows more about his battlefield has the upper hand. Now go back and get the treasure."

I touched my nose again, finding myself back in the quiet wood with a man holding a revolver pointed at us.

"Get diggin' boy," Duane yelled angrily. "I ain't got all night. Dig!"

"You heard him," I said confidently. "Dig, as hard and as fast as you can."

Without saying another word, I pushed my shovel into the dark soil and threw the dirt up to Julia. Julia and John didn't despair, they worked alongside me without saying another word. We toiled in silence for about 30 minutes until my shovel pounded onto something hollow.

"I was worried when yeh got so quiet all the sudden," Duane sneered. "But now you've found the casket I'm happy you were just doin' yehr best to make me happy. Sorry I'm so hard to please. Do yeh remember when I said you were goin' to take the gold from the casket? I lied. Me and me boys are doin' that part. So get out of the hole, nice and easy, and let the professionals do their work."

John and I hopped out of the hole, and stood by Julia, as Billy Clubbard and Gavin Robbins jumped in. After clearing out a little more dirt, Tuug handed down a bag full of battery-powered tools. The sounds of a drill and a power saw rang through the trees as they carved into the top of the casket.

"What'd yeh see down there?" Duane grimaced. "Yeh through yet?"

"Almost," Gavin, answered, knocking the wood with his foot. A loud snapping sound echoed through the graveyard.

"Quiet there!" Duane said fearfully. "Do yeh want ta bring the Coppers down on us?"

"Sorry about that," Billy whispered. "We just broke through the top a the casket. We found his skull with the rest a his bones curled up all the way to his dusty nose hairs. There might be something hidin' under his skull, I can't tell. I'm checking."

I couldn't believe Billy had the guts to reach his hand under the skull of Jacob Marley. He might have thought twice about it if he knew what would happen. As soon as he touched the bones of the dead man, Marley's tormented spirit rose from his body, shrieking and moaning like he had been shot a second time.

"Touch not my bones!" Marley roared like a young lion dressed in a black mien, whipping his chains around in circles.

"It's death itself!" Billy yelled. He pulled his hand out of the casket still holding onto Marley's skull.

"Put down my skull!" The ghost demanded, whipping his chains around and through the petrified grave robber. He rose above them all, howling and threatening as ominous as death.

Gavin whelped in horror, dropped his tool bag on the casket and tried to crawl out of the deep hole. Every time Marley's ghostly boxes passed through Gavin's body he let out a grunt, as if the boxes, or the gold inside of them fueled his fears.

"Just give the specter what he wants," Tuug growled from above the grave, ignoring the repeated attempts by the hooded Jacob Marley to wrap the heavy boxes around him. "Return the skull to the coffin and he'll leave us alone. The dead do not like being touched."

Billy dropped the skull into the coffin and jumped to the other side of the grave, joining Gavin in his attempt to escape.

Even Duane had seen the ghost and, although he wasn't in the grave, he tried to keep away from Marley's angry advances.

"You are all babies," Tuug smirked while shoveling more dirt above the grave. "See, he is almost gone. In my language "Tuug Qabri" means robber of the dead. I have experience in these matters. The dead must be respected or they will fight back."

Tuug was right. Marley was being blown away by the Winds of Doom as he spoke. The heavy boxes and chains circled around the helpless apparition, wrapping him up in a cocoon, lifting him into the air. No matter how hard he tried to stay, even to defend his own human remains, the winds finally overcame him, blowing him away.

"Is he gone now?" Billy whimpered.

"Yes, he is gone," Tuug shot back unsympathetically. "Just don't touch his bones again and he won't come back."

"I ain't touching no more nasty bones," Billy cursed. "I'm gettin' out of this place as soon as I can!"

"Then get back to work, yeh manky blighter!" Duane demanded, pretending he wasn't scared by the ghost. "We ain't been caught robbin' a grave yet and we ain't about to start now."

"I think I heard something," Gavin warned.

"Is it the ghost again?" Billy cried.

"I don't think so," Gavin answered, straining his ears. "It sounds like someone's trying to open the front gate."

"I hate this place," Billy complained. "Always cold, the graves are too close together, haunting spirits and—"

"Shut yer trap and keep workin'," Duane snarled, looking anxious. "But I thought I heard something, too. I'll check it out."

Duane closed his eyes, focusing his ears on the distant sound. Moments later footsteps broke the silence, along with more rattling chains, and the creaking of a large rusty gate.

"Someone's coming!" Duane whispered.

"It's the cops," Tuug announced in a panic. "We must get out of here."

"Calm down, yeh manky git," Duane cursed. "They ain't got us yet. We ain't leavin' the treasure for those blokes to steal. When we have it, we can go."

"I found it," Billy sang triumphantly, breaking through the last board on the other side of the casket. "Five metal boxes. We're rich!"

"Hand them up, quickly!" Duane demanded.

"Not unless you increase our cut," Billy insisted fiendishly. "The three of us want half, you can keep the other half for yourself."

"And why should I do that?" Duane spat, raising his revolver at the greedy criminal.

"Call it Revolver Democracy," Billy smiled, pulling out his own weapon. "You cut us in or we kill you!"

Another clicking sound came from behind, Tuug gave a fiendish grin, brandishing another gun. Before Duane knew it he had three guns pointed at him.

"Fine, take half then," he grimaced, screwing a silencer on his weapon. "But we're getting' nothing if the cops catch us. So get to work!"

John, Julia, and I watched helplessly as five heavy boxes were thrown to the dirt above the hole. A few minutes later Gavin climbed down the ladder and produced a heavy wheelbarrow.

"Well, this is goodbye then," Duane smirked, pointing his gun at Julia. "We'll ne'er get away with you three nutters slowing us down. Sorry it had to end this way."

"But you said you'd let us live!" I shouted.

'I lied," he snarled, pointing his gun at me and pulling the trigger.

Chapter Twenty

A Shot in the Night

It all happened so fast, I didn't have time to think. The impact of the bullet hit me, throwing me into the grave. I landed on a wall of dirt, sliding into the casket and onto the bones of Jacob Marley. As soon as I touched his bones he appeared above me, looking down with pity.

"Your nose," he moaned gently, before disappearing. "Touch your nose!"

My eye sight was fading along with my strength. In my last moments of consciousness, I reached up and touched my nose. The second I did, time stopped, along with my beating heart.

For a moment I didn't know if I were dead or alive. My coat was already soaked in blood and my shirt was even worse. Although in agony, I realized in time-warp I could move around without losing more blood. At that moment I knew I was still alive.

Intense pain continued rippling through my body, kicking off my fight or flight response. I ignored the desire to run away and chose to stay and fight for my friends. I clawed my way out of the grave and saw the ghostly war waging around me.

Mr. Grant and his men had formed a shield wall around the Circle of Lebanon while the enemy forces were pressing in. I could hear Prince Gregor MacGregor inciting his followers from above. The spirit world was alive with action, but the mortal world had stopped dead in its tracks.

Duane was frozen in time, still holding his gun and smiling devilishly. He had already aimed his weapon at John, planning to finish him off next. I was too weak to think of a complicated plan so I clicked John and Julia into time-warp with me and collapsed to the earth.

The action only took a second, but that gave Duane just enough time to pull the trigger a second time. The bullet had already left the barrel, but it didn't hit its mark. Time-warp made the piece of metal hang in the air like it was part of a deadly magic trick.

Julia gasped, seeing me covered in blood and fell to her knees in tears. John was too shocked to say anything and just stood there helplessly.

"He... he shot me!" I stammered, speaking first.

"Are you hurt badly?" Julia blurted above the confusion of the war around us.

"I think so," I answered, still on my knees, unable to stand because of the pain. "I think I'm dying."

"Don't talk like that!" Julia blurted, holding back her tears. "I can't believe he just shot you! And he was just about to shoot us, too! What a horrible man."

"This is nuts!" John gasped. "How are you even able to move?"

"Blood doesn't pump outside of time," I wheezed, ignoring the fight storming around us. "But it hurts like crazy. I'll stay alive as long as we stay in time-warp, but if we leave, I'm doomed."

"Mr. Grant!" Julia called frantically. "Mason's been shot!"

"That's impossible!" Robert Grant responded, instantly coming to our aid. "We've pushed the demons back... Oh, I see! He's been shot in your world! I'm terribly sorry, my boy."

"What do we do?" Julia begged.

"Ha! I have just the man!" he answered heroically. "A fellow Victoria Cross recipient from the Indian Mutiny, Surgeon General Sir Anthony Dickson Home. Sir Home. Report!"

"Who called my name?" a disagreeable old man responded, appearing by the tree. "What do you want? Can't you see I'm fighting a war here?"

"My apologies," Mr. Grant replied hastily. "I need your medical expertise. Mr. Howell, our coin bearer, has been shot."

"Oh, I see," he said, kneeling down to examine my injuries. "It's a clean wound. It appears the bullet went right through his body. It's a miracle it missed so many vital arteries, organs, bones, and the like."

"So does that mean you can save him?" Julia pleaded.

"He may live if we can stop the bleeding," the doctor said "If not, he'll die in a few minutes if left alone in the mortal realm."

"Stop the bleeding!" Julia begged. "He's my fiancé. Please don't let him die!"

"And how can I do that?" the surgeon balked. "I'm a spirit and he's a mortal."

"I'm a mortal," she begged. "Show me what to do!"

"Would you be willing to do everything I say? This will be gruesome."

"Anything," she begged. "What do we do first?"

"We'll need basic medical supplies," Dr. Home said urgently. "We'll need antiseptics to clean the wound, gauze, bandages, and a needle and thread for sutures, seeing how much damage has been done."

"Wait right here," John offered, running for his car. "I think I can help. St. Nicholas told me to prepare for a dangerous mission. I packed a full medical kit in my car just to be on the safe side."

"I don't know what we would do without you!" Julia praised as John ran to the car. She looked back at me with pity in her eyes, weeping and brushing my hair with her fingers. "What were you thinking?" she begged. "Why would you stand in front of a bullet like that?"

"I don't know," I answered, shock taking its toll on my attention span. "I didn't think. I was just trying to protect... you. Fiancé', huh? I like the sound of that. Are you sure you want to be married to someone as reckless as me?"

"Shut up!" she said "I've been your Mrs. Claus for four years now, I'm not about to stop now. If I'm not your fiancée, then we have bigger problems to talk about."

"Julia wouldn't be your only problem, dude," John added, coming back with a large medical bag. "If you die I'll never forgive you."

"I'm glad I'm so loved," I smiled painfully.

"No problem," John said seriously, "Thanks for saving us, man. That took guts."

"No problem. I'm fireproof, right?" I tried to joke, wincing at the pain.

"Did you think you were bulletproof, too?" Julia chided, wiping the tears from her eyes.

Sir Home had Julia rummage through the medical bag and started setting up his operating room. John helped Julia take off my coat and shirt and put a blanket under my back to keep me out of the dirt.

John stood around helplessly for a minute or so until he couldn't stand it anymore. "I'm not doing any good here, hovering around like a vulture," he groaned, "While you and Sir Home are working, I'm going to load the gold in the trunk of the car. But before I do," John fumed, "I'm taking all the guns away from those goons. I'm tired of being pushed around. I wish I could shoot them all myself!"

John gathered up all the guns and threw them into the grave where he knew the robbers couldn't find them. Next he tried to pick up one of the gold boxes, but it was too heavy to move more than a few steps. He ended up dragging them, one-at-a time, to the car.

While John was moving Jacob's treasure, Sir Home set up a front line "sterile" field, as good as could be done under the circumstances, and prepared to help Julia save my life.

"Are you sure you can to do this?" Surgeon General Home asked Julia. "It won't be easy."

"Yes," she responded firmly, "just tell me what to do."

"Begin by cleaning the wound with betadine, this will hurt him, a lot…"

I don't know what else they said because he was right, it did hurt and I passed out from the pain. By the time I woke up my shoulder was bandaged up with tape wrapped firmly around my whole upper body.

"You did amazingly well," the doctor said to Julia with admiration. "You could be a surgeon if you put your mind to it. The world is always in need of skilled hands like yours."

"Thank you, sir," she sighed, cleaning the blood off her fingers with a bottle of water. "How long do you think he will be out?"

"He is just waking up now," Sir Home said graciously. "And a good thing, too. Your friend has just about finished loading the car with the treasure."

"Hey, Mason," John announced, trying to lighten the mood. "I knew you had a plan to get out of all the work. Well done!"

"I do my best," I said weakly. "How is the war going?"

"I think we're winning, but Mr. Grant tells me they are regrouping for another try. Would you like something to drink? You might be thirsty after losing so much blood."

"That would be great," I said weakly. I was thirsty. As I put my parched lips to the lip of the water bottle, an image of the Ghost of Christmas Present flashed in my mind, giving me an idea. "Julia, could you pull out my pouch and mix some Christmas Ambrosia in my water? I could use a little Christmas cheer right now."

"That's a great idea," she agreed, generously filling my water bottle with more Ambrosia dust than I would have. "The Spirit said not to skimp. I hope this helps."

I thanked her, and took a sip from the simple plastic bottle. A rainbow couldn't have been more refreshing. The fluid tasted like sweet tart orange juice, begging me to drink again. A few moments after enjoying the second swallow, I felt a powerful sense of purpose come over me. Ideas streaked through my head and every bit of despair left my body. I took another sip, the flavor becoming pure grape juice, revitalizing my body, causing my wound to tingle and sizzle with relief. By the time the drink was gone, the pain was manageable, and I could sit up unassisted.

"I think you should both have some of this," I suggested, "I feel much better."

"Keep him down as much as possible, Miss Martin," Dr. Home suggested. "Don't let him rip out the stitches."

"Thank you so much for your help," Julia beamed, light literally shining through her skin. "I think you may have saved his life."

"No trouble at all," he smiled, bowing deeply. "Now back to the front lines. Good luck to you Mr. Howell, your fiancée is charming beyond words. You are a lucky man."

"Yes I am," I agreed, as he disappeared into the night.

"Do you really feel better?" Julia asked hopefully as she cleaned up around the operating sight.

"I do," I answered truthfully. "You saved my life!"

"I'd do it over again, if I needed to," she said gently, handing me another bottle of Christmas Ambrosia.

The temporary peace that had surrounded us now gave way to confusion again. The grunting and scraping sounds of the shield wall broke into the shrill noise of metal striking metal. Suddenly Robert Grant appeared under the tree.

"Take the gold and fly away," he ordered. "They're beginning to break through our lines again."

"I'd love too," John insisted. "But the last box won't fit in the trunk. We'll have to put it on the front seat next to me."

"Be quick about it!" Mr. Grant commanded, then disappeared.

"I'll help you," Julia cried. "We have to get out of here."

"No kidding?" John responded frantically, lifting the treasure with all his might. "Just hold the door open for me. I think I can get it."

He spoke too soon. As Julia opened the door, John tripped on a slippery root, causing the old box to hit the trunk of the cedar tree and slam to the ground, scattering gold coins all over the loose dirt.

Chapter Twenty-One

The Race Against Time

The latch of the old metal box must had rusted through. When it crashed into the tree, it couldn't hide its secret treasure any longer. The lid burst open, every unholy spirit took notice, leaping to catch a glimmer of the spilled treasure.

"Crap!" John cursed. "Crap! Crap! Crap!"

"Gold!" a ghost screeched over the suddenly quiet battlefield. "I see the gold!"

"The fortune is real!" another cried. "I want it. Give it to me now!"

A great roar rose over the battlefield, followed by a surge of warriors, pushing forward, squeezing our defenders into a smaller circle. Suddenly the ground beneath us started to shake.

"What's going on?" I begged, clutching my aching shoulder while sitting up on the blanket outside the car.

"The fiends are entering into the graves from below us," Mr. Grant yelled, "once they do they'll crawl up through the ground to get to the gold. We have them mostly mostly blocked off but you'd better gather up that treasure quickly. I don't know how long we can hold them off."

"Hurry up," I pleaded to John and Julia while fumbling to take another deep drink of my Christmas Ambrosia. "We're about to have company!"

John and Julia had about half of the gold gathered in when a patch of earth started boiling right in front of me. Grasping, scratching hands rose up followed by a head and shoulders, trying to pull itself out of the ground. The leather clad phantom looked at me and then at the gold with wide eyes. I leaned forward and kicked him in the head, causing him to roll all the way to the shield wall. I was more powerful than I thought, even in my weakened condition.

With that knowledge I got up, joining the other defenders. I only fought when I had to, but each time I did, the pain nearly overwhelmed me. Luckily my actions gave John and Julia more time to gather up the treasure.

The London Fire Brigade firemen caught most of the intruders as they popped up from the ground but one managed to avoid our detection and snatched up a golden coin, grasping it in his ghostly hands.

"I have the treasure," he screeched, "It's mine!"

"Not anymore," I insisted, grabbing the coin from his hands while a fireman threw him over the wall.

"That's my treasure!" he howled, transforming mid-flight into a flaming knight, his whole body glowing with fiery red flame which he rolled together and threw at me. Just as the fireball was about to strike one of the defenders blocked its way, deflecting the plasma.

Unfortunately, the other greedy ghosts now realized they could summon up body armor and shoot fireballs and hundreds of them morphed in front of our eyes, leaping into the air and beginning an all-out firestorm.

"Your training is complete," Prince Gregor roared from somewhere above us. "Harness your rage and transform into instruments of doom. Attack from the air with fire!"

Following his orders, the enemy soldiers morphed into whatever terrifying warrior they could imagine. Some became wild Vikings with leather goat skins girded around their chests. Others changed into bold Roman legionnaires with dull black armor and black feathers on their helmets.

They became an army of warriors from every age of English history, holding maces, ball and chains and every kind of sword imaginable. All of them rose into the air in a controlled tornado of power and threw fireballs and lightning bolts at us. They swept down in organized advances, slamming into the shield wall, using their own bodies as battering rams.

Miraculously the shield wall withstood their attacks. Our defenders drew in tighter to keep the enemy arrows and fireballs from breaking through, allowing John and Julia to gather up the remaining gold coins. By now the whole cemetery was at war and everyone in it was forced to take sides.

Commander Ashforth and Berg, along with the other heroes of the London Fire Brigade flung enemy soldiers all over the cemetery with their long fire axes as Lt. Col Earl and Private Sewell, with their valiant soldiers from the Commonwealth and Screenwall Brigades assembled an anti-aircraft gun and blasted flying legionnaires out of the sky by the dozens.

Mr. George Wombwell had full use of his powerful menagerie including Nero, his trusted lion who attacked without mercy. Elephants, bears, lions, tigers, and all sorts of other creatures bit, clawed, and tormented the ghastly army.

Percy Lambert was in the fight, flying his ferocious Talbot Star all through the skies, running over enemy ghosts in the fastest car of his age.

Michael Faraday and his Christmas Lecture guests pitched in by electrocuting the enemy with a large electromagnetic inductor.

Douglas Adams appeared in his starship, The Heart of Gold, and flew back and forth, knocking flying enemy soldiers out of the sky.

Even Miss Elizabeth Jackson, now dressed in glorious white battle armor, had two gigantic hounds with glowing red eyes at her side, who fought fiercely at her direction. In charge of it all was the acting General, Robert Grant, the Defender of Highgate Cemetery, commanding a most unlikely army against a near unstoppable foe.

But it was soon apparent, that even with the help of so many heroic people the treasure was still about to be stolen by greedy ghosts, clawing up from the ground. No matter how many we captured and threw over the shield wall they just kept coming.

"We need to create a distraction," Julia said with frustration. "If we don't, we're done for."

Chapter Twenty-Two

Dangerous Distractions

"What kind of distraction are you talking about?" I asked while helping a fireman toss out another grasping ghost.

"One good enough to give John the time to gather up the rest of the gold," she answered. "If we could just draw their attention off with something they wanted more than treasure…"

"There's nothing they want more than gold," I complained.

"Oh, yes there is," she assured me, smiling triumphantly. "But I need two things to pull this off. I need John's backpack and your watch."

She crawled into the back of the car and came up with the backpack and began rummaging through the assorted water bottles and chips.

"What are you looking for?" I asked.

"This," she said happily, holding up four chocolate bars. "If ghosts love chocolate as much as Robert Grant says they do, we have our distraction."

"Mr. Grant," Julia ordered. "We're about to run onto the battlefield. Cover us!"

Mr. Grant directed a group of WW I soldiers to defend us as Julia ran up to the immobile Gavin and began putting chocolate pieces in his shirt and trouser pockets. The grave robber was frozen in time, and although he was a dangerous and powerful man in the mortal dimension, in this dimension he was helpless to defend himself from what little 115-pound Julia was about to do to him.

As soon as her defending guards saw what she was doing they turned pale from a desperate desire to have the chocolate.

"Don't worry boys," Julia assured them, finishing up with Gavin. "Keep the other ghosts at bay for a just a just a few more minutes and I'll let you be the first ones to have a chance at the chocolate."

"Yes ma'am," they all said in unison, eager for her to complete the mission.

With Gavin's pockets loaded with chocolate Julia now began working on Billy's as I stuffed Tuug's pockets with pieces of chocolate at the same time. The more pieces we broke off the more the aroma swept through the battlefield.

Our work was an immediate success. Our defenders were already starting to fight off ghosts who had come up from the ground under the tree. Instead of turning to the gold as they rose from the tombs below they turned their attention to the chocolate being carried by the grave robbers.

"It's working," I said, as even flying ghosts took notice of the smell.

When we got to Duane I shuddered at his cold dark eyes. John had removed the gun from his hand but his eyes still held the bloodlust of a murderer. Julia put a couple of squares of chocolate into his hands in place of the guns and put the other pieces in his pockets.

"Now let me have your watch so I can click them into time-warp," she asked urgently.

"Be careful," I warned and handed over the watch. I was too weak to run around the battlefield, but Julia was eager and able to dart around, avoiding the worst of the fighting. She ran over to where Gavin was standing and prepared our men.

"As soon as I click these men into time-warp," she instructed our defending soldiers, "you can have all the chocolate you can get your hands on. Just make sure to let Prince Gregor's men have some."

"Hurrah!" they exclaimed. "Just tell us when to let Prince Gregor's men through!"

When Julia clicked Gavin into time-warp his surprise was immediate. He stepped back in shock as soldiers from both sides of the war attacked him at the same time making him slip and tumble into the open grave.

Julia brought Billy and Tuug into time-warp the same way. The moment they left time they gasped in shock as the war raged around them.

"It's the ghost war!" Tuug cried, swatting the ghost's grasping fingers away and leaping off the lip of the Circle of

Lebanon and onto the pile of dirt below. "You have awakened the dead. We are all doomed!"

Dozens of Prince Gregor's men abandoned their positions and chased after Tuug, his wretched cries adding to the confusion of the battlefield.

"I think your plan is working," I yelled over at Julia. "They've left John alone completely."

"That's a relief," she sighed. "Let's give him a little more time by getting Duane into time-warp."

She darted through fighting men to where Duane was standing, frozen in time. Julia clicked him into time- warp and we stepped back to stay clear of his brutal reaction.

What?" Duane asked in confusion as the scene around him instantly changed. He fumbled around for his gun but couldn't find it. "How did you get over there? Where's my gun?"

"I guess Revolver Democracy doesn't work so well without a revolver," I said defiantly.

"I don't need a gun to work you over boy," Duane snarled, running in our direction like a freight train.

Duane was a huge man, with arms like stones and a will of stubborn iron. I thought we were doomed until a wall of WW I soldiers blocked his path, knocking him to the ground. I had seen how hard they fought to defend their home, but that was nothing compared to how they fought for a chance to have a piece of sweet chocolate.

"Impossible," Duane exclaimed as he picked himself off the dirt. He spun around in terror for a moment but saw John's car loaded with the boxes of gold. He looked at the treasure, then looked at the men standing in his way and growled.

"You can't stop me so easily," Duane spat. "That's my treasure! Billy, Gavin, help me get it back."

"But... but... it's the ghost war," Billy Clubbard stammered. "Tuug says we awakened the dead!"

"Forget about Tuug," Duane ordered. "I want my treasure. Gavin, get out of that hole and stop playing around."

"I'm not playing around," Gavin cried, fighting off a horde of ghosts trying to steal the hidden chocolate pieces. "It's the walking dead! They're scratching me, biting me, beating me... help me! Get 'em off me. Get 'em off me!"

"You're fired," Duane snarled, grabbing two soldiers and tossing them aside. "They're just stupid ghosts. Billy, I'm given' you Tuug and Gavin's share, now do what you're told. Get the gold out of the trunk of that car. I didn't hire you to look stupid."

Billy was still just as afraid as before, but the lust for gold drove him forward. He trembled uncontrollably as he marched towards John who was busily gathering up the last few coins. As he walked under the tree a horde of Prince Gregor's men swooped down from the branches and began tearing at his clothes to steal the chocolate.

"They've got me!" Billy wailed pathetically, his feet literally coming off the ground from their aerial attack. "Get the blighter's away! Leave me alone!"

"I'm not giving up that easily," Duane growled at me, ignoring his friend being tossed around in the air and his other partner being beat up in the grave. "Somehow this is your doing, boy. I'll take my gold even if I have ta bash all three of yeh to death!"

"That's not going to happen," I said defiantly. "You don't know your battlefield very well, do you?"

He ignored my words and charged at me again. He didn't get far. Just as our soldiers attacked him from one side, a group of Prince Gregor's men attacked him from the other. As big and powerful as the murderous grave robber was, he didn't stand a chance. They grasped and clawed, bit and scratched, until after only a few seconds he was already beaten to his knees.

"Stay away from me," Duane yelped, as frenzied ghosts tried to take the chocolate from his pockets.

"Give me the chocolate!" a horrible Viking snarled, ripping Duane's shirt apart to get at it.

"Take it!" Duane yelled frantically, throwing all the chocolate he could find at the greedy soldiers. The Viking dove for the pieces of candy, fighting with his rabid friends for control of the brown chocolate squares. Duane was clawed and scratched until there was nothing left of his shirt but rags. Gold is nice, but chocolate is… well, let's just say, to die for.

Gavin was finally able to crawl out of the grave and jumped for the ladder. Half crawling, half falling down it, he landed on the road below and ran screaming into the night drawing another 20 greedy ghosts after him.

"I surrender! I surrender!" Billy begged under the tree, finally breaking free of his attackers and rolling up into a ball. "I give up, just get them off me."

Julia and I ignored Billy's pleas for the moment and ran over to where John was kicking the dirt around searching for the last coin.

"That's it," John said triumphantly, picking up a coin and throwing it into the box resting on the front passenger seat of the Nova. "That's the last one." All the gold glowed for a second, giving us the confidence we had gathered in the whole treasure. "Let's get out of here."

"What about the grave robbers?" I asked with pain returning to haunt me.

"Stand back and I'll click them back into time," Julia answered. In no more time than it takes to blink twice, she had Billy and Duane transported back to the mortal dimension.

"It's time for you to leave," Robert Grant insisted, appearing next to Julia. "Your job is done here."

"But what about Prince Gregor and his men?" I asked concerned.

"Don't worry about them," he assured us, "We'll continue the fight for as long as it takes. We have all the time in the world."

"It's been an honor fighting with you," George Wombwell said merrily, appearing with Nero the Lion by his side. "And an honor to fight for the cause of the Santa Claus League. Fly north my friends. Complete the mission!"

"We will," I said, believing we might be able to really do it.

"Thank you so much for everything you've done," Julia added, with a curtsy. "I hope we all get to meet again!"

I stood up straight and saluted the noble warriors. With Julia's hand in mine and John's hand on my shoulder, I clicked the watch. The moment we entered back into time the battlefield scene was gone. But then, a less pleasant reality took its place as a wave of intense pain swept over me.

"Are you okay?" John asked, sensing my troubles.

"Not at all," I admitted. "I feel horrible."

"Let's get you back in the car," Julia ordered. "Have a few sips of ambrosia, that seems to help."

"Where are the other two grave robbers?" John asked as he noticed Billy whimpering by the tree and Duane laying close by like a pile of ripped up clothes.

"I don't know," I answered, struggling to get into the backseat of the car.

"Tuug and Gavin both jumped down into the lower circle and ran away," Julia exclaimed. "I don't know where they are."

"That's fine by me," John smiled. "Let's go before the police get here."

"No," Julia insisted. "We just can't leave them in time-warp."

"Sure we can," said John. "Some people deserve eternal torment."

"We have to take them out of time-warp," I insisted, grasping my shoulder in pain. "But I don't think I'm going to be much help this time. I think I ripped something moving around so much."

"Stay with him Julia," John ordered, pulling out a pocket knife and opening the blade. "I'll take care of Gavin and Tuug!"

"Don't you dare!" Julia gasped, looking at the glimmering steel.

"Don't I dare do what?" John asked, stabbing the front passenger tire of his car. "Oh, stab them with my pocket knife? Nah, but I'd like to. No, I have to deflate the tire get rid of this stupid tire-boot before we can fly out of here. I hate boots!"

"That's a relief," she said, getting into the car with me.

"So is this!" John yelled, ripping the tire boot off the tire and throwing it down onto the circular path below. "Try stopping me now, you, stupid boot!"

"Do you feel better now?" Julia said, buckling me in.

"Yes, I do!" he shot back. "Now let's go before something else happens!"

"I don't feel so good," I groaned weakly, as Julia slid me into my safety harness. I was bleeding again and lightheaded.

Duane Slotham could barely lift his head out of the dirt, but he had seen my weakened condition and laughed at John. "He won't make it around the block with that hole I shot in him. Your boy here's gonna die and the police are coming to carry his carcass away. You'll go to jail with the rest of us!"

"I don't think so," John said with determination, revving the Nova's engine. "Call this American Ingenuity! Say hello to the police for us. Peace out!"

A Mission of Mercy

John levitated the car, stowing all four tires inside the wheel well with a satisfying clunk. We circled around the tree, pitching the front of the car to face the ground and maneuvered it into the path of the Circle of Lebanon.

"Where do you think they are?" John said. "I can't see them."

"We'll have to go into time-warp to see them," I groaned, handing him my magic watch. "They might be hiding near where we first parked the car. You can click them back into time with my watch."

"Cool," John grinned. "I get to use the watch of power!"

Julia and I touched John's back when he clicked the watch a single time, taking us all into time-warp. The battle was still waging even this far away from the tree. Off in the distance we noticed an area of densely packed tombstones with a concentration of even more soldiers, surrounding two glowing lights.

"I think I found them," Julia announced, pointing over at the mob. "Fly over there so we can rescue them."

"They were happy to leave us for dead," John said "I still think we should leave them here."

"Are you serious?" Julia chastened. "Remember what side you're on. The Santa Claus League rescues everyone, the good and the bad alike!"

"I guess you're right," John scowled, flying the Nova toward the mob. "I just wish we could punish the bad a little more thoroughly."

When we hovered over the swarm we found both Gavin and Tuug in the middle of the fight, standing back to back desperately trying to defend themselves.

"There they are!" John exclaimed, swatting the Roman Legionnaires away with his car and tilting it so he could reach out a hand to them.

"Gavin! Tuug! Take my hand!"

"Stay away!" Gavin cried pathetically.

"Leave us alone," Tuug added, trying to fight off the remaining soldiers.

"If you don't take my hand now I'll leave you trapped with the dead forever," John ordered again. "You have no idea how much I want you to refuse this offer."

"Anything to be free of this place!" Gavin sobbed, thrusting his hand up to meet John's.

"Don't leave me here!" Tuug pleaded, reaching up his hand as well.

"You better do it fast," Julia warned, as the legionnaires regrouped for another attack. "Here comes Prince Gregor and his men."

As soon as John clicked my magic watch we were all immediately taken back into time, free of ghostly tormentors.

"I ought to run you guys over," John yelled at the cowering men in the dark.

"Go ahead," Tuug wailed, covering his eyes with pieces of his shredded shirt. "Just don't let the demons come back!"

John lifted his Chevy Nova away from the tombstones just as a special police unit dressed in riot gear came storming onto the path with their guns drawn. "Come out of there with your hands up!" a police officer yelled at Gavin and Tuug."

"Don't shoot," Gavin whimpered, kneeling and putting his hands behind his head. "I surrender!"

Tuug followed his lead, surrendering to the police as well.

"What's that above your head, sir?" one of the men called, shooting at us on sight.

Hold your fire, Sgt. Evans!" the commanding officer ordered. "Wait for my orders!"

"Get us out of here," Julia begged, just as the bullets made a sickening thud in the undercarriage.

"Will everyone stop shooting at us," John said annoyed, pulling the Nova into the sky and darting into the night.

John headed directly North at full throttle, gaining speed by the second. The North star illuminated our path, letting us know we succeeded in escaping the cemetery. Step one was complete, now for step two: fly north and survive the journey!

Chapter Twenty-Four

Life or Death Decisions

I was raw with pain as we approached the speed of sound, my shoulder bleeding again. All Julia could do was apply pressure to the wet bandages. My chest pounded like a thousand drums and my eyes felt heavy. We all had flight helmets on, allowing Julia to look directly into my eyes as if the helmet didn't exist.

"Stay with me, Mason," she demanded fiercely.

"The pain is getting worse," I warned, "I don't know how much more of this I can take."

"Take us back into time-warp!" Julia begged. "This is killing him!"

"I can't," John insisted. "Not yet at least. I don't dare until we put some distance between us and the cemetery. I'm turning on the afterburners. We're going supersonic."

"Heaven help us," Julia moaned.

The car shuddered as we passed through the sound barrier and I shuddered, too. The pain relieving effect of the Christmas Ambrosia had worn off, causing my shoulder to throb with pain as never before.

"Are you feeling better or worse?" Julia asked, checking my dressing for more blood loss.

"Worse," I admitted. "I feel dizzy."

"How fast can we go without flying hypersonic?" Julia asked, holding onto my hand.

"About Mach 3.5," John said, flipping more switches around."

"Don't you think Mach 3.5 is fast enough to outrun them?" Julia asked, hating the thought of engaging the scramjet.

"Maybe so," John answered, "but at this burn rate we'll run out of fuel before we get to the North Pole. I think engaging the scramjet might be our best option."

"If we must," she sighed, hating to agree.

John was concentrating on his airspeed indicator as we approached the needed airspeed to engage the scramjet. He was about to flip on the switch when a large bump rocked the car, followed by a hissing sound.

"What was that?" Julia screamed, startled by the change in our fortunes.

"I don't know," John panicked, looking around the vehicle with his special holographic helmet. "I can't see anything ahead of us. Wait a minute," he groaned. "One of our fuel lines is ruptured. I'm guessing that policeman shot through it before I was able to get the shields up. We're already down to three-quarters of a tank, and losing fuel fast."

"What will we do?" Julia cried.

"We can light the scramjet's pre-burners if I can reach Mach 2.5," he offered. "They'll take us to Mach 4 where the true scramjet will kick in. I just don't know if I can get us to Mach 2.5 without going into time-warp."

"We'll just have to take our chances in time-warp," I said weakly. "Let's at least check it out!"

"Here goes nothing," John conceded, getting things ready for the transition. John flipped the car into time-warp, immediately revealing a swarm of flying ghosts surrounding us.

"I don't think that's fog," Julia panicked, watching as a dark purple ball of energy rushed toward us causing the windshield's "heads up" display to glow red and the emergency alarm to blare.

"That's Prince Gregor and his horde. We're doomed."

"No we're not," I insisted weakly. "Not with John at the wheel. He'll figure something out."

"Thanks Mason," John smiled, darting out of the way of the purple energy blast. "It's nice to have you appreciate my brilliance."

"And humility?" I jested, still grimacing in pain.

"We'll work on that later," he muttered, gritting his teeth while dodging another purple energy ball. "For now just keep praising my brilliance."

"What are you doing?" Julia panicked. "You're flying right into them!"

"Yep," John smiled, accelerating past Mach 2. "Just hold on to Mason. There's nothing to worry about."

"Nothing to worry about?" Julia gasped, seeing a cluster of red circles pop up on the heads up display as soon as he did. "Prince Gregor's men are back! Turn away!"

"I can't," said John, watching his airspeed indicator approach Mach 2.5. "We're almost out of gas."

"Out of gas?"

"Just hold on and pray this works."

"You're doomed," Prince Gregor said, racing towards us and causing our collision alarm to sound off again. "If you stay in my dimension my followers will destroy you, if you escape to yours, Mason will die! You are out of options. Attack boys!"

Prince Gregor MacGregor joined his minions, hands outstretched, leading an assault meant to tear us apart. The ungrateful ghosts formed into a net formation at his command, rushing forward to meet us. Just as we were about to slam into his ghostly barricade, John flipped a switch, causing the lights in the car to go dark! "Take that, you, rabid vampire!" John said, slamming his fists on the dashboard. "I beat you! I beat you again! Go suck out some other guy's dreams, parasite! You're not sucking out mine!"

"What just happened?" I asked, the pain overwhelming me again.

"We just left time-warp and passed right through his whole army," John yelled triumphantly.

"That's what I thought!" I groaned. "I can barely breathe."

"John, do we have any fuel left?"

"Not much," he admitted.

"So we're going to fall into the Arctic Ocean instead?"

"Explode would be a better description." John exclaimed. "Hold on, I'm flipping on the scram jet!"

John flipped the switch, but nothing happened. The airspeed indicator hovered around Mach 2.499... then finally hit 2.5.

"I thought you said this would work!" Julia cried. "It will!" John yelled, flipping the switch again and banging his hand on the control panel. "It just needs encouragement!"

He was about to try for a third time when a roar burst from the tail of the car, thrusting us straight down, taking us to Mach 3 and gaining speed by the second.

"Pull up, pull up!" I begged.

"I'm on it!" John shot back, pulling up on the wheel as hard as he could. The ocean got closer and the car still refused to budge. "I think the steering hydraulics might be damaged as well." he yelled over the roar. "But I think I can get it straightened out!"

The direction of the car slowly changed as he forcefully pulled us out of the dive. The car shuttered as he finally pulled it level, aiming us for the North Pole again.

"Are you alright, Mason?" John begged, setting our course for the North Pole.

"I don't think so," I admitted quietly. "I don't know what's happening to me."

For some reason it was getting harder to breathe than before. I could feel blood leaking down my chest and onto the leather seats. For the first time in my life I considered the reality of my death without fear. A peace came over me and I realized I might not make it to the North Pole alive, but somehow, it didn't matter. I was tired. Sleeping was the only thing that mattered. I closed my eyes and enjoyed complete relaxation despite the pain.

"Snap out of it!" Julia demanded, shaking my whole body. "Don't close your eyes. Come back to me! Come back to me!"

"It's okay," I think I said, but maybe I just thought it. "I'll wake up in a little wh—"

Julia was crying, screaming, trying to revive me, but I couldn't stay awake to see what happened next.

I wish I could say that what happened next was horrible, but I felt liberated from all my pain. I was finally at peace. Nothing but light and unbelievable beauty surrounded me. I looked down at my body for a few moments then floated upwards above the earth and enjoyed the warmth of the sun on my face.

I was only constrained by my own imagination and I experienced the incredible freedom to fly wherever I wanted to go. Soon, I found myself sitting on the edge of a large satellite, with someone, who could have been my twin sitting next to me.

"Hello Mason," my visitor said cheerfully. "You've had quite a day, haven't you?"

"Yeah," I agreed, unalarmed at his question. "Who are you?"

"Someone who cares about you very much," he smiled. "How do you like my Santa Claus suit?"

"It's wonderful," I answered, suddenly recognizing my Grandpa Adams as a young man.

"I'm glad to hear that," he said serenely. "I'm not the first one in the family to wear it. It's been passed down from generation to generation for a long time. I'd like to keep it in the family if possible... and you and Julia could keep this inheritance going, if you wanted to. So, I have a favor to ask of you."

"Anything!" I insisted.

"Go back and live!" he yelled, pushing me off the satellite.

I didn't float downwards softly; I fell furiously like I was propelled by a rocket. Gravity tugged at me with a vengeance, pulling me down, slapping me in the face with its cold winds. I picked up speed, falling faster and faster, until, looking down I could see a flying car approaching with equal velocity. I instantly knew what I had to do. I imagined myself as a flying squirrel and made myself a wingsuit. With complete control, I prepared myself to collide with John's car—back into my body, back to Julia, and back to pain.

The closer I got to my body, the more pain I felt. The urge to miss my mark grew the closer I got, but I fought it. Something was stinging my face over and over, and my shoulder ached with near unbearable torment, but I was determined to complete my mission. The car was in front of me now and I had one more chance to turn away, but I couldn't bring myself to do it. I hit the car's ceiling and then crashed into my body.

"Wake up!" Julia screamed, slapping my face.

She had already taken my flight helmet off and was forcing something sweet into my mouth. I gagged on it at first, but a few drops of life-giving liquid made it into my stomach. A feeling of calm, almost as intense as I felt with my grandpa, filled my soul and I felt blood pumping back into my limbs again.

"That tastes good," I said weakly, choking a bit on the sweet Christmas Ambrosia. "But that's all I want."

"Keep drinking," Julia demanded, forcing the tangy liquid into my mouth and putting the helmet back on my head to keep me oxygenated. After a few minutes the taste changed flavor, becoming a delicious grape elixir and I gulped the rest of the drink down eagerly.

"Thanks, Julia," I said gratefully, gaining my energy back, "I lost it there for a minute."

"Don't you dare quit on me. If you start getting sleepy, you tell me about it. We have a long flight ahead!"

"Yes dear," I said gratefully, letting her secure my flight helmet back on tight.

While I was fighting for my life, John had managed to hold our course and engage the full scram jet engines. We were at maximum velocity, cruising at about Mach 10 and maintaining altitude.

"That was a close one," Julia panted. "Do you have full control of the steering yet, John?"

"As long as I don't have to make any major turns," John said breathing heavily as well. "I did not see that coming. Is Mason alright?"

"He's stable," she confided. "If I can keep him drinking his Christmas Ambrosia, I think we can keep him alive."

"That's good," John said relieved. "Keep him as high as a kite if you have to."

"You better let the League know what's going on," Julia suggested. "Although I'm sure the North Pole has powerful defenses."

"I was thinking the same thing," John agreed, clicking on the radio microphone in his flight helmet.

"Greenland Radar, Santa Claus League, two zero one, flight level one zero, Mach 10.4-niner, we have an emergency situation…"

"Santa Claus League two zero one, radar contact, state your emergency."

"We have escaped Highgate Cemetery, but have attracted a whole army of flying ghosts, led by Prince Gregor MacGregor. We are flying hypersonic, with minimal controls and carrying a wounded passenger. At cruising speed and altitude, our ETA is 23 minutes, repeat 23 minutes. Request emergency landing protocols."

"Roger, Santa Claus League two zero one... one moment, I have an urgent transmission from North Pole Tower coming through... connecting."

"John, is that you?" a familiar voice sounded over the scratchy radio transmission.

"Rudolph?" John blurted. "It's me. I'm so glad to hear your voice. The mission's a disaster. I've got blood all over my upholstery and we have a whole army of nasty ghosts chasing after us. What do we do now?"

"Just get here as fast as you can," he ordered. "I've called for St. Nicholas to come back to the North Pole for you. He's in Argentina." He paused for a moment then asked a harder question. "Why is there blood all over your upholstery? Don't you know how hard it is to get blood out?"

"I know, man!" John agreed, "but Mason's been shot and is fading fast. He's bleeding everywhere. It's pretty bad. He almost died a minute ago."

"I'm speechless," he gasped. "Who would do such a thing? I'll have a team of First Responders ready to patch him up as soon as you land."

"There's one more thing," John blurted, "my steering lines are freezing up. I think the hydraulics were damaged along with my primary fuel lines. What should I do?"

"Fly straight, yah," Rudolph answered, "and don't crash. I suggest you stay out of time-warp for as long as possible to keep from running into more ghosts. I'll see you in about 22 minutes."

"Roger," John confirmed. "Santa Claus League two zero one out!"

"Well, you heard the man," John grimaced, muting the radio microphone. "We've got 22 minutes to try and stay alive. I wish I had a way of eating sunflower seeds through my flight helmet. That's going to be my next invention."

"Only you would think of that!" Julia said. "Just stay awake for us. We'll hang out back here and keep from freaking out any more than we have to."

"Keep him drinking that spiked punch," John suggested. I could use some myself, but I have to drive!"

Julia and I had nothing to do for the 22 minutes but keep my heart pumping. We were flying in regular time, but I could tell we were being attacked from every angle. I was on the border between life and death. Even though I couldn't see them, I felt sick to my stomach every time we passed through a wall of invisible ghosts. I could feel them attacking me, sucking all the joy from my soul.

Julia kept me going, rubbing my hands and legs to keep me awake. I have to admit, all I wanted to do was sleep. The only thing that kept me alive was the thought of disappointing my Grandpa and the determination of Julia coaxing me to breath. Of course regular sips of my magic Christmas Ambrosia helped, too.

After what seemed like days we crossed over the polar ice cap. What a relief. All we had to do now was turn around and land at the North Pole. Unfortunately, when John tried to turn the car it refused to respond.

"Mayday, Mayday, Mayday," John announced quickly. "Greenland Radar, Santa Claus League two zero one with complications. Steering mechanism frozen. Entering into time-warp to make turn. Expect immediate attack by Prince Gregor and minions. Request assistance. Again... request assistance!"

"Affirmative," Greenland Radar responded smartly "Assistance present and engaged. Passing you off to North Pole Tower. Enter into time-warp at will."

"Here goes nothing," John grimaced, flipping the switch and taking us back into time-warp, setting off the emergency alarm and filling the whole heads up display with red circles.

The clear night sky exploded with action. Hundreds of sleighs, flying coaches, cars and airplanes buzzed around us, shielding us from harm. The whole of Prince Gregor's flying minions were attacking the defenders of the Christmas City with flaming knights tossing balls of fire at old-fashioned flying sleighs, barely missing their marks. Vikings threw lightning bolts from their swords, trying to burn up soaring cars and airplanes. So much was going on I don't know how John could keep everything straight, let alone know where to land.

"North Pole Tower, Santa Claus League two zero one," John said into the radio coolly. "Requesting an emergency landing!"

"Emergency landing cleared, ISL approach, runway zero one zero," North Pole Tower responded.

"Roger," John said without missing a beat, "making the approach now."

I don't know how John could understand anything. The radio was filled with chatter. Instructions were being given to more aircraft than I could keep track of, but John was perfectly calm, taking it all in as the fight around us intensified.

"Give me a status report," Rudolph said over the radio, dispensing with official control tower protocols.

"I don't have enough fuel to slow us down to a safe landing speed," John explained, as he turned us around in a huge arc, heading back to the North Pole. "I'm missing a front tire, so I'll be coming in nose up and bottom heavy. Not to mention a thousand ghosts trying to knock me out of the sky. Prepare your crews for a belly-landing. I'm comin' in hot!"

"How hot is hot?" Julia groaned.

"Oh, pretty hot," John muttered softly, flipping switches wildly. "Setting the air brakes, check. Engaging reverse thrusters, check, deploying emergency chute, check. Concentrate on hitting the runway, check!"

"Hitting the runway?" Julia stammered.

"At about 210 miles an hour," John said, extending the landing gear. "I just hope I can control her with only two tires."

I relaxed enough to see John emitting sparks of lightning from his fingertips, his emotions were in complete control. I loved him for that. Julia on the other hand was leaning forward with red thunderbolts swirling around her.

"Just sit back and be with me," I said calmly. "There's nothing we can do, so just brace yourself."

"That's easy for you to say," she complained, you're stone cold drunk! "We're going to hit the ground, we're gonna hit—"

"That's okay," I insisted weakly, happy to be in time-warp. "We're going to be alright. Just hold my hand. If this is the end, I want to end it with you."

She relaxed and took my hand. The scene around us was pandemonium. A flying armored knight rammed into the car, causing her to squeeze my hand in a death grip. But she looked straight ahead, trying to stay calm.

"Why do you even like me?" she asked gritting her teeth as John passed through the Christmas City's defense shield.

"I don't just like you," I replied earnestly. "I love you. I always have. It's like you're programed into my DNA. I don't want to spend another minute without you."

Our conversation was interrupted as we hit the runway going about 220 miles an hour, even with the emergency chute engaged. The back two tires smoked like they were on fire as we hit the ground, which is good, because at least they didn't explode on impact. They did their job to a point, slowing us down somewhat before blowing up, making our return a true belly landing. The emergency crews prepared for us by throwing up a safety net, but hitting the metal cables of the net as fast as we were going would have torn us to bits for sure.

Julia held on to my hand, and I forced her to look into my eyes. "I love you," I said again. Her terrorrized look met my intense gaze which helped her calm down again. Unfortunately, John interrupted our moment of solitude.

"We're coming in too fast!" he yelled, his countenance turning a fiery red for the first time. His color is normally a cool blue, even in the most desperate situations. By his flaming reaction, I knew we were in danger, and might not survive. But somehow I held out hope, even as we slid uncontrollably toward the metal barricade with sparks flying from the Nova's belly.

Prince Gregor MacGregor must have seen us ready to explode with his gold. He swept down, clutching the roof of the Nova and lifted us off the ground. With all his power he slowed us down, acting like a third parachute. He may have been powerful enough to carry us away, but he lost his grip at the last moment, dropping us into the safety barricade.

Emergency sirens, collision alarms, airbags, fire suppression foam and intense pain all worked together in one terrible symphony. I felt the force of all the windows being blown out by our impact against the barricade and I didn't remember anything after that. Luckily we were outside of time, preventing me from bleeding to death... but unfortunately, the gold in the trunk didn't fare as well.

The War at the North Pole

I must have been unconscious for a while, because by the time I opened my eyes a hundred Vikings, and flaming Knights were landing on the runway, picking up pieces of gold and swooping them away. Apparently, once a treasure was taken outside of time, it was available for the spirits of the dead to take. I'm not sure who they were fighting with the most, our forces or each other.

A hundred defenders surrounded the car, most of them were mechanics and crew members from other planes who had given up defending their own destroyed aircraft. A dozen 747's and another five or six Airbus A380's were strewn in pieces on the runway, most on fire while greedy ghosts were ripping apart smaller airplanes and even some older-looking magical sleighs.

The North Pole was not inhabited by hearty warriors as was the cemetery. They were toymakers, accountants, teachers, and computer operators. The city had no standing Army, Navy or Air Force because their defense was ice, snow, and 2,000 miles of arctic wind. I was still hanging upside down in my seat belt harness when St. Nicholas rushed to my side, loosening me from my bonds.

"Are you alright, son?" he asked, helping me down from the seat and removing my helmet.

"I don't think so," I answered honestly, rolling on my side. "I've been shot."

"And I thought your crash landing was the worst of your troubles," he said gently, checking out my wounds. "Just stay where you are and rest for a moment."

"Where's Julia?" I groaned, trying to sit up.

"I'm right here," Julia said with concern, scooting next to me. "St. Nicholas helped me get out of the car before he could get to you. Just stay still. John's with Rudolph and the emergency responders, trying to keep Prince Gregor's soldiers from stealing more of the gold and causing more damage to his car."

"I can see you're in good hands," St. Nicholas said, tucking something white and bone-like deeper into his coat pocket. He finished standing up when Rudolph ran toward him with his hat on his chest, his head bowed down in despair.

"What have you done?" St. Nicholas asked with a booming voice, changing his demeanor and shaking the whole city.

"I failed you, sir," Rudolph confessed loudly. "I let the shields down to allow John and his friends to make their emergency landing. They aren't official members of the League, so they couldn't land with the shields up."

"So rather than protect my city, you chose to allow them to land instead?"

"Yes, sir," Rudolph shouted again, almost robotically, "and allowed the enemy to enter in as well. We can't stop them, they are everywhere. We are defenseless."

Rudolph was right. Leather-clad Vikings and flying knights were flying around the whole city, tearing apart buildings, clawing at, and beating up people. Armored soldiers marched through the streets, breaking glass and ripping off doors. The whole city of the North Pole was under attack with apparently nothing to stop the onslaught.

"It's too late to change that now!" St. Nicholas boomed, his voice shaking the whole city. "What's done is done."

"What are your orders?" Rudolf asked.

"Defend the city!" St. Nicholas insisted loudly, then dropping to an earnest whisper, "Well done. Help John and the other men protect as much of the gold as possible. We'll need the treasure as a bargaining chip!"

"Yes, sir," Rudolph yelled as he ran to join John and the other defenders.

However, there wasn't much left of the car to defend. When Prince Gregor tried to snatch us away, he twisted and nearly ripped the car apart. The windows were all blown out, the top of the car shredded, and the front grill smashed from the hard landing into the emergency cables. The ghost's dark shadow was above us that very moment, ordering his ungrateful swarm to attack from all sides.

I watched as St. Nicholas put his fists on his waist and surveyed the scene before him. His city was on fire, his friends were in peril, and the organization he had built for over a thousand years was under attack. His countenance became grim as he came to a decision. "It's time to put an end to all of this nonsense," he said, speaking quietly to himself.

Standing even taller than before, he commanded the attention of his foe. "Prince Gregor MacGregor," he called with a voice that shook the whole city.

Everyone and everything stopped at his command, his voice freezing the actions of the entire population. I hoped the powerful man would freeze the entire horde, and order his men to take them out like garbage bags; I held my breath in suspense.

"Your Royal Highness," he called again, his voice piercing and driving fear into every ghostly heart. "I surrender!"

The defenders of the North Pole gasped in horror. "I surrender!" he repeated again fiercely. "Therefore, call off your horde and order them to cease harming my people. Let us come to acceptable terms."

"Such a wise choice," Prince Gregor replied gleefully. "Noble Warriors," he ordered softly over the battlefield. "Report to your Commander!"

A roar of disapproval sounded from his minions, followed by growls of defiance as they continued terrorizing the city, refusing to obey Prince Gregor's command, and destroying everything they could find.

"Call them off now," St. Nicholas roared, causing the very ground to tremble. "Call them off or I will order my men to continue the fight. I may not seem powerful to you at this moment, caught off guard within the soft heart of my home, but when I call my tens of thousands from around the world to avenge me, you will know my wrath!"

"As you wish," Prince Gregor roared, projecting his voice like a spear. "Warriors! Come to me now!"

The malice of his words gripped my heart, sending bolts of excruciating pain through my shoulder. The Vikings, Legionnaires, and Fiery Knights must have felt the same fear, for

210

in one unified motion they all flew to form a line of unwilling servants, turning back to their civilian forms as they touched the ground. His minions were now black and listless, their light extinguished as well as their ability to act for themselves.

"I'm glad you've decided to surrender," a familiar Scottish voice rang through the night. "What's the point of fightin' when we can solve our problems peacefully, isn't that right, St. Nicholas?"

"That's right," St. Nicholas agreed. "So show yourself and we can start the negotiations."

"Not so fast!" the Prince spat, still flying above us. "I canna trust a powerful man like yourself to keep his word. The rich never keep their word."

"I am a man of honor," St. Nicholas objected fiercely. "I always keep my word."

"Doubtful," Prince Gregor mocked. "Honor is a fantasy, remember that me warriors, and remember the second truth as well, the rich never keep their word."

His followers, reduced to dimly lit spirits, laughed and clapped their hands. Obviously, Prince Gregor wasn't talking to St. Nicholas at all, but only using him as a puppet to feed his own cruel army.

"Enough of this chatter!" St. Nicholas ordered. "We negotiate or I order my men to continue our defense!"

"Touchy, touchy," Prince Gregor mocked calmly, swooping out of the night sky like a bat, and touching down. "I'm happy to negotiate your surrender."

As soon as his feet met the ground his dark armor transformed into the attire of a Scottish gentleman, complete with a blue waistcoat, white shirt, perfectly tailored pants and dark shiny boots.

"And if this is a surrender," he said cautiously. "Would ye be so kind as to be bound in cords ta keep your hands from touchin' anything... let's say, magical."

"As you wish," St. Nicholas stated calmly holding his hands out, offering them to be tied.

"Bind him!" Prince Gregor ordered one of his men. The cruel soldier didn't waste any time tying St. Nicholas' hands together while chuckling to himself.

"And your friends too, of course," Prince Gregor insisted, pointing to John, Julia, and me. "They'll have to be tied up as well. I've had an exhausting night fightin' these three."

"By all means," the Saint concurred.

The soldier tied up John first, snarling, laughing, and snorting with delight. When he got to Julia and me, the soldier realized he had miscounted, only one strap was left to bind us with, addition wasn't his strong point. Cursing under his breath he turned to return for another cord when Julia interrupted him.

"You'll be whipped for not bringing the right number of ropes," she whispered, "being as clever as you are, I'm sure you'll decide to use one cord and tie us both together."

The soldier nodded with a grunt, then crossing our wrists over each other and he wrapped the single cord over our wrists.

"It's now or never," I whispered fiercely, looking firmly into her eyes. "Julia May Martin, I'm tired of messing around, will you marry me?"

I held my breath. My heart had taken charge of my head. I had uttered words I could scarcely even imagine. An angry ghost was tying us together to be likely sentenced to death, and I couldn't breathe because of a marriage proposal. I searched my own soul for a feeling of doom that would tell me I was doing the wrong thing, but no matter where I searched, I found peace instead.

"Are you sure?" she gasped, noting how I hadn't even breathed since I made the proposal.

"Yeah, I really mean it," I insisted, after exhaling. "Ring or no ring, your father's permission or not, will you marry me?"

"Yes, yes," she sang. "Wealth doesn't matter to me, you're all that matters. I've always been willing to marry you, fortune or not."

"Now I feel like a dork," I answered happily. "I've been killing myself trying to figure out how to ask you to marry me. I didn't think you'd say yes."

"You are a dork then," she said winking. "It takes a strong man to marry a trouble making woman like me. But you've made me so happy... finally a proper proposal and a hand-fasting ceremony as well. How romantic is that?"

"I'm sorry I waited until we were about to be executed," I apologized. "I wanted this moment to be unforgettably romantic, not offered as we faced our deaths."

"I find this unforgettably romantic," she said happily, "who needs a ring when you have a rope!"

"Stop talking," the nasty soldier snarled, finishing up the knot.

"Careful there," I complained, "that's my fiancée you're tying up."

"We're in this together now," she whispered as he shoved us forward. We joined St. Nicholas, Rudolph, John, and a half dozen other bound men I didn't know.

"You two look committed," St. Nicholas noted. "Look, I'm engaged!" Julia smiled happily, showing him her bindings. "And even Prince Gregor MacGregor and all his horde can't divide us, not in life or in death."

"Aye, in death is such an appealing thought after the trouble ye've given me this night," Prince Gregor snarled, fidgeting his fingers on the handle of his blade.

"A thought you'll take out of your head this instant," St. Nicholas warned. "We still haven't settled on the terms of our surrender."

"I hardly see ye in a strong bargaining position!" Prince Gregor roared. "Ye would do well to obey me demands."

"You wouldn't be so arrogant if you knew the safety of your treasure was at stake," the old Saint said fiercely. "You still want the gold I assume?"

"Of course I want the gold," Prince Gregor fumed, pulling his sword from its scabbard. "It's mine!"

"I'm afraid it's not yours," St. Nicholas stated calmly. "The treasure belongs to Jacob Marley. The gold is cursed, and the curse can only be lifted under certain conditions, which these three have yet to meet. So, if you kill them now you will never get your treasure."

Purple energy burst from Prince Gregor's hands, destroying nearby trees and tearing bricks from buildings. The energy attacked St. Nicholas as well but failed to cause him any harm.

"Don't do that again," St. Nicholas warned dangerously. "I want the remains of my city and my people untouched, including my three young apprentices. The gold is cursed, and my men still surround most of it. We will defend it until help comes."

"Without me treasure I will tear your city apart, them included," the evil spirit responded.

"I thought as much," Saint Nicholas whispered. "So I have a secret to tell you. All my young friends have to do to break the curse is to present the treasure to me while standing on the Heart Stones of Christmas."

"Present 'em where?" the victor growled. "What're the Heart Stones of Christmas?"

"The power supply of my Christmas magic of course," St. Nicholas answered with surprise. "I thought you knew that. But no matter, they are not far from here. Once the transfer of ownership is completed, the treasure will be yours. I can't think of a more historically significant place to hold such an important event... the location has one other key advantage."

"And what is that, pray tell?" Prince Gregor asked cruelly.

"Privacy, Your Highness," he whispered. "You probably want the surrender performed without so many greedy eyes looking on, right? How many others do you want to share your gold with anyway? I've seen how your followers act when gold is around."

Prince Gregor MacGregor paused for a few moments as he tried to think of a down side to this new option. He had planned this surrender for so long even the slightest deviation had to be considered carefully. Gradually a wicked smile formed on his face.

"I won't be disrespected," he roared loudly, changing tactics so all could hear. "We'll not hold the surrender ceremony on the field of battle, but at the Heart Stones of Christmas, bringin' ultimate shame to ye and everyone in your League." He turned to his followers and raised his hands in triumph. "We are victorious! The poor and ignorant have won at last!"

Prince Gregor's army responded with cheers of victory. They leapt into the air, turning back into flying warriors and circling the Christmas City.

"Lead me ta the Heart Stones of Christmas," Prince Gregor demanded, transforming into a dark knight and joining his army in the air. "I'll be monitorin' your actions from above. If ye try anythin' tricky, I'll order me army to descend upon ye and this city and tear it to the ground."

You May Kiss the Bride

"Follow me," St. Nicholas ordered, leading the way. We walked for about ten minutes, passing destroyed houses with broken glass and trampled furniture tossed into the street. Toys were equally abused, with plastic trains dashed to pieces and dolls torn limb from limb. Even though he walked briskly, he always made sure the three of us were able to keep up.

St. Nicholas acknowledged the wanton destruction by walking even faster, causing the guards to fall behind. The five guards who carried the boxes of gold were especially abused, walking with difficulty and grunting with their heavy burdens.

Walking was hard for Julia and me, bound to each other and having to twist our arms to walk side by side. My shoulder still hurt like crazy, but without blood flowing in my veins, I wasn't bleeding anymore. As painful as it was, the fast pace did give us the opportunity to talk more freely than if we were surrounded by guards."

"Why did you agree to marry me?" I asked quietly, trying to keep from being heard. "I'm… penniless!"

"I thought so too, until four years ago when Mrs. Warner talked to me. Do you remember that night when she warned us not to join the Santa Claus League?"

"I remember. She said we had to wait for a personal invitation from St. Nicholas. I also remember she talked to you separately, so what else did she say?"

Julia paused for a moment then revealed her private conversation. "Mrs. Warner said, 'If time is money, how wealthy is a man who can share an unlimited amount of time with you?' I've thought about her words every day for the last four years. Yeah, my dad's a billionaire, but how much time does he get to spend with my mother? If she measured his wealth based on how on much time he really spent with her, she might call him a pauper. I don't want to be married to a pauper, I want to be married to a king."

"A king, huh?" I smiled. "Do you see me as rich as a king?"

"Richer than a king!" she insisted. "You're fireproof, you know the past, the present, and shadows of the future for everyone you meet. You can also stop time with the touch of your nose; however, I wish you were bulletproof, that would have come in handy."

"But besides all of that," she continued, "you have attributes I hold even more dear. I love your kindness, your wonderful way with children and, most of all, your generosity. I feel selfish agreeing to your proposal but I can't help it, I don't want to let any other girl in the world have you. I'm not backing out now."

"I don't want to be a bother," John spoke up as he tripped along behind us, "but we are marching to our death. We're about to die for a League we don't even officially belong to!"

"That is true," St. Nicholas confirmed, joining in our conversation. "And Mrs. Warner was right; you weren't allowed to join my League unless the invitation came personally from me. I'm thinking the time has come to make that invitation. Seeing that the circumstances are dire, and may not give us another opportunity, therefore, I'd like to make an exception to protocol, and formally invite you all to join the Santa Claus League, the American Chapter."

"You could make an exception?" John blurted, tripping over a torn up stuffed doll.

"Well of course," St. Nicholas retorted. "You are all far too young to enter the League otherwise. But look at them, hand-fasted together in true love, looking so happy and ready to die for the cause of Christmas. How could I resist inviting you all to join with me at a time like this? All that needs to happen now is a marriage."

"A marriage?" John whispered incredulously. "When do you plan on performing a marriage?"

"Right now!" he said. "If we wait any longer it might be too late."

"Now? We've surrendered to a mad man!"

"Don't ruin the moment, Mr. Patten," St. Nicholas rebuked. "Do you want to join the League or not?"

"Well of course I do, but I don't want to have to get married today to do it!"

"Don't be ridiculous," St Nicholas said merrily. "Only Mason and Julia will have to get married today. You'll have plenty of time to find the right girl. Take your time!"

"If that's the case," John pondered. "I'm all for it! I've been pushing these guys to get hitched for months."

"Then the point is settled," St. Nicholas insisted, keeping up his quick pace to avoid interruption from our captors. "Mason Wells Howell and Julia May Martin, have you come here freely and without reservation to give yourselves to each other in marriage?"

"Yes," we both said together.

"Will you love and honor each other as man and wife for the rest of your lives?"

"Yes," we sang together again.

"Will you accept children from God and bring them up lovingly?"

I thought about my Grandpa Adams and his desire for me to pass on the Santa Claus suit to the next generation. I enthusiastically agreed. I don't know what Julia was thinking, but she agreed, too.

"Since it is your intention to enter into marriage, join your right hands, Oh," St. Nicholas said. "I see you already have. Therefore, before God and these witnesses, declare your consent."

"I, Mason Wells Howell," I said resolutely, knowing the words by heart. "Take you, Julia May Martin, to be my lawfully wedded wife, to have and to hold, from this day forward, for better, for worse, for richer, for poorer, in sickness and in health, for as long as we both shall live."

"What about my father?" Julia asked timidly. "He wouldn't approve of an elopement."

"I'm positive he won't," I assured her. "He'll probably charge me with kidnapping. But it's not his decision, it's yours and mine. A new world needs a new government. I want to share the rest of my world with you."

"Like Thomas Paine said," she agreed "It's absurd for an island to rule a continent!"

"Well said," St. Nicholas smiled. "Children should learn from their fathers, but not be ruled by them. Which brings us to you Miss Martin. Are you willing to give your consent to this union?"

"Yes, I am," she beamed, looking into my eyes. "I, Julia May Martin, take you, Mason Wells Howell, to be my lawfully wedded husband, to have and to hold, from this day forward, for better, for worse, for richer, for poorer, in sickness and in health, for as long as we both shall live."

"You have declared your consent before me," St. Nicholas stated boldly. "Therefore, by the power vested in me, I now pronounce you man and wife, legally and lawfully wedded. You may kiss the bride."

I slowed down a little and pulled her close to me, kissing her as my wife. The moment's delay caused the guard to catch up to us, whipping me on the back with a thick leather strap. The bandages shielded most of the blow and the pain faded quickly. I didn't care though; it was worth it.

"No more of that!" St. Nicholas demanded, causing the guard to shrink back in fear. "There's no need to flog the newlyweds. The terms of surrender have not been agreed upon. Rudolph, are you a witness to their marriage?"

"Yes, sir," Rudolph confirmed. "I'll mark John down as the other witness. That's alright with you isn't it, John?"

"No problem," John answered, stumbling down a quaint paved trail. "I'll sign as a witness to a marriage, just don't let me sign my own death warrant by mistake." The guards caught up with us again and smacked John on the back of the head for yelling.

They smacked me too, but I didn't care, I just got married, I couldn't have been happier!

The Surrender

We walked down a grassy path and entered into a little grove of trees which hid a beautiful stone cottage. Prince Gregor MacGregor swept down from the sky and joined us, transforming back into a Scottish Gentleman. Standing in front of the cottage door was a woman I knew well, Mrs. Claus. She stood resolute, guarding her domain, with one hand holding a broom stick and the door knob with the other.

"That monster is not entering into my home." she announced angrily.

"I canna hardly be called a monster," Prince Gregor said smoothly. "I'm just a humble general, acceptin' what's rightfully mine."

"You're not accepting anything in my home," she said hotly.

"It's alright," St. Nicholas whispered, giving his wife a kiss on the forehead, "we were defeated. I had no choice. Please allow us to come in."

She fearfully stood her ground, but after looking into his eyes she noticed a sparkle of hope. "Come in then," she said exasperated, putting her broom down and opening the door.

St. Nicholas entered the cottage first, followed by Julia and I, still tied together, then John, and Prince Gregor's men carrying all five chests of gold. The last one to enter was Prince Gregor MacGregor who ordered his guards to leave the house and wait outside to guard Rudolph and the other prisoners.

"The gold," Prince Gregor said with urgency. "I want the gold."

"Don't you want to go over the terms of our surrender first?" St. Nicholas asked dryly.

"Nay," he whispered cruelly. "I want the gold now or I'll tear this house down, stone by stone!"

"Very well," St Nicholas said stoically, motioning for John, Julia, and I to come forward. "Please stand on the Heart Stones of Christmas in front of my fireplace."

We obeyed his directions and stood on a circle of decorative stones. The stones were placed together like pieces of a stained glass window with each stone a different color, natural and uncut. Some were almost transparent and sparkled like jewels while others looked like common field stones. The pattern was simple and bore a striking resemblance to a snowflake.

"Mr. Howell, please tell me why you and your friends are here?" St. Nicholas asked calmly as the stones began to glow.

"I came... we came to deliver Jacob Marley's treasure to you."

"Could you please describe the nature of the treasure?"

"Five boxes of gold coins," I answered as the stones began to throw sparks all around the room.

"And why are you bringing them to me?"

"Jacob Marley asked us to dig it up and give the treasure to you," I began, looking at the colorful explosions all around us. "We had to fly to—"

"No, no," St. Nicholas interrupted me politely, waving his hands in the air. "I don't need to know the details. I accept your delivery. You all performed admirably and you are dismissed."

We backed off the stones, causing them to go dark and dull again.

"Now for you, Your Royal Highness," St. Nicholas motioned courteously. "Please stand on the stones to have the ownership of the gold transferred to you."

Prince Gregor MacGregor walked to the center of the circle, reverently bowed to St. Nicholas and stood up straight again. The Heart Stones of Christmas began to glow at his presence, sending more sparks flying through the room.

"Bowing was a nice touch," St. Nicholas noted. "Even the Heart Stones of Christmas were impressed. I wish you were always this polite. But since you've come with an army to destroy my home it does seem rather deceptive."

"Give me my gold," Prince Gregor growled, causing his shape to shift into a terrifying dark knight with an enormous sword that shone with green power.

"Now that's more like it," St. Nicholas complimented, walking over to the chests one by one and opening them up with his bound hands. As he reached the last chest he pulled something white from his sleeve and thrust it deeply into the last cache of coins.

"I expected you to look like a monster acting the way you do," he chastened, "nonetheless, as per our agreement, I, St. Nicholas Claus, being of sound mind and acting as trustor, do transfer title of this fortune to his Royal Highness, Prince Gregor MacGregor, and recognize him as the sole owner of said treasure. The treasure is yours."

The moment St. Nicholas proclaimed Prince Gregor the owner, the stones sent a fireball spinning all over the room. It circled around as if trying to find a reason to exist then split up into five balls, crashing into the boxes of gold, causing the coins to sparkle with power.

"It's finally mine!" Prince Gregor shrieked even louder, shaking the house with his voice and causing pots and pans to fall off their hooks in the kitchen.

"It's all yours." St. Nicholas whispered back with relief. "Now get out of my house."

"Ye mean my house," the Prince said darkly, pulling out his sword and pointing it at St. Nicholas. "I warned ye ta never trust a rich man. In me terms of surrender, you give me your house, your city at the North Pole and the life of everyone here ta do as I see fit. I take it all."

"Actually you don't get anything but the treasure," St. Nicholas said calmly, breaking his bonds as if they were made of butter.

"Aye, ye had better stand down," Prince Gregor growled triumphantly. "I'm the one with the sword at your chest and a battalion of loyal troops at me command. So I suggest you do what I say!"

"I'm afraid I won't," St. Nicholas said, standing his ground. "The Winds of Doom will take care of you."

"The Winds of Doom have no power over me," he bragged. "I've withstood their powers for almost 200 years and I can withstand them now!"

"The Winds may have something else to say about that," St. Nicholas replied dryly. "After all, you are a very wealthy man with nothing good to show for it. Ah, here comes your treasure now!"

"Ye can't trick me so easily," Prince Gregor snarled. "You'll regret your insubordination after I cut your friends inta little pieces."

Prince Gregor pulled his sword from its scabbard and slashed it in the air violently. He leapt off the stones and bolted in our direction. Julia screamed and I threw her behind me, expecting him to do his worst. John acted quickly in our defense as well and grabbed a chair and stood with it raised while Prince Gregor continued lunging our way.

But before he got any closer, ghostly chains floated into the room connected to five heavy metal boxes. They swirled and tumbled around looking for their new owner. The floating boxes recognized Prince Gregor and attacked, forcing him to use his sword to defend himself against the chains.

"What's happening?" Prince Gregor begged, fighting off the heavy chains and boxes.

"Your treasure has arrived," St. Nicholas proclaimed. "Enjoy your gold!"

"But that's impossible!" he growled, becoming more angry as he fought off the chains and boxes. "I don't believe you. Guards, storm the cottage. Seize them. Contain them. Kill them."

"They can't hear you," St. Nicholas answered calmly. "The walls to my cottage are two feet thick. You're on your own now, so take your gold and leave."

The treasure was relentless, countering his every move and attacking with even more violence. One by one the leg irons attached themselves to his body, followed by irons on his wrists. The chains wrapped around his arm, breaking his grip on the sword and throwing it to the ground.

"While the Winds are still gentle," St. Nicholas said earnestly, pointing at the five boxes of gold, "I suggest you come enjoy what you fought so hard to get for a few minutes while you still can."

Prince Gregor dragged the ghostly chains connected to his arms and legs and stood in front of the physical metal boxes filled with gold, relishing the ownership of each one. He passed by each box and sifted his fingers through their golden coins.

Despite the ghostly shackles, elation filled his greedy eyes until he got to the last box. As soon as he put his hand into its gold he touched something that electrocuted him like a live wire, causing him gasp in agony.

"What was that?" he asked, fear replacing his confident air. "Something just stabbed me. Something deadly is stuck in my gold?"

"A bone," St. Nicholas confirmed. "One of your bones to be precise. It's a floating rib, number 12, on the left to be exact. I was in Venezuela making a few deliveries when I got an emergency call from Rudolph telling me about your impending attack. Digging up your grave was the logical thing to do."

"You dug up my grave?" Prince Gregor cried, noticing a wind, beginning to swirl around the room, causing the chains to clang together.

"Yes," Saint Nicholas explained. "This curse requires the recipient to be buried with the treasure, but getting you buried with Jacob Marley's cursed treasure was the tricky part. That being the case, instead of burying the treasure with you, I buried you in the treasure. When I said I was giving you the treasure, I meant it."

"How could this happen?" the pathetic ghost wailed, with the boxes banging into him without mercy. "My plan was perfect. I studied this out for more than a hundred years."

"And I've practiced my art for over 1600 years," he reminded the Prince. "Age before beauty, I always say, but back to the plan. In order for my plan to work, you had to believe you successfully invaded my heavily guarded home. My friend, Mrs. Warner came up with the idea to allow Mason, Julia, and John to be initiated into the League, but not to allow them full fellowship. This meant that when the Chevy Nova came crashing into the Christmas City, Rudolph had to let our defensive shields down to let them in. I simply instructed Rudolph to not put the shields back up until all of your soldiers were safely inside."

"But we defeated your forces," he stammered, as the winds began to tear at his clothing and the chains wrapped around him.

"No," St. Nicholas assured him. "We let you win. I was worried you would see through Rudolf's poor acting job, but you didn't. In fact, you didn't even notice how poorly our men fought at Highgate Cemetery. I begged my fellow League members, Mr. Grant, Mr. Wombwell, and Mr. Faraday to take it easy on you to keep your enthusiasm up. I didn't count on Mason being shot, but I did provide the Christmas Ambrosia to keep him alive. I hoped he would have the good sense to use it and he did."

"Ye tricked me!" Prince Gregor condemned as the Winds lifted the ghostly boxes into the air, tugging the spirit around with them. "How do ye pretend ta be called a Saint and deal so treacherously?"

"I tricked you?" St. Nicholas said with indignation. "Alright I'll prove I am not treacherous; I will give you one chance to avoid this curse. Give your treasure to anyone in this room and you will be free of its power."

"Give up me treasure?" Prince Gregor asked furiously. "I won't give it up, nay, not in a thousand years. The treasure's mine, all mine!"

"As I expected," St. Nicholas replied. "Your greed has tricked you, not me. Farewell, Prince Gregor MacGregor. In life you stole from the poor and the ignorant, and even in death you demanded power over them. Now you will pay the price for your evil success. You are doomed to wander the earth as a vagabond, witnessing the suffering of the poor and ignorant, without the ability to help them. May God have mercy on your soul."

The link between the haunted treasure and the physical gold was forged. The five boxes on the table were spread out like corpses, tangible but without their spirit. Now Prince Gregor owned the doomed spirit of the treasure and it tossed him around ruthlessly.

The prince screamed in agony as the Winds of Doom spun the haunted boxes and chains around his body, banging into him, choking, tugging, and pulling him away. Finally, the power of the Winds overcame him, flinging the victor and his treasure through the window, leaving the physical boxes behind.

Redemption at Last

As soon as Prince Gregor was blown from the room the swirling air died down returning to normal. Mrs. Claus ran to her husband and gave him a grateful embrace. "I thought you had lost your mind for a moment," she sighed. "Thank goodness you had it all under control."

"Thank you for trusting me, dear," he smiled broadly. "Beside every good man is an even better woman."

"You're a sweet man," she complimented. "What's the plan now?" she said with a twinkle in her eye.

"First of all, we invite Jacob Marley to come join us," he said with deep satisfaction. "Jacob Marley, please enter our humble home."

At his invitation a cloaked figure appeared in the room, standing motionless and erect. For nearly 200 years he had been tormented by the chains of his own selfishness but now he was free. He lifted his feet and they obeyed his commands. He pulled back his dark hood, showing the face of a handsome young man instead of a tormented corpse.

As he removed the black cloak, the clothes and style of a younger, happier man were revealed. His suit was bright blue, his tall boots shiny and clean. His shirt was as white as a new crisp Sunday shirt, and his hands were clean and soft again.

"I am redeemed!" he said joyfully. "How is this possible?"

"With the magic from the Heart Stones of Christmas, of course," St. Nicholas smiled. "But the true source of that magic comes from the love of a small babe born in Bethlehem. You should thank Him for your freedom."

"That I will do," Jacob said solemnly, bowing his head. "What else would you have me do?"

"Let me think about that," St. Nicholas pondered. "I know there's something important... ah yes, you have a cloak to return. The Spirit of Christmas Future will get very upset if I lose that."

"Yes of course," The redeemed Jacob Marley said, handing over the magical cloak. Energy and sparks of light shot from the black material as St. Nicholas took it and set it aside carefully.

"Now, your next task will be much more meaningful to you," St. Nicholas exclaimed. "Please stand on the Heart Stones of Christmas."

The moment Jacob had both feet squarely planted on the magical stones, a light glowed from their depths. A gentle breeze filled the room, swirling around the ancient yet young man, rushing through his clothes and lifting his hair.

"What's happening?" Marley asked in amazement.

"You are being summoned," St. Nicholas answered kindly. "Many generations of your fathers are anxious to be joined with you again, and one very pretty Baroness as well."

In an instant the room burst with color and light. The cozy living room became a glowing green field with an enormous cedar of Lebanon tree in the center. A sturdy branch held up a rope swing occupied by a beautiful woman.

"Sarah!" Jacob called, falling on his knees and bursting into tears of happiness.

As soon as his knees touched the ground the room exploded in light, blinding me for a moment. When I could finally focus again, the room was filled with magic embers, swirling around them. As the vision faded, so did the light from the Heart Stones of Christmas. Jacob Marley was gone.

"That was exciting," St. Nicholas said merrily, closing the lid of the last chest of gold. "You don't see that every day, not even here."

"What are you planning to do with the gold?" I asked, still dazzled by Jacob's transformation and departure.

"I don't have any plans for it," he answered. "It's not my gold. It belongs to Prince Gregor MacGregor. A cursed treasure has a split soul and is nothing to trifle with. One day he may have a change of heart, and we will help him direct it in more positive ways. But the only way to remove the curse is for him to give the gold away… for now, I'll just keep it safe."

"But what about the rest of Prince Gregor's army?" Julia asked timidly. "They're standing ready to destroy your city."

"I think we got off on the wrong foot with them," St. Nicholas chuckled. "It's so hard to be welcoming when your guests insist on tearing apart your city. However, I believe the Spirit of Christmas Present left Mason with a gift of Christmas Ambrosia that could put the mob in a better mood. Would you be able to spare a drop or two?"

"Oh yeah," I agreed, reaching for my pocket and pulling out my magic bag. "They look like they could use a generous helping of Christmas joy."

"We have plenty of apple cider," Mrs. Claus offered, getting up from the table and rolling up her sleeves. "Let's get mixing!"

"May I help?" Julia offered.

"Of course you can," she smiled. "I could use a little muscle as well. John, Mason, could you help me move a few barrels around?"

"I don't think Mason can help," Julia apologized. "He was shot today. He's lucky to be alive at all."

"I haven't heard any complaints lately," St. Nicholas mused. "How does your shoulder feel, Mason?"

"I haven't even thought about it since Julia and I were married," I admitted, rolling my arm up and down. "It feels great."

"Take the bandage off and let's get a look at that wound," St. Nicholas suggested, helping Julia unwrap my long bandages.

When the bloody gauze was finally removed, clean healed flesh met our gaze. "Just as I expected," he said. "You've become bulletproof!"

"Bulletproof?" Julia marveled, feeling the perfectly healed wound. "When did that happen?"

"The moment he became an official member of the Santa Claus League," he explained cheerfully. "Mason's powers didn't come all at once. An ability like being fireproof or bulletproof only came as a reward for extraordinary loyalty."

"So if Mason didn't stand in the way of that bullet he wouldn't be bulletproof right now?" John asked.

"You are correct," Saint Nick answered. "Awesome!" John replied.

"Truly awesome, as you would say," he agreed. "Especially when you consider how rarely members of my League ever get such powers. The three of you must share a deep bond of friendship for that level of magic to exist. In time, he may become even more powerful than his grandfather, and they called him the Man of Steel."

A few minutes later we walked outside carrying a pitcher of spiced cider and eight thick glasses. The eight ghastly lieutenants were dutifully guarding Rudolph and the other leaders in our company.

"The negotiations are over boys," St. Nicholas smiled, pouring all the guards a drink. "You won quite a victory today!"

They cheered, taking the cups and gulping down the contents until it was all gone.

"That was the best drink I've had in centuries," one of the men complimented.

"You can say that again," another guard agreed. "It actually tastes like a memory. It reminded me of a Christmas with me grandmother and for a second there, I could feel the warmth tingle right down to me toes."

"I had the same sensation," the Captain of the Guard said, trying to coax another drop out of the cup. "But where's Prince Gregor?"

"I'm not sure," St. Nicholas smiled. "Enjoying the fruits of his victory I assume, but he would want you to share in the spoils of war with him. Please take these kegs to your army and share it with them equally."

"Can we have another drink?" another soldier asked eagerly, his skin becoming lighter by the second. "Drink as much as you like," St. Nicholas encouraged.

"Just make sure everyone gets a generous amount... you know how angry Prince Gregor can get."

"Aye, that man has a temper," the Captain agreed.

"Aren't we going to tell Rudolph and the rest of your men what is going on?" I asked, after the eight had left with a cart full of Christmas Ambrosia. "They still think we've surrendered the North Pole."

230

"I've already told all of our people," St. Nicholas said. "They're only pretending to be defeated at this point. While the three of you have been standing here, I've held a war council, organized a reconstruction party and finished my deliveries to Argentina. The war has been over for days for me. I just haven't let you or Prince Gregor's army know it."

"Won't his army be upset when they find out they've lost the war?" John asked.

"Who says they lost the war?" St. Nicholas declared, motioning for Mrs. Claus to pour us all out a drink. "One taste of this and they'll be convinced they won the war!"

"I'll drink to that," John said, in between gulps. "This stuff is fantastic."

After a few rounds of drinks, St. Nicholas was able to make peace with the foreign invaders. It wasn't long before the whole army got their humanity back, leaving them with no desire to fight against the Christmas City. They begged to return to their mother country as soon as possible, and St. Nicholas obliged, arranging comfortable transportation for all 1,000 combatants, who headed back to London as happily as they could go.

That evening St. Nicholas invited Julia, John, and I to a private victory feast. When it was done, St. Nicholas held up a glass of Christmas Ambrosia and proposed a toast.

"To Mason, Julia and John," St. Nicholas called out, "long live the youngest members of the Santa Claus League."

"Here, here!" Mrs. Claus cheered, drinking to our success.

"Now that you're all official members of the League," he stated, having another deep drink of spiked hot chocolate, "I'm assigning you to continue serving in the Central Washington area. Your official duties will begin after Mason and Julia get back from their honeymoon. Congratulations newlyweds!"

"About the honeymoon," I said uncomfortably, "Julia and I are a bit worried about the legality of our marriage in the mortal world."

"Oh, of course," St. Nicholas chortled, pulling out an ornate official document inscribed on vellum. "I haven't given you the marriage license yet. Here it is, signed by me, the officiating priest, and by Rudolph and John as witnesses."

"That is lovely, but..." Julia paused, looking at the illuminated manuscript with helpless eyes, "but Mason and I can't live together as man and wife unless our marriage license is recorded in our own County Courthouse. As lovely as this marriage certificate is, no one will ever believe the legality of a hand-written document signed by St. Nicholas, with Rudolph Reinman and John Patten as witnesses."

"You poor dear," Mrs. Claus said kindly, putting her arms around Julia and giving her a hug. "And what about you Mr. Patten? You look miserable as well."

"I can't get my car fixed," John blurted, "it's totaled. To make matters worse, I have a parking ticket in London to worry about. I'm doomed."

"I'm so sorry," Mrs. Claus consoled, squeezing his hand with kindness. "What do you suggest, Nicholas?"

"It's a complicated situation," St. Nicholas answered honestly. "The car is a total loss, I'm afraid. Even Rudolph can't straighten out the frame. He was about to order a new one, but I stopped him. I have another plan I think you might like better."

"What is it?" John asked, cheering up considerably.

"It's hard to explain, some things are better just to experience." St. Nicholas answered mysteriously. "As for your traffic ticket problem, I've already had one of my men return the tire boot back to the London Police Department and removed the record of the ticket from their computer system. You also have nothing to fear from the police or the grave robbers, they won't say a word for fear of sounding crazy."

"But what about our marriage license?" Julia begged, still holding my hand. "I'm a married woman, I want to live like one."

"Have a little patience," St. Nicholas reassured her, pushing a salt shaker around the table in a mindless way, "everything will work out."

"Stop teasing them, Nicholas," his wife chided, "for a saint you can be very annoying."

"That's true, I can be," he agreed, "but if you knew the past, present and future of every person on the planet, you might want to have a little fun as well. I like to solve problems in the cleverest way possible. It's my coping mechanism."

"I love you, dear," she smiled, clearing a few things off the table. "But sometimes you drive me to drink."

"Now, if you'd let me smoke my pipe once in a while, I might not be so hard to live with."

"Don't even start with me, Nicholas Claus," she warned. "Saint or no, you'll be sleeping with the chickens."

"Did you hear that?" he praised, "she's my perfect match. She balances me in every way. I believe the two of you are just as blessed."

"So you do have a solution for us?" I rejoiced. "We can remain married in the mortal world?"

"Of course, my boy," St. Nicholas said heartily. "So step back. I'm about to perform a bit of Christmas magic, and I'm not sure what to expect. Jacob Marley, enter my humble home."

The Heart Stones of Christmas glowed again, filling the whole room with light. Out of the beam stepped a gloriously robed angelic being.

"That doesn't happen very often," St. Nicholas muttered, reaching around the corner and pulling out the magic cloak of the Spirit of Christmas Future. "Even I am surprised by the wonders of Christmas magic from time to time. Mr. Jacob Marley, would you be willing to finish your duties as the Spirit of Christmas Yet to Come?"

"I would," the Spirit nodded, taking the powerful robe and throwing it over his white clothes. As soon as he did he became as black as night.

"Why are you dressed in black again?" Julia gasped, stepping back from the cloaked man.

"My cloak is not black," the Ghost of Christmas Yet to Come insisted. "I am the reflection of the uncreated. I am the future, unmade, and unknown. I have no form and no substance. I am only shadows of what may be. Do not fear me. Whatever the future may hold will be of your own making. There is nothing to fear unless you create a reason to fear it."

"Are you ready to show these three a glimpse of Christmas yet to come?" St. Nicholas asked.

"I am prepared," the mysterious Jacob Marley answered, the cloak beginning to pulse with power. "Does the coin bearer have the coin?"

"Yes, I do," I insisted, pulling the shilling from my pocket and showing it to the Spirit; he didn't flinch at its sight this time. I put it back in my pocket, glad I had taken care of it so well.

St. Nicholas smiled at me and explained, "When I borrowed the cloak from the Spirit of Christmas Future I didn't realize all the magic had to be used before it could be given back. It's nice to know I still have things to learn. It's kind of refreshing really. Please stand on the Heart Stones of Christmas, and Mr. Marley will do the rest."

I pulled Julia and John close to me and we stood on the stones, causing them to glow until they reached a brilliant white. At the moment when I didn't think the room could get any brighter, Jacob Marley raised his arms, causing the room to blow apart in an explosion of color.

Chapter Twenty-Nine

Haunted Again

When the colors reassembled we were no longer standing on the Heart Stones of Christmas, instead we were standing in a futuristic room with flowing LED lights flickering up the walls. I couldn't tell if the floor was made of tile or metal, but there were rows of flimsy-looking chairs surrounding one large soft chair.

"Where are we?" I asked.

"Your potential future," Jacob Marley spoke, causing his robes to fly around him again.

"Why have you taken us here?" asked Julia.

"I only have enough magic to show you one scene from your potential future," he explained, "And I believe this one event sums up your future joy the best."

The door to the room opened, allowing a hundred children with their parents to rush in. The youth were giddy with excitement and they seemed to be waiting for someone.

As I wandered about the children, I could sense their joy and dreams; but some of their futures I couldn't even comprehend, as they pondered on professions I didn't know even existed. I saw what they wanted for Christmas—toys I had never imagined, using technologies undiscovered in my frame of reference.

"How far into the future do you think we are?" Julia asked.

"I don't know," I replied.

"I'd say about 80 years," John offered, from across the room.

"Why would you say that?"

"Because I think the Santa Claus walking down the hall is you," he answered. "And dude, you look like you're a hundred years old."

"He is correct," the Ghost of Christmas Future confirmed. "This is your future self. Do you recognize the woman he has brought with him?"

"It's Julia," I answered, looking past the old woman's wrinkles and shrunken frame, peering into her bright eyes. She was at least a hundred years old, too, but full of life and fun... I couldn't help but laugh.

"Why are you laughing at me?" she said.

"I'm not laughing at you," I assured her. "I'm laughing because I can't believe how beautiful you still look. You are absolutely adorable."

"I do look good don't I?" she agreed modestly. "But look at you, Santa Claus, you're such a jolly old man, no wonder the children are bouncing off the walls to sit on your lap. Who couldn't fall in love with you?"

I watched in wonder as one child after another sat on my future lap, telling me their Christmas wishes and getting a Christmas present from my magic toy bag. My love for Julia increased as each child received a candy cane from my beautiful little Mrs. Santa Claus.

I saw rainbows, sparkles, and firecrackers coming from the little girls, and raging waters, whirlwinds, and lightning bolts coming from the little boys. I saw dreams and love and ambition in most of the children, but despair and sadness in others.

I noted how the ancient Mrs. Claus wrote down the names of certain children we both instinctively identified as needing our help. We were old, but the dreams and the needs of the children surrounding us were still young and real. I could tell even after all the years that had passed, we still loved every second of what we did.

About two-thirds of the way through the line a little seven-year-old girl sat on my future lap and opened up her synthetic fur-lined coat. As she did a bolt of lightning flashed from a beautiful necklace she was wearing. The fast forward motion of the vision stopped, slowing down to real-time.

"That's an amazing necklace," my future self said kindly. "Have you ever seen such a beautiful thing, Mrs. Claus?"

"Oh my goodness," both the old Julia and the young one standing next to her exclaimed at the exact same time.

236

"It's a gift from my grandmother!" she beamed, causing the necklace to shine even brighter. "It's magic. To most people it looks like a cheap piece of plastic, but to someone who can see how special I am, they see a beautiful sparkling diamond. Can you see it?"

"I see it," old Santa cried, causing the stone to shoot rainbows all over the room. "What about you Mrs. Claus?"

"I see the diamond," she confirmed, covering her teary eyes to shield them from the light. "But I see you shine even brighter. What's your name?"

"Victoria," she said with spirit. "My grandmother calls me her Little Victory."

"That's so sweet," Julia sniffled. "Where is your grandmother now? We knew her when she was a just a girl. Is she still alive?"

"Oh yes," Victoria beamed. "I talk to her on the Holo every other day. She's too old to come visit me in person. She gave me this necklace as a present. She said a bright young lady like me needs to know how important she is. I have a lovely secret too; do you want to hear it?"

"If it's okay with your mother," I answered.

"It's alright," her mother smiled cheerfully. "I already know it. She tells everyone she trusts."

"I have two fathers," the little girl whispered in Santa's ear.

"You have two fathers?" the old Santa repeated with his lip quivering.

"I do," she replied happily. "And you wouldn't believe who the second one is? But I know Him and He loves me. I must be the luckiest girl alive."

"I'm sure you are," Santa Claus said, trying to keep control of his emotions. "That must be why I have such a special gift for you. I've been curious all night long who would get this one."

"Can I open it here?" she begged, taking the brightly wrapped gift from me, and looking at Julia.

"If it's okay with your mother," Julia answered, tears falling down her face as well.

"Of course," her mother smiled.

The seven-year-old girl opened the present carefully, revealing two stunning diamond earrings and a diamond bracelet embedded with the same Christmas magic.

"Oh, these are lovely," she beamed, holding them out into the light. "These are just what I was hoping for. Grandmother will be so happy."

"Could you do a favor for me, please?" Mrs. Santa Claus asked. "When you show these gifts to your grandmother, please give her our love."

"I will," Victoria laughed, hopping off of old Santa Claus's lap and taking her mother by the hand. "I'll pass these treasures down to my own kids. This gift will never end."

"I don't think you know this," the little girl's mother confided before walking away. "But my mother, Carolyn, is the most kind and gracious woman in the world. I don't know how she does it, but the sun doesn't shine on her, it shines through her. She tells me Santa Claus saved her life when she was young. It must have been you she was talking about."

"Oh, no, it wasn't me," the old Santa insisted. "You can thank her Heavenly Father for that."

The little girl skipped out of the room holding her mother's hand, causing everything to go into fast forward again.

"I think we just witnessed another Christmas miracle," Julia said to me, drying her eyes with her shirt sleeve.

"And you're still more precious to me than all the diamonds in the world," I insisted, holding her close while her aura radiated as brightly as the diamonds that sparkled.

Julia, John, and I watched in amazement as the few remaining children were loved and brightened by the magic of Christmas, but it wasn't long before Mr. and Mrs. Santa Claus were the only ones left in the large hall with the lights dimming.

"Are you ready to go home?" an old, but familiar voice echoed as its owner entered the room.

"Ready when you are," the old Santa answered. "Did you get the gyros stabilized in the Nova, or are we riding home sideways again?"

"Ha, ha," the ancient John said sarcastically, "if it wasn't for me you'd have to ride the Commercial Spacelines, and I don't remember them making Christmas Eve house calls."

"I'm serious," the old me responded, "if we have to ride sideways again, we will fly coach."

"Nah, I got it fixed," the old John said. "I just like messin' with you."

The three old friends walked out of the room, down a hall and onto a large platform outside of the building as Jacob Marley motioned for us to follow. When we stepped onto the platform, the reality of our surroundings came into full view. We were not on a city sidewalk, but standing on a spaceport landing bay.

The space station wrapped around us in a huge circle and the earth spun above our heads like a blue sapphire floating in a star-studded sea of black. The sun was at our back, shining on us warmly. John gasped as the older version of himself opened the passenger side door of a 1979 cherry red Chevy Nova, no different from the one we had been so fond of driving around.

"St. Nicholas fixed it!" John exploded. "Look at it, over a hundred years old and still purring like a kitten."

"With gyro problems apparently," Julia added. "I hope you get working on that when we get home."

"You better believe it," John said without hesitation. "If I get her back, I'll be the happiest guy in the galaxy."

We watched the old couple get into the car and John lifted the old Chevy off the pad, blasting off into the darkness toward the earth. In just a few seconds the old car disappeared, leaving behind a trail of sparks.

"Did you see that?" John blurted. "Did you see it go into time-warp? What a beautiful car. That was awesome."

"I love this life you've given to me," Julia said lovingly, giving me a kiss.

In my peripheral vision I noticed the magic power of Jacob Marley's cloak go out. The magic was gone. He pulled the hood off his face, revealing his bright countenance. He smiled at me and bowed his head in deep respect, vanishing into the night.

When I started out on this adventure I honestly thought I was supposed to redeem Jacob Marley. At that moment I understood the truth: he had redeemed me. I wish I had shown my gratitude better, but when I'm being kissed by a beautiful girl, I tend to forget about everything and just enjoy the moment.

When I finally opened my eyes, I expected to see Julia standing in front of me, instead I was standing alone in my parents' living room, staring into our Christmas tree!

Chapter Thirty

Vanished in the Night

I looked at the clock in a panic as it struck 6 a.m. Looking at the calendar on my phone, it said December 25th. The Spirit of Christmas Future had returned me to my own reality, just like Ebenezer Scrooge was returned to his.

I was stunned and fell to my knees devastated with the fear of losing Julia. I looked down and saw my own fingertips creating dark purple sparks of anxious energy. Was it all a dream? Would she remember anything?

"Merry Christmas, Mason," my two sisters, Sage and Myia sang, bouncing down the stairs. My parents came creeping after them, as if they had been up half the night, wrapping and putting presents under the tree.

"Are you alright?" my mother asked.

"No!" I blurted, standing back up in a daze. "She was right here! I was kissing her... and then she vanished."

"Who vanished?" my mother asked confused.

"My wife!" I answered emphatically just as my cell phone began ringing.

"My car's fixed, my car's fixed!" John shouted over the phone. "St. Nicholas pulled it off. I can't believe it! I was looking at you and Julia smooching when the next thing you know I was in my garage looking at my car. What just happened?"

"I don't know," I answered confused. "The Ghost of Christmas Future must have taken us back home, but hey, Julia's calling me, I'm putting you on hold."

"Hello, Julia?" I asked. "Are you alright?"

"No," she cried over the receiver. "I was kissing my husband a moment ago, and now I'm in my bedroom staring at a wall. Do you even know what I'm talking about? Am I going crazy?"

"No, no!" I insisted. "You're not going crazy. The same thing happened to me, and John too. I remember everything, but most of all, I remember getting married to you!"

"Thank goodness!" she cried. "But now it's all gone. It was nothing but a dream!"

"No, it wasn't," I said emphatically. "I don't believe that. Dreams have meaning and I won't allow mine to be taken from me. Julia May Howell, pack your bags, we're going on a honeymoon."

"What?" both of my parents blurted out at the same time, joining their blue and purple flaming aura into one.

"I'm serious," I insisted, ignoring my parents as they seemingly suffered from a joint heart attack. "You know we're married and I know we're married. I don't need any more proof than that. Will you come with me?"

"Of course," she cooed over the phone. "Tell John to come get me. I'm waiting impatiently. If he can't make it here in 15 seconds, I'm honeymooning with some other guy."

"I heard that," my mom protested as Julia hung up. "You can't elope, we have a wedding to plan, invitations to send out—

"I'm not eloping," I clarified. "I already did that... hold on."

"Hello, John?" I interrupted my mother's frantic pleas. "Can you please go to Julia's house and pick her up? Because if you can't bring her to me in 10 seconds you're not the John Patten I know."

"I'm on it," John blurted, hanging up the phone.

"Fifteen seconds, 10 seconds?" my dad complained with blue flames surrounding him like a gas stove. "What are you talking about?"

"It's a long story," I insisted, as I counted backwards. "Four, three, two," and when I got to one the doorbell rang.

"They're here!" I sang, opening the door and getting on one knee. "Julia May Howell," I begged as she flew through the door. "Will you stay with me forever?"

"Yes," she sang, jumping into my open arms, making us both roll onto the ground.

"That's what I'm talking about," John yelped, slapping me on the back."

"Alright!" my dad said, his aura changing to popping red firecrackers. "What is going on here?"

"Julia and I were married this morning," I said happily, springing to my feet and helping Julia up. "We wanted you all to be the first to know."

"It was a grand affair," Julia said, wiping the tears from her eyes and kissing me again. "We were bound together, marching to our deaths with a burning city all around us."

"St. Nicholas was the officiator," I added. "And gave us our vows as we prepared to surrender the North Pole to a madman."

"And I was a witness," John insisted. "It was the best wedding I've ever been to!"

"I think we should call the police," my mother gasped, reaching for the phone with her body swirling with orange flames. "They must have been drugged!"

"Hey Mason," my little sister, Myia cried, "there's a present here for Julia. Can she open it here, now she's my new sister?"

"Sure," I said, taking the phone from my mother's hand and hanging up the receiver.

"The note says to Mrs. Julia May Howell," I read, handing the box to Julia, "the newest member of the Santa Claus League. Please accept these tokens of my appreciation. Thank you for your heartfelt service. With love, St. Nicholas."

"St. Nicholas just called me, Mrs. Howell," Julia sniffled with little white sparks dancing around her. "Isn't that sweet…"

"What's inside?" Seven-year-old Myia asked, bouncing up and down, setting off fireworks with each jump. "It looks like a piece of rope!"

"It's my engagement rope!" Julia gasped, bursting into tears again. "He thinks of everything!"

"What else is in there?" Sage asked, her own countenance washed in all the colors of the rainbow.

Julia reached in and pulled out an official Grant County wedding certificate, signed by the judge and stamped by the Grant County Recorder, along with the larger parchment signed by St. Nicholas, with Rudolph and John as witnesses.

"It's official!" Julia beamed, showing the marriage certificate to my mother. "I'm Mrs. Julia May Howell. I'm married to your son!"

Julia reached into the box again, pulling out a full Mrs. Santa Claus dress, complete with glasses, apron, and shoes. A sleek space suit with a hood, socks and gloves came out with it.

"Look at this?" she gasped, holding the beautiful red dress and shimmering space suit next to her. "I get my own Christmas uniform, too!"

"Wow," Myia exclaimed, shooting off more sparks. "That little box holds a lot of stuff."

When Julia pulled out the last gift from the package, a little note was attached. "To Mr. and Mrs. Howell," it read. "May these rings act as a symbol of your love for each other. Happy Christmas!"

When she opened the ornate wooden box it revealed a brilliant diamond ring alongside a men's band cast in gold. "It's our wedding rings!" Julia cried. "It's the ring I fell in love with at Miller's Jewelry store!"

The diamond ring sparkled like Christmas tree lights, reflecting all the joy Julia was feeling and it was the same ring I tried to buy for her a few days earlier. The two carat marque was surrounded by smaller diamonds, looking like stars surrounding the sun. I took the brilliant ring out of the box and drew near to my wife.

"Now it's official," I said, placing it on her finger. "With this ring, I thee wed!"

She looked at the ring on her finger and began to cry. She took out my ring and placed it on my finger as well. "With this ring, I thee wed," she repeated.

"I now pronounce you man and wife!" Myia said, taking a few packing peanuts from the box, and throwing them above our heads like flower pedals.

We kissed in front of everyone while Sage joined in the fun, dumping the rest of the packing peanuts on our heads and dancing around the room. Even my mother cried at the realization we were really married.

"Hey, there's a present from St. Nicholas over here for John, too!" Sage sang, holding it up.

"Let me see that," John yelled with glee, sparking embers like a bonfire. He jumped next to Sage by the Christmas tree and in a flash, ripped off the wrapping paper and opened the box. Inside was a set of stylish early 20th century motoring clothes complete with shirt, tie, coat, pants, hat, goggles, and boots. Along with the clothes came a similar shimmering suit made to fit his lanky dimensions.

"I love my life!" he said, turning white with joy and jumping up from the Christmas tree. He rushed for the guest bathroom and moments later an explosion rattled the whole house.

"It's okay, Dad," I insisted, attempting to calm his panicked look. "I've seen this happen before. The bathroom will be alright and John isn't dead!"

"Hello everyone," John smiled, appearing by the Christmas tree, wearing his new motoring clothes with his finger by his nose. "Wait, what just happened? How did I get over here?" he bragged disappearing and popping up by the refrigerator in the kitchen. "It's like magic, how am I doing that?"

"Show off," Julia exclaimed, ignoring his appearing and disappearing act.

What damage John didn't do to the bathroom, Julia finished off, fusing the Christmas magic of the Mrs. Santa Claus suit into her body. After getting dressed again, Julia touched her nose, bringing me into time- warp with her own magical powers.

"We're a perfect match, Santa Claus," she cooed, kissing me warmly. "I really am married to a king!"

"And you're my queen, Mrs. Claus," I replied, kissing her back. "All the success in the world couldn't make me as happy as you do. Without love, success just turns to greed."

The light of happiness coming from my family was more colorful than the Christmas tree. We opened Christmas presents together while my mother cried. I had to shield my eyes as she burst into tears of joy, sending shooting stars all over the room. Later, she cried even harder when we drove off for our honeymoon.

Julia and I were so happy we could barely contain our emotions. As eager as we were to set off for our honeymoon we still had one more stop to make. Julia had to tell her mother she eloped, and I had to face her father.

Merry Christmas to All...

John drove Julia and I to her house at around eight in the morning. Julia's favorite security guard was manning the front gate when we drove up to the compound entrance.

"Hello Mr. Gibbins," Julia said sweetly. "Could you please let us in? And oh, Merry Christmas."

"Of course," he said courteously, opening the heavy metal gates. "Welcome home Miss Martin."

"I'm not Miss Martin anymore," Julia bragged, showing off her ring. "I'm Mrs. Howell now. I was just married this morning. But please, allow me to break the news to my parents. They don't know yet!"

"Of course," he said courteously. "Congratulations on your marriage. I'll let your father know you've arrived. And Merry Christmas to you as well."

I suspected Mr. Martin wouldn't be happy about Julia showing up with me this early in the morning, but I knew he would explode once he found out we were married. Still, I hoped for the best. As soon as we drove up her driveway he stormed out of the house in a frenzy. "How did you get out of the compound without my knowledge?" he yelled, red flames shooting from his aura. "Who helped you sneak out?"

"Calm down, Dad," Julia insisted. "I didn't ask for help from anyone. I left through the front door. Mason needs to talk to you about something really important. I've been with him all morning."

"All morning?" he gasped, his flames burning even more intense. "I installed the most secure security system in the world this week and you just evaded it without so much as a backward glance? Tell your friends to go home. You're coming with me!"

He took Julia by the arm and marched her toward the huge front doors. She looked back at me as they walked away with pleading in her eyes.

"This is all yours, Mason," John said emphatically. "I'll just sit here and wait for you to come out."

"I've got this," I said, stopping time and slipping through the front door before it slammed closed. I looked around for my new wife and her father, luckily they hadn't made it far.

Mr. Martin was frozen-in-time ready to walk up the stairs, dragging Julia with him. Mrs. Martin was frozen as well, coming out of the kitchen, caught in mid-step with a shocked look on her face. I stood on the second stair right above him, and touched my nose.

"Please, sir," I begged, appearing in front of him like a ghost. "Just talk to me. Don't jump to conclusions! There's no danger here!"

"What in the world!" he exclaimed, erupting in flames again and taking a surprised step back. "Where did you come from? Never mind. Guards! We have an intruder. Guards!"

The next moment Julia appeared, standing next to me in her own time-warp bubble. "It's no use, Mason," she said sadly. "He's not going to listen to you until he calms down."

"Maybe not," I said hopefully. "But I at least want him to know we're married. I don't want him to be worried sick for two weeks while we're on our honeymoon. I like your Mom and Dad, and I know you won't be happy unless they're happy, too."

"You really are a sweet man," she smiled, kissing me softly. "I'm glad I married you. I have an idea then. You block off the door to keep the guards out, and then help me set things up. I may need a pinch or two of your Christmas Ambrosia as well."

We worked for about a half an hour outside of time getting our meeting place set up as comfortably as possible. When Julia released them out of time-warp, both of her parents were sitting across the kitchen table from us. Set in front of them were two mugs of hot chocolate with a generous amount of Ambrosia mixed in.

"Mom, Dad," Julia began, "before you say a single word, please have a sip of hot chocolate, it will help you feel better. Don't panic. I'm married. Mason and I eloped last night. We're about to leave for our honeymoon."

"Impossible," her father said, his aura sparking with menacing lighting bolts.

"Just listen to them, dear," Mrs. Martin insisted as she took a sip of the hot chocolate. The moment she did her aura danced with a curious yellow glow. "Oh my, this is tasty."

"This isn't real," he fumed, unknowingly striking me with red energy bolts.

"I don't care!" Mrs. Martin demanded as determined yellow sparks began shooting from her own countenance "Take a sip of that hot chocolate and let them talk."

Julia's mother stared at Mr. Martin until he reluctantly picked up the cup and gave it a sip. "Wow," he stammered, taking a deeper drink. "This is good! Where did you get it?"

"Thanks for listening, sir," I began, hoping he would keep drinking the spiked hot chocolate. "It's an old family recipe. I understand how much you love Julia, and I'm grateful for the sacrifice you've made to protect her all these years."

"She's my whole world!" he insisted, his aura cooling down as took another deep drink. "For years now I've watched her getting closer and closer to you, and now..."

"Dad, I still love you," Julia exclaimed with tears in her eyes. "I'll always be your little girl. You've just gained the son you always wanted to have."

Mr. Martin didn't say a word for at least a minute. He sat calmly, holding back his deep emotions while sipping on his hot chocolate. I could see his aura change from flames of anger to the blue waves of deep loss and sorrow. Mrs. Martin became impatient after a while and took him by the hand, giving him a pleading look.

"Oh, alright!" he finally agreed, his personal energy bursting into a rainbow of colors and releasing all the tension in the room. "Welcome to the family!"

"Congratulations sweetheart," Mrs. Martin cried. I could see light streaming from her whole body as she leapt from her chair, giving us both a hug. "I have no idea what's going on, but I couldn't be happier."

"I love you too, Mom," Julia wept. "See my ring? Isn't it beautiful?"

"I'm impressed!" she beamed. "I love that cut."

"I'm sorry we didn't get to have our official talk before we were married," I apologized to Mr. Martin. "I should have tried harder."

"Don't worry about that," he said, giving me an equally hearty hug, "you did your best. I'm embarrassed how badly I treated you. I wasn't thinking about her happiness at the time, only my own. I'm sorry for my rude behavior."

"There's one thing we have to talk about," Mrs. Martin scolded, with little yellow lights zinging around her. "You may have escaped the big wedding, but if you think you're getting out of the reception, you have another think coming!"

"She has you on that one," Mr. Martin insisted. "She's been saving up for your wedding for years."

"I have," she agreed, her yellow zingers only getting more intense. "What's your mother's phone number, Mason? We're going to throw the biggest, loudest wedding reception Central Washington has ever seen!"

After giving Mrs. Martin my mother's cell phone number we loaded Julia's stuff into John's car. With a few words of counsel and lots of tears we finally drove out of the compound.

"Where to?" John said eagerly, his own countenance bursting with fireworks.

"The Greek Isles," Julia blurted. "Can we honeymoon there, please Mason?"

"You bet," I agreed, "anywhere you want to go."

"The Greek Isles it is," John said while tapping on his scramjet switch. "I could get you there fast."

"Not fast enough," I insisted, pulling Jacob Marley's silver shilling out of my pocket and carelessly tossing it to him. The coin spun around and around, glowing with magic and bursting with sparks the moment it hit his hand.

"A tip for the coachman," Julia cried, buckling herself in and giving me a kiss. "Warm up those scram jet engines and show me how fast this thing can go!"

"Now you're talking!" John exclaimed. "It's up you now, Mason. Say the magic words."

"You bet," I agreed, holding onto my new wife. "Now, Dasher! now, Dancer! now, Prancer! and Vixen! On, Comet! on,

Cupid! on Donner and Blitzen! To the top of the porch, to the top of the wall! Now dash away, dash away, dash away all!"

"Merry Christmas!" Julia called out happily, holding on for dear life.

"And God bless us, every one!" John added, blasting us off toward the moon and into the new adventure of our lives.

The End

Stephen Miller was born in Provo, Utah in 1962. In high school he excelled at debate winning several statewide competitions. He also met his wife in high school and they were later married when they re-met attending college and have had seven wonderful children.

Stephen has served in the Utah Air National Guard and an LDS Mission in Rio de Janeiro. He holds a BA from BYU and an MBA from the University of Phoenix.

His first book, Captain Justo from the Planet Is was first told as a bedtime story to his children. They loved it so much they wanted him to write it down for his first foray into being an author. It has slowly grown into a fantasy adventure for all ages. The second is called Captain Justo The Valley of Bones and he is now creating the third installment.

The Santa Claus League was inspired by the legend of his grandfather, Loran Wells Duke. Although he never met his grandfather, Stephen's life has been shaped by his example, especially at Christmas time. His grandfather loved playing Santa Claus. This book is dedicated to his honor.

Christmas is a magical holiday and Stephen's children had many common questions about Christmas and Santa Claus.

How does Santa Claus bring toys to the whole world in one night? Why do so many men pretend to be Santa Claus? If Santa knows who is naughty or nice then why doesn't he do something about it? Stephen answers all these questions in his charming new novel, The Santa Claus League.

Stephen now lives in Orem, Utah with his beautiful wife Edna and is surrounded in love not only by children but grandchildren as well.

Other Books by Stephen Miller

The Santa Claus League: 'Twas the Night Before Christmas

Captain Justo Saga in two formats:

Captain Justo From the Planet Is
Captain Justo: Valley of Bones

Or

Captain Justo Log 1.1: Gold From the Sky
Captain Justo Log 1.2: Dangerous Training
Captain Justo Log 1.3: Homeland Attack
Captain Justo Log 2.1: Into the Deep
Captain Justo Log 2.2: The Serratian Betrayal
Captain Justo Log 2.3: Valley of Bones

Find these books at www.worldofstephenmiller.com

www.ingramcontent.com/pod-product-compliance
Lightning Source LLC
Chambersburg PA
CBHW060541260626
47161CB00003B/1004